ACCLAIM FOR DEAN KOONTZ'S FRANKENSTEIN SERIES

BOOK ONE: PRODIGAL SON

"Like [an] expert plate-spinner, the [author sets] up a dizzying array of narrative viewpoints and cycle[s] through them effortlessly. . . . The odd juxtaposition of a police procedural with a neo-gothic, mad scientist plot gives this novel a wickedly unusual and intriguing feel. . . . A compelling read, with an elegant cliffhanger ending."
—*Publishers Weekly*

"Koontz realizes his original concept for a cable TV effort from which he withdrew. It was TV's loss, for, filmed utterly faithfully, *Prodigal Son* could be the best horror thriller and, hands down, would be the best Frankenstein movie, ever. This is a book that helps restore horror's good name."
—*Booklist* (starred review)

"This rich and complex tale is not only an ambitious project, but one of the most enjoyable monster stories in years. . . . This is classic Koontz at his best."
—*Fangoria*

"This first book in a multipart saga features fascinating characters and an intriguing premise."
—*Library Journal*

"Koontz . . . examine[s] society's present milieu under the lens of traditional western mores and in so doing has presented the public with works that are perfectly entertaining and, more importantly, prescient. . . . In [*Prodigal Son*] the dimensions of the universe are in collision. We are brought to the door of chaos, anarchy, and destruction. In chilling, vivid detail, the author will keep the reader on the edge of his chair, as they begin the journey toward the ultimate blasphemy." —*California Literary Review*

BOOK TWO: CITY OF NIGHT

"Relax, Dean Koontz's Frankenstein, volume one of which, *Prodigal Son,* was a pulse-pounder all the way, is going to be a trilogy. But don't expect to relax all that much. This book cooks, no second-volume doldrums anywhere in it. . . . Smart dialogue and cutting-edge scientific notions are the oh-so-sweet icing on this delectable thriller's irresistible, devour-able cake." —*Booklist* (starred review)

"Dean Koontz gives us another major dose of all the great things we received in the first book. It is filled with sharp narration, imaginative situations, and a thrilling suspense-filled adventure. . . . This book is not only an insightful and an intellectual delight,

but it is also a fun and exciting read. . . . Koontz has given a fresh new feel to an old story."
—Associated Content

BOOK THREE: DEAD AND ALIVE

"Spinning the old Mary Shelley classic on its head, Koontz has a grand time making the 'monster' his noble hero and the scientist the immoral, heartless villain. He does this with amazing skill. [He] understands that in a world of sinners and saints, we don't need special effects to make monsters."
—INDenver Times

BOOK FOUR: LOST SOULS

"Koontz does his dance of . . . suspense, wry dialogue, sharp characterization . . . charming (and well-integrated) comic relief, and cultural criticism more adroitly than almost ever before."
—*Booklist* (starred review)

"This successful mix of crime-inspired detective story and sf adventure is ideal for Koontz devotees as well as readers who enjoy genre crossovers."
—**Library Journal**

"[Koontz] sets the scene, tantalizes and goads us to want more." —Bookreporter.com

ACCLAIM FOR DEAN KOONTZ

"Of all bestselling authors, Koontz may be the most underestimated by the literary establishment. Book after book, year after year, this author climbs to the top of the charts. Why? His readers know: because he is a master storyteller and a daring writer, and because, in his novels, he gives readers bright hope in a dark world." —*Publishers Weekly* (starred review)

"A modern Swift . . . a master satirist."
—*Entertainment Weekly*

"A rarity among bestselling writers, Koontz continues to pursue new ways of telling stories, never content with repeating himself. He writes of hope and love in the midst of evil in profoundly inspiring and moving ways." —*Chicago Sun-Times*

"Koontz is a superb plotter and wordsmith. He chronicles the hopes and fears of our time in broad strokes and fine detail, using popular fiction to explore the human condition [and] demonstrating that the real horror of life is found not in monsters, but within the human psyche." —*USA Today*

"Perhaps more than any other author, Koontz writes fiction perfectly suited to the mood of America: novels that acknowledge the reality and tenacity of evil but also the power of good; that celebrate the

common man and woman; that at their best enter-tain vastly as they uplift."
—*Publishers Weekly* (starred review)

"If Stephen King is the Rolling Stones of novels, Koontz is the Beatles." —***Playboy***

"[Koontz is] far more than a genre writer. Characters and the search for meaning, exquisitely crafted, are the soul of his work. This is why his novels will be read long after the ghosts and monsters of most genre writers have been consigned to the attic. One of the master storytellers of this or any age."
—***The Tampa Tribune***

"Dean Koontz is not just a master of our darkest dreams, but also a literary juggler."
—*The Times* (London)

"Dean Koontz writes page-turners, middle-of-the-night-sneak-up-behind-you suspense thrillers. He touches our hearts and tingles our spines."
—***The Washington Post Book World***

"Dean Koontz almost occupies a genre of his own. He is a master at building suspense and holding the reader spellbound." —***Richmond Times-Dispatch***

"Demanding much of itself, Koontz's style bleaches out clichés while showing a genius for details. He leaves his competitors buried in the dust."
—***Kirkus Reviews***

Dean Koontz

Doubleday Large Print
Home Library Edition

Bantam Books New York

FRANKENSTEIN

the dead town

A Novel

This Large Print Edition, prepared especially for
Doubleday Large Print Home Library, contains the
complete, unabridged text of the original Publisher's
Edition.

ISBN 978-1-61129-666-2

Cover art and design: Scott Biel
Title page art from an original photograph by
Margaret Young

Printed in the United States of America

**This Large Print Book carries the
Seal of Approval of N.A.V.H.**

To the memory of Gilbert K. Chesterton,
who presented wisdom and hard truths
in a most appealing package, changing
countless lives with kindness and a smile

Men can always be blind to a thing so long as it is big enough. It is so difficult to see the world in which we live.

—G. K. CHESTERTON

FRANKENSTEIN

the dead town

Owl-eyed and terrified, Warren Snyder occupied an armchair in his living room. He sat stiff, erect, his hands upturned in his lap. Now and then his right hand shook. His mouth hung slightly open, and his lower lip trembled almost continuously.

On his left temple, a silvery bead gleamed. As rounded and as polished as the head of a decorative upholstery tack, it looked like a misplaced earring.

The bead was in fact packed with electronics, nanocircuitry, and was rather like the head of a nail in that it was the visible portion of a needle-thin probe that had been fired into his brain by a pistol-like device. Instantaneous chemical cauterization of flesh and bone prevented bleeding.

Warren said nothing. He had been ordered to remain silent, and he had lost the power to disobey. Except for his twitching fingers and the tremors, which were both involuntary, he did not move, not even to change position in the chair, because he had been told to be still.

His gaze shifted back and forth between two points of interest: his wives.

With a silver bead on her left temple and her eyes glazed like those of an amped-out meth junkie, Judy Snyder perched on the sofa, knees together, hands folded serenely in her lap. She didn't twitch or tremble like her husband. She seemed to be without fear, perhaps because the probe had damaged her brain in ways not intended.

The other Judy stood by one of the living-room windows that faced the street, alternately studying the snowy night and regarding her two prisoners with contempt. Their kind were the spoilers of the earth. Soon these two would be led away like a couple of sheep, to be rendered and processed. And one day, when the last human beings were eradicated, the world would be as much of a paradise as it had ever been or ever could be.

This Judy was not a clone of the one on the sofa, nothing as disgusting as a mere meat machine, which was all that human beings were. She had been designed to pass for the original Judy, but the illusion would not hold up if her internal structure and the nature of her flesh were to be studied by physicians. She had been created in a couple of months, programmed and extruded—"born"—as an adult in the Hive, deep underground, with no tao other than her program, with no illusion that she possessed free will, with no obligation whatsoever to any higher power other than her creator, Victor Leben, whose true last name was Frankenstein, and with no life after this one to which she needed to aspire.

Through the parted draperies, she watched a tall man crossing the snow-mantled street, hands in his coat pockets, face turned to the sky as if delighting in the weather. He approached the house on the front walkway, playfully kicking up little clouds of snow. Judy couldn't see his face, but she assumed he must be Andrew Snyder, the nineteen-year-old son of the family. His parents expected him to return home from work about this time.

She let the draperies fall into place and stepped out of the living room, into the foyer. When she heard Andrew's footsteps on the porch, she opened the door.

"Andy," she said, "I was so worried."

Shucking off his boots to leave them on the porch, Andrew smiled and shook his head. "You worry too much, Mom. I'm not late."

"No, you're not, but terrible things have been happening in town tonight."

"What terrible things?"

As Andrew stepped into the foyer in his stocking feet, the Judy replicant closed the door, turned to him, and began to unbutton his peacoat. In the best imitation of motherly concern that she could manage, she said, "You'll catch your death in this weather."

Pulling a scarf from around his neck, he asked again, "What terrible things?" He frowned with confusion and annoyance, as if her fussing with his coat must be out of character for her.

As she opened the buttons, she maneuvered him until the doorway to the study lay beyond even his peripheral vision.

"All the killings," she said, "it's horrible."

Intent upon her to an extent he had not been until now, Andrew said, "Killings? What killings?"

As he spoke, his replicant glided silently out of the study, directly to him, and pulled the trigger instantly upon pressing the muzzle of the brain-probe pistol to Andrew's left temple.

The young man's face wrenched with pain but for only a moment. Then his eyes widened with terror even as his face relaxed into an expression that was hardly more readable than that of someone in a coma.

"Come with me," said the replicant Andrew, and led his namesake into the living room. "Sit on the sofa."

Silvery bead shimmering like a drop of mercury on his temple, Andrew Snyder did as he was told.

If the replicant Andrew had chosen to sit opposite the real one and squeeze the trigger again, the pistol wouldn't have fired another skull-piercing dart. The second shot would have been a telemetric command initiating transmission from the embedded needle to a data-storage module in the replicant's inorganic brain. In ninety minutes or less, the essence of the young man's life experience—acquired knowledge, memories, faces, torrents of sights and sounds—would be downloaded to his impersonator.

The replicant had no need, however, to pass for Andrew Snyder in more than appearance. By this time the night after next, all the citizens of Rainbow Falls would have been killed, rendered, and processed; no one who had known the real Andrew would remain alive to be deceived by his laboratory-bred double.

Ninety minutes devoted to memory downloading would be, in this instance, a waste of time. Replicants despised waste and distraction. Focus and efficiency were important principles. The only morality was efficiency, and the only immorality was inefficiency.

The Community, as creatures born in the Hive called their new civilization, would soon possess a secret base from which to move outward relentlessly across the continent and then swiftly across the world. Communitarians were the embodiment of progress, the end of history, the end of all the repulsive messiness of human delusions and random events, the beginning of a planned future that, according to a precise timetable, would lead one day to the absolute perfection of all things.

The Communitarian Andrew Snyder, already dressed for the winter night, left the living room to join the Communitarian Warren Snyder, who waited for him in the Ford Explorer that was parked in the garage. The real Warren, paralyzed in the living-room armchair, was the general manager and the program director of KBOW, the only radio station in town.

Early in every violent revolution, those who would overthrow the current order must seize control of all means of communication in order to deny the enemy a command structure that might facilitate resistance. Everyone working the evening shift at KBOW must be controlled and then conveyed to one of the centers where the people of Rainbow Falls were being vigorously processed.

The replicant Judy remained behind with

the Judy whom she had replaced and with
the two males sitting docilely in the living
room. Her assignment was to wait here
until a transport arrived to collect the
brain-pierced trio and take them to their
destruction.

Even if the members of the Snyder family had been in control of their faculties,
they would not have been acceptable
company. Human beings were, after all,
not merely base animals like any creatures
of the fields and woods; they were by far
the worst of all species in the world, so
vain as to claim exceptional status among
all living things, so utterly deranged as to
believe that they were born with souls and
were meant to live with meaning so as to
fulfill a cosmic destiny, when in fact they
were a cancer in the bosom of Nature.

In spite of their pretensions, they were
meat. Just meat. Blood and bone and meat.
And insane. Mad. They were mad meat
and nothing more.

Communitarian Judy despised them.
She loathed the way they lived, too, with no
concern for the numerous imperfections of
their surroundings.

The living-room carpet was only the

most immediate example of their inferiority in this regard. Lint. She counted six bits of lint just in the area bordered by the two armchairs and the coffee table in front of the sofa. And not merely specks of lint. Cat hairs, as well. The cat had fled through a pet flap in the kitchen door, but its hairs were everywhere.

Order was an important principle, no less important than focus and efficiency. Indeed, efficiency was not achievable in a state of disorder. Order must be imposed before perfect efficiency could be achieved. This was a truth deeply programmed into her.

Waiting for the transport that would haul away the Snyders was not an efficient use of time. As Judy paced back and forth across the filthy carpet, stopping now and then to part the poorly hung draperies and search the street for a sign of the scheduled truck, she was acutely aware that progress waited to be made on countless fronts, that there was a world to be conquered and changed, and that she was at the moment contributing nothing to the heroic efforts of the Community.

She felt somewhat better when she got

the vacuum cleaner out of the closet and swept all the exposed areas of carpet until she could see no lint, no stray thread, no single cat hair. But then, through the glass top of the coffee table, she glimpsed what might have been a peanut that had been dropped by one of the Snyders and had rolled under the furniture.

Agitated, she dragged the coffee table away from the sofa where two of her prisoners obediently waited, and she exposed the carpet under it for closer inspection. In addition to the peanut, she found a dead fly. The insect appeared to be dry, brittle, as if it had been under the table for days and would crumble to flakes and dust upon being touched.

The peanut and the fly were not the sum of it. There were cat hairs, too, and a crumb of something that she could not identify.

"Lift your feet! *Lift them!*" she ordered Andrew and his mother, and with no change of expression in their slack faces, they obeyed, raising their knees high and their feet off the floor.

With Communitarian fervor, Judy vacuumed the carpet in front of the sofa. When she saw that Warren, in the armchair, had raised his feet, she also swept that area.

Inevitably, she began to wonder what dust and debris might have built up on the baseboard behind the sofa and on the carpet under it. She had visions of extreme disorder.

She went to the window and parted the draperies, in which the folds had not been ironed with sufficient care to ensure that they would hang uniformly. She looked left and right along the wintry street. A patrol car cruised slowly past the house. All the police in town were already Communitarians, had been for the better part of the day, but that fact did not calm Judy in the least. Only one thing would assure her that the planned takeover of the town was proceeding in an efficient manner: the arrival of the transport and the crew that would collect the Snyder family.

Turning away from the window, she surveyed the room and judged the entire space a disaster.

chapter 2

Silent legions of snow marched softly through the night, laying siege to Rainbow Falls, Montana, conquering the black streets. Like clouds of battle smoke, the blizzard faded the red-brick buildings and the towering evergreens. Soon street-scapes and landscapes would be ghostly and bleak, apocalyptic visions of a dead future.

Oblivious of the cold, Deucalion roamed the snowswept town as only he, in all the world, could travel. The terrible lightning that shocked him to life in Victor's original laboratory, more than two hundred years previously, also brought him other gifts, including a profound understanding of the quantum structure of reality, an intuitive awareness of the weave in the foundation fabric of all things. He knew that the universe was immeasurably vast and yet a strangely intimate place, that distance was both a fact and an illusion, that in truth every point in the universe was next door to every other point. A Tibetan monastery on the opposite side of the world from Rainbow Falls was in another sense only one step away, if you knew how to take that step.

Deucalion knew how, and in an instant he transitioned from an alleyway behind Jim James Bakery to the roof of the Rainbow Theater. This town of fifteen thousand souls had an Old West feel because many of its buildings dated to the late nineteenth and early twentieth centuries; they had flat roofs with parapets of the kind that bad guys and sheriffs hid behind during gunfights in old movies.

No building in town rose above four stories, and the theater ranked among the tallest structures. From this vantage point high in the falling snow, Deucalion could see east and west along Cody Street. Most businesses were closing early because of the storm, but the restaurants and bars remained brightly lighted. Only a few vehicles were parked along the curbs; and traffic had fallen to a fraction of what it had been just half an hour earlier.

The large panel truck with midnight-blue cab and white cargo section was one of only four vehicles moving along Cody Street. Other identical trucks operated elsewhere in the town. Earlier Deucalion had learned the nature of the task in which the hard-eyed, two-man crews were engaged: transporting subdued citizens of Rainbow Falls to facilities where they would be killed.

The victims had been replaced by lookalikes created in Victor's facility somewhere along State Route 311, which locals called the End Times Highway, a twenty-four-mile loop of wide two-lane blacktop that dated back to the Cold War. That road apparently served nothing along its remote wooded route except for an array of missile silos that had been decommissioned after the fall of the Soviet Union and had been in some cases abandoned and in other cases sold off to corporations for use as low-humidity, high-security storage vaults for sensitive records. Many locals were convinced that the silos were but a small part of what lay hidden along the End Times Highway, that other secret subterranean facilities had been built deep to withstand multiple direct nuclear strikes. Finding Victor's lair this time would not be easy.

No doubt the first people to be replaced by replicants and murdered had been those in the police department and in elected offices. Victor would take control of the town from the top and work down to the last unsuspecting citizen. Deucalion had already seen captive employees of the telephone company being herded into one of the blue-and-white transports, whereafter they were taken to a warehouse for disposal.

When the truck down on Cody turned north on Russell Street, Deucalion stepped off the roof of the theater and directly, boldly, magically onto the corrugated-steel step that served the passenger door of the vehicle. Surprised, the man riding shotgun turned his head. Holding fast to an assist bar on the wall of the cab, Deucalion

wrenched open the door, which barely
cleared his great bulk, reached inside with
one hand, seized the passenger by the
throat, crushed his windpipe, pulled him
off the seat, and threw him into the snowswept street as if he weighed no more than
a hollow plastic department-store manne-
quin.

"Always wear your seat belt," he muttered.

Earlier this night, he discovered that the
current generation of Victor's creations were
not as hardy as the New Race specimens
that the would-be god produced years previously in New Orleans. Those individuals
had been difficult to take down even with an
Urban Sniper, a police-only shotgun that
fired slugs instead of buckshot. These Montana replicants were nevertheless tougher
than human beings, though they were easy
prey for Deucalion, whose strength consid-
erably exceeded theirs.

The truck's forward movement threw the
door back against Deucalion, but he had a
great capacity to endure pain. He pushed
it open again and swung into the passenger seat, pulling the door shut behind him.

Taking out one of the two-man crew and

boarding the vehicle required mere seconds, and the confused driver only half braked when he saw his partner snatched from the cab. Deucalion reached for the key, switched off the engine. Surprised but not afraid—these new replicants seemed fearless—the snarling driver swung his right fist, but Deucalion seized it in mid-strike, twisted it, and broke the wrist.

The driver grunted but didn't cry out in pain. As the truck coasted along the street, Deucalion clamped his left hand to the back of his adversary's head, slamming the replicant's face into the steering wheel. He slammed it again and again, and yet again, only twice sounding the horn.

The weaving truck swiftly lost momentum, the front tire on the port side met a curb that it barely managed to climb, and the driver stopped resisting. As the vehicle came to a full stop, the front bumper thumped gently against a lamppost. Deucalion was certain the replicant must be dead, but for insurance he got the man in a choke hold and broke his neck.

These two killings could not be called murder. True murder was strictly a crime against humanity. Except for outward appearances, these specimens from Victor's current laboratory were not human in any sense. Abominations. Monsters. Lab rats.

Deucalion felt no guilt for having terminated them, because he was, after all, another monster, the earliest model in Victor's product line. Perhaps he had been somewhat sanctified by contrition for his long-ago crimes and by his centuries of suffering. He might even be a monster on a sacred mission, although still in essence a monster, a product of Victor's hubris, created from the bodies of hanged criminals as an affront to God.

He could be as brutal and ruthless as any of his maker's newer creations. If the war against the natural world had begun, humanity would need a monster of its own to have any hope of survival.

Leaving the corpse behind the wheel, Deucalion got out of the truck. Even in the breathless night, the storm still seemed to qualify as a blizzard, so thickly did the snow fall.

Suddenly, it seemed to him that the flakes of falling snow did not take light from the streetlamp but, instead, were illuminated from within their crystalline structures, as if they were shavings of the lost moon, each filled with its measure of the lunar glow. The longer that Deucalion lived, the more magical he found this precious world.

Russell Street, a secondary thoroughfare, was deserted, free of both other traffic and pedestrians. No shops were open in this block. But a witness might appear at any moment.

Deucalion walked back along the tire tracks and stopped beside the individual whom he had thrown from the truck. In spite of its crushed throat, the lab rat still tried to draw breath and clawed at the tire-compacted snow in a feeble attempt to drag itself onto its knees. With the hard stamp of a boot to the back of its neck, he put an end to the creature's suffering.

He carried the corpse to the truck and opened the rear door. The cargo space was empty; the next batch of luckless people destined for extermination had not yet been collected. He tossed the body into the truck.

He pulled the driver from the cab, carried him to the back of the vehicle, threw him into the cargo box with the other corpse, and closed the door.

Behind the steering wheel, he started the engine. He backed the truck away from the lamppost, off the curb, into the street.

The display screen in the dashboard brightened with a map of a small portion of Rainbow Falls. A blinking red GPS indicator showed the current position of the truck. A green line traced a route that the driver was evidently meant to follow. At the top of the screen were the words TRANS-PORT #3 SCHEDULE. Beside those words, two boxes offered options, one labeled LIST, the other MAP. The second box was currently highlighted.

Deucalion pressed a forefinger to LIST. The map vanished from the screen, and an assignment list appeared in its place. The third address was highlighted—THE FALLS INN—at the corner of Beartooth Avenue and Falls Road. Evidently that would have been the truck's next stop.

Along the right side of the touch screen, in a vertical line, were five boxes, each labeled with a number. The 3 was highlighted.

When Deucalion put a forefinger to the 1, the list on the screen was replaced with a different series of addresses. The legend at the top now read TRANSPORT #1 SCHEDULE.

Here, too, the third line was highlighted. The two-man crew of Transport #1 had evidently successfully collected the people at the first two addresses and perhaps conveyed them to their doom. Their next stop appeared to be KBOW, the radio station that served not only Rainbow Falls but also the entire surrounding county.

Having replaced the employees of the telephone company with identical replicants earlier in the evening, thereby seizing control of all land-line phones and cell-phone towers, Victor's army would next take control of KBOW, preventing the transmission of a warning either to residents of the town or to the people in the smaller surrounding communities.

Deucalion switched to MAP and saw that the radio station was on River Road, toward the northeastern end of the city limits, about two miles from his current position. Transport #1 was scheduled to arrive there in less than four minutes to collect KBOW's evening staff. This suggested that the assault on the radio station might already have begun. If the route he followed to KBOW was the one that the truck's navigation system recommended, the show would be over by the time he arrived there.

He opened the driver's door, swung out of the truck—and stepped from Russell Street onto the radio-station parking lot.

chapter **3**

Mr. Lyss drove around going nowhere in the snow while he tried to think what to do next. Nummy O'Bannon rode with him, going to the same nowhere, because Nummy didn't drive but he was good at riding.

Nummy felt kind of bad about riding in this car because Mr. Lyss stole it, and stealing was never good. Mr. Lyss said the keys were in the ignition, so the owner wanted anyone to use it who might need it. But they had hardly gone a mile before Nummy realized that was a lie.

"Grandmama she used to say, if you

can't buy what somebody else has or either make it for your own self, then you shouldn't keep on always wanting it. That kind of wanting is called envy, and envy can make you into a thief faster than butter melts in a hot skillet."

"Well, excuse me for being too damn stupid to build us a car from scratch," Mr. Lyss said.

"I didn't say you was stupid. I don't call nobody names. That's not nice. I been called enough myself."

"I like calling people names," Mr. Lyss said. "I get a thrill out of it. I *delight* in calling people names. I been known to make little children cry, the names I call them. Nobody's going to tell me I can't do something that gives me so much innocent pleasure."

Mr. Lyss wasn't as scary as he looked earlier in the day. His short-chopped gray hair still stood out every which way, like it was shocked by all the mean thoughts in his head. His face was squinched as if he just bit hard into a lemon, his eyes were as dangerous-blue as gas flames, shreds of dry skin curled on his cracked lips, and his teeth were gray. He seemed like he could get along fine without food or water, just so he had his anger to feed on. But some of the scary had gone out of him. Sometimes you could almost like him.

Nummy was never angry. He was too dumb to be angry. That was one of the best things about being really dumb, so dumb they didn't even make you go to school: You just couldn't think about anything hard enough to get angry over it.

He and Mr. Lyss were an odd couple, like odd couples in some movies that Nummy had seen. In those kind of movies, the odd-couple guys were always cops, one of them calm and nice, the other one crazy and funny. Nummy and Mr. Lyss weren't cops at all, but they were really different from each other. Mr. Lyss was the crazy and funny one, except that he wasn't that funny.

Nummy was thirty, but Mr. Lyss must be older than anyone else who was still alive. Nummy was pudgy and round-faced and freckled, but Mr. Lyss seemed to be made mostly of bone and gristle and thick skin with a million creases in it like some beat-up old leather jacket.

Sometimes Mr. Lyss was so interesting you couldn't stop looking at him, kind of like in a movie when the little red numbers were counting down on the bomb clock. But at other times, staring at him too much could wear you out, and you had to turn away to give your eyes a rest. The snow was soft and cool to look at, floating down through the dark like tiny angels all in white.

"The snow's real pretty," Nummy said. "It's a pretty night."

"Oh, yeah," Mr. Lyss said, "it's a magical night, breathtaking beauty everywhere you look, prettier than all the prettiness in all the pretty Christmas cards ever made—except for the ravenous monster Martians all over town *eating people faster than a wood-chipper could chew up a damn potato*!"

"I didn't forget them Martians," Nummy said, "if that's what they are. But the night's pretty anyway. So what do you want to do, you want to drive out to the end of town, maybe see are the cops and the roadblock still there?"

"They're not cops, boy. They're monsters pretending to be cops, and they'll be there till they've eaten everyone in town."

Although Mr. Lyss drove slowly, sometimes the back end of the car fishtailed or it slid toward one curb or the other. He always got control again before they hit anything, but already they needed a car with tire chains or winter tires.

If Mr. Lyss stole another car, one with tire chains, and if Nummy went with him, knowing from the start it was stealing, he would probably be a thief himself. Grandmama raised him, so the bad things he did would bring shame on her in front of God, where she was now.

Nummy said, "You don't really know the monster cops are still there till you go look."

"I know, all right."

"How do you know?"

"Because I'm a freaking genius," Mr. Lyss said, spraying spit, gripping the steering wheel so hard that his knuckles looked as sharp as knives. "I just *know* things, my brain is so damn big. Back there in jail this morning, we hadn't known each other two minutes till I knew you were a dummy, didn't I?"

"That's true," Nummy admitted.

On the cross street ahead of them, a police car passed south to north, and Mr. Lyss said, "This is no good. We'll never get out of town in a car. We've got to find another way."

"Maybe we could go out the same way you come in. I always wanted to take me a ride on a train."

"A cold, empty boxcar isn't the glamorous fun it sounds like. Anyway, they'll have the train yard covered."

"Well, we can't fly."

"Oh, I don't know," Mr. Lyss said. "If your skull is as hollow as it seems to be, I could tie a basket to your feet, blow hot air up your nose, and ride you out of here like you were a big old balloon."

For a block or so, Nummy thought about that as the old man switched on the defroster and as the windshield, which had started to cloud at the edges, became clear once more. Then he said, "That don't make no sense unless it was just you being mean."

"You may be right."

"I don't know why you have to be mean."

"I do it well. A man likes to do something if he's good at it."

"You aren't as mean to me now as you was at first, back when we just met."

After a silence, Mr. Lyss said, "Well, Peaches, I have my ups and downs. Nobody can be a hundred percent good at something 24/7."

Mr. Lyss sometimes called him Peaches. Nummy wasn't sure why.

"A couple times," Nummy said, "I even sort of thought maybe we was getting to be friends."

"I don't want any friends," Mr. Lyss said. "You take a Kleenex and blow that thought out of your head right now. Blow it out like the snot it is. I'm a loner and a rambler. Friends just weigh a man down. Friends are nothing but enemies waiting to happen. There's nothing worse in this world than friendship."

"Grandmama she always said friendship and love is what life is all about."

"You just reminded me there *is* one thing worse than friendship. Love. Nothing will bring you down faster than love. It's poison. Love kills."

"I don't see no way that's true," Nummy said.

"Well, it is true."

"No, it's not."

"Don't you call me a liar, boy. I've torn the throats out of men who called me a liar.

I've cut their tongues out and fried them with onions for breakfast. I'm a dangerous sonofabitch when I'm riled."

"I didn't say liar. You're just wrong about love, just wrong is all. Grandmama loved me, and love never killed me."

"*She's* dead, isn't she?"

"Love didn't kill her, it was the sickness. If I could've took her cancer into me and then died for her, I'd be dead now, and she'd be alive here with you."

They rode in silence for a minute, and then Mr. Lyss said, "You shouldn't always listen to me, boy, or take what I say too seriously. Not everything I say is genius."

"Probably most of it is, but not what you said just now. You know what? Maybe we could skidoo."

"Could what?"

"You know, like a snowmobile."

Mr. Lyss steered the car carefully to the curb and stopped. "We could go overland. But is there enough snow for that? It's like an inch on the ground."

"Deeper than an inch," Nummy said, "and lots more coming fast."

"Where would we get a snowmobile?"

"People they have them all over town.

And then there's the snowmobile place they sell them over on Beartrack."

"Another damn street with *bear* in its name. Whoever named the streets in this godforsaken jerkwater had about as much imagination as a stump."

"Like I said, there's a bunch of bears in the general area. We don't got no tigers or zebras to name our streets after."

The old man sat quietly for maybe two minutes, just watching the snow fall, as if he decided it was pretty, after all. This was a long silence for Mr. Lyss, who always had something to say about everything. Nummy was usually okay with people being silent with each other, but this much quiet from Mr. Lyss was worrisome because it made Nummy wonder what he was scheming.

Finally, Mr. Lyss said, "Peaches, you actually know anyone who has a snowmobile?"

"I know a couple."

"Like who?"

"Like the Boze."

"Boze?"

"Officer Barry Bozeman. People call him the Boze. He races off-road all year 'round in one or another thing."

"Officer?"

"He's a policeman. He laughs a lot. He makes you feel you're as good as anyone."

"He's dead," Mr. Lyss said bluntly. "If he's a cop, they killed him and replaced him with one of their lookalikes."

Nummy should have known the Boze was dead, because even the police chief, Rafael Jarmillo, was one of the aliens, so every cop was for sure one of them, too. All the real police were dead and eaten like happened that morning to all the people in the jail cells next to the one from which Nummy and Mr. Lyss escaped.

Grandmama always said no matter how sad something was, still you needed to keep in mind that you would be happy again someday, and you needed to go on. Going on was important, she said, going on and being happy and doing the right thing, because if you went on long enough and were happy enough and did the right thing often enough, you would get to go live with God. But God really didn't like quitters.

"Is he married?" Mr. Lyss asked.

"Is who?"

"Tarnation, boy, there's so much vacant space in your head, you should rent it out, there's a whole damn *warehouse* full of empty racks between your ears. The Boze! Who else would I be asking about? Is the Boze married?"

"Kiku her head blowed up, she went to quiet, and it just buzzed away, so you never know."

Mr. Lyss made a big bony fist, and Nummy flinched because he thought Mr. Lyss was going to hit him. But then the old man took a deep breath, opened the fist, patted Nummy's shoulder, and said, "Maybe you could say that again but in English this time."

Puzzled, Nummy said, "That there was English."

"Tell it to me in different English."

"I only know but one kind of English."

Mr. Lyss's knobby hand fisted again, but he still didn't hit Nummy. He brought the fist to his mouth, and he chewed on a knuckle for a while, and then he said, "What is Kiku?"

"That's Mrs. Bozeman, like I said. She was a nice Japanese lady."

"What did you mean—her head blew up?"

"From the bee sting on her neck. She

had the allergies but never knew till the sting. Her face they say it blowed up like a balloon."

"What do you mean—'she went to quiet'?"

"Quiet Meadows. The cemetery up on Brown Bear Road. The bee it stung and just buzzed away, but Kiku she died, so you never know."

"They have any kids?"

"The Boze and Kiku? No. That's good because now Boze is dead, too, the kids would be orphans, all sad and everything."

"No, they'd be monster food, just like the Boze was. And since he's a cop, now a monster cop," Mr. Lyss continued, "we'll be able to get at his snowmobile, because he won't be home to stop us. All the cops will be out and busy, killing people and building those cocoons like we saw and doing whatever other filthy stuff their stinking alien kind does."

"I didn't notice they stink," Nummy said.

"Oh, they stink. They stink big-time."

"Must be something wrong with my nose."

chapter 4

Behind the wheel of the Jeep Grand Cherokee, squinting through the snow, Carson O'Connor-Maddison—with Michael Maddison—cruised Rainbow Falls on a monster hunt.

Earlier, Deucalion had told them about the large unmarked panel trucks with midnight-blue cabs and white cargo sections, which were essentially on an Auschwitz mission, collecting citizens who had been forcibly subdued and delivering them to an extermination facility in a warehouse. They had found one of the trucks and had tried to take the two-man crew captive for interrogation by pretending also to be Victor's creations. But the driver quickly recognized the deception, said "You're not Communitarians," and then it was just kill or be killed.

From an earlier encounter, Carson had learned that these newest golems of Victor's were harder to take down than an ordinary man or woman but were far less tough than his previous creatures in New Orleans. She didn't know why he had stopped producing the nearly invincible specimens that he had called the New Race, unless perhaps his failure to be able to control them completely and at all times had instilled in him some fear of his own creations.

Because they couldn't think of anything else to do, they were looking now for another blue-and-white truck with the hope of being able to wound rather than kill the crew. With the right techniques of enhanced interrogation, maybe the wounded could be persuaded to reveal Victor's current center of operations.

The snow complicated the search, diminishing visibility and hampering mobility even for a four-wheel-drive vehicle. Carson was a need-for-speed driver, but these road conditions inhibited her. Snow sucked.

Carson had been born on the Bayou. She was a Louisiana girl who loved Cajun food and danced to zydeco. As a New Orleans homicide detective, she had chased down Victor Helios, aka Frankenstein, and once he and all his creations in the Big Easy were dead, she had been able to look back on the case as an exhilarating adventure. In fact, even at the height of the terror, she and her partner, Michael, now her husband, had been having fun. Police work was always fun. Taking down bad guys was the best fun there was. Guns were fun. Even being shot at was fun as long as the shooters kept missing.

They were no longer cops, they were private investigators, and they lived in San Francisco. Here in Montana, they were out of their element *and* without authority, though not without big guns, including Urban Sniper shotguns that fired slugs capable of dropping a grizzly bear. A weapon of this power was its own kind of authority. In spite of the guns and even though they were decked out in ultracool black Gore-Tex/Thermolite storm suits, the situation in Rainbow Falls was so desperate that they hadn't had a laugh since before sundown, and the prospects for fun seemed bleak.

"Snow sucks," Carson said.

"That's like the tenth time you've made that observation," Michael noted.

"Am I boring you? Is our marriage over? Do you want some woman who has nothing but good things to say about snow?"

"Actually, boring turns me on. I've had enough excitement for a lifetime. The more boring you are, the hotter I get."

"You're just barely walking the line, Johnny Cash. Better watch your ass."

In this residential neighborhood on the south side of town, the properties were half acres or larger. The evergreens soared so high that their upper branches seemed to weave into the substance of the sky, and the houses under them appeared, by contrast, to be smaller than they were. There was a Black Forest feeling here, the atmosphere of a fairy tale but one in which a troll with sinister appetites might appear at any moment. Seen through the tremulous curtain of densely falling snow, the lights of every home seemed to twinkle with a promise of mystery and magic.

One house, set farther back from the street than many of the others, on at least an acre, was the locus of considerable activity. Several pickups and SUVs were on the driveway, near the house, parked at different angles from one another, engines running and headlights set high. Exhaust vapors smoked up through the snow and pairs of bright beams tunneled the dark, pierced the storm, and revealed at various distances the fissured trunks of trees.

As there were no sidewalks or streetlamps in this neighborhood, Carson pulled onto the shoulder of the roadway and stopped to better assess the activity. A few people were standing around the cars, and a man—a mere silhouette from this distance—stood at the head of the front-porch steps as if guarding entrance to the house. The rooms were bright behind every window, and bustling figures could be glimpsed beyond those panes.

"Us or them?" Michael wondered.

Looking past him at the house, Carson said, "Hard to tell."

A sharp tap on the window in the driver's door redirected her attention. A man with a walrus mustache, wearing a Stetson and a greatcoat, had rapped the glass with the muzzle of a shotgun, which was aimed at Carson's face.

chapter 5

Transport #1 had not yet arrived when Deucalion stepped out of distant Russell Street and into the KBOW parking lot. Four vehicles were in a row to the left of the building, and a Ford Explorer stood in a no-parking zone near the front door. Judging by the steam rising from the falling snow that melted on the hood of the Ford, the engine of the SUV had been switched off only a moment earlier.

A single-story brick building housed the radio station. The open-girder transmission tower rose behind it, topped by an array of red lights blinking high in the snowy night.

Two men, evidently from the Explorer, approached the front door. They had their backs to Deucalion, and they were unaware of him as he approached. Most likely they were Victor's people, the advance team leading the assault on the station's night staff. But he could not attack them without some evidence of their intent.

In a single step, Deucalion transitioned from the parking lot to the reception lounge beyond the front door. The lights were low, and no one manned the desk.

When he heard a key in the front door, Deucalion turned on his heel and, in the same instant, pivoted out of the lounge and into a hallway beyond a closed door. He was following the men by preceding them, which required that he guess correctly where they would go next.

At low volume, ceiling speakers carried the voice of the current on-air personality. Judging by his words and by his slight Montana accent, he must be a local talk-show host in these lower-rated hours when a nationally syndicated program would be an unwise use of prime programming.

The first door on the left was labeled MEN. Deucalion stepped into the small restroom, which smelled of pine-scented urinal cakes. He didn't switch on the light but held the door ajar an inch to watch the corridor.

He heard them enter from the reception lounge, and a moment later they passed him without glancing in his direction. They looked solemn and determined.

Farther back in the building, they opened a door, and someone in that other room said, "Warren? Didn't you go home?"

Because the lavatory door had operated soundlessly when he entered, Deucalion boldly opened it now and stepped into the hallway behind Warren and the other man. They had already disappeared into a room farther along the corridor, where the door stood wide.

The same voice that greeted Warren became suddenly alarmed—"Hey, hey, what the hell?"—and there were sounds of a struggle.

Crossing the threshold, Deucalion saw two men dressed in snow gear—the pair from the Explorer—and a third who wore jeans and a sweatshirt. The guy in jeans sat in a chair at an L-shaped control board covered with indicator lights, gauges, and switches. One of his assailants pinned him down, pressing the right side of his face hard into the board as the other man withdrew a small pistol-like instrument from a pocket of his ski jacket. That device would no doubt fire one of those silvery, round-headed needles that robbed people of their free will and that perhaps had other functions no less horrifying.

Shadow-silent, Deucalion moved, surprising this drone from Victor's hive. He seized the wrist of the hand that held the brain probe, broke fingers as if they were breadsticks, twisted the weapon out of the other's grip, jammed the muzzle to the replicant's temple, and pulled the trigger.

Face-to-face, Deucalion saw the drone's pupils briefly widen, then shrink to pinpoints, as if the room lights had first dimmed and then flared brighter than the sun. He collapsed to the floor no less emphatically than if the glimmering bead on his temple had possessed the mass of a boulder, bearing him down.

Reacting perhaps more quickly than would the average human being but as a tortoise to a hare when compared to Deucalion, the second drone released the engineer whose face he'd slammed into the control board. He reached into a pocket of his ski jacket. His confidence came from his programmed identity, which declared members of Victor's newest race to be superior to anyone they would ever meet. But like any ideology based upon a lie, it would fail to sustain him in a confrontation with hard reality. The hardest reality this creature would ever face was the speed and power that Deucalion had received from the strange thunderbolt that had brought him life—and far more than life—out of the storm.

Deucalion's fists were the size of sledge-hammers. Blow by brutal blow, the startled drone reeled backward. A flurry of punches to the throat crushed his airway. He gasped for breath, drew none. Without breath, he had no strength to escape a choke hold. In that vise grip, his cervical spine shattered, and he collapsed in his executioner's embrace and then out of it to the floor, as loose and limp and inanimate as a knotted mass of rags.

The first drone was not affected by the brain probe in the same way as were real people. He remained alive, twitching on the floor like a beetle with a broken shell, clawing at the carpet with his hands. Tremors rattled his teeth together. His eyes rolled wildly in their sockets. Plumes of pale blue vapor issued from his nose, not in rhythmic exhalations but in continuous streams.

Deucalion pressed one boot against the creature's neck, pinning it in place. He bore down harder, with all his weight, until a snap and crunch of vertebrae, like the click of a switch, put an end to the spastic movements and to the plumes of vapor.

When he looked up from the dead drone, he found the engineer regarding him with terror. Deucalion's size was not the only thing about him that could inspire crippling fear in even the most fearless men.

With one exception, his wounds healed rapidly, and he was never ill, but the ruined half of his face, ravaged in a confrontation with his maker centuries earlier, served as a constant reminder that he, too, was ultimately mortal. Perhaps only Victor, in all the world, had the power to destroy him, but that was a theory for which he avoided seeking proofs. The broken planes and grotesque concavities of that half of his countenance were partly concealed by an intricate tattoo in many colors, administered by a monk in a Tibetan monastery. The design was genius, distracting the eye from the grievous scars and the hideous contours over which the bright inks seemed to be in constant motion. Yet still Deucalion lived mostly in the night and shadows, because anyone could see through the tattoo to the truth if they stared long enough—just as this radio engineer saw through it.

Periodically, as well, subtle pulses of light throbbed through his eyes, as if the lightning that had brought him to life remained within him, endlessly traveling the circuits of his nerves. He had seen this phenomenon in numerous mirrors over the centuries; and even he could be disturbed by it, although not for the same reason that it spooked others.

Having been stitched together from cadavers, he sometimes wondered if the light within might be evidence that, when lightning animated him, he had been given not only his various powers but also a soul and perhaps a soul of a unique kind. Although he had come to love this intricately woven world with all its grace and beauty, he was weary of the strife that was as well an element in the weave. And he was weary of the loneliness unique to one who had not been born of man and woman. He hoped for a better world beyond this place, a realm of peace and charity . . . and perfect tenderness. But he was also *disquieted* by the possibility that he possessed a soul, because the rage and murderous violence of his early years, when he had been so bitter and confused, left him with a daunting weight of guilt from which he must be redeemed. Perhaps a realm of peace was not a reward that he could earn. His inner light might be an inevitable hellfire.

Having risen from his chair, the engineer stood in the corner formed by the L-shaped control board, regarding Deucalion as if he were indeed a demon. His round face and rubbery features would more readily shape themselves to smiles and laughter. His expression of shock and terror was so at odds with the nature of his fundamental appearance that it seemed comic, like the exaggerated look of fright that a mime might wear as he strove mightily to sell his emotion to the audience without benefit of a voice.

"They weren't human," Deucalion said. "And regardless of how I may appear, I'm not one of them. But more of them are coming, and they'll be here soon."

The engineer's mouth moved, though no sound issued from him. With both trembling hands, he gestured so aimlessly that no sign he made conveyed the slightest meaning.

"Pull yourself together, man. You've got to fight or die. There is no other choice. How many of you are in the building?"

The engineer clutched one hand with the other, as if to still them both, and when at last he spoke, his voice was unexpectedly calm. "Four. There's just four of us."

chapter 6

Jocko on the brink of greatness. In the study of the pretty little house he shared with Erika Five. Beyond the town limits of Rainbow Falls. Snow at the window.

Sometimes Jocko sat on the swiveling desk chair in front of the computer. Sometimes knelt on it. Sometimes stood on it. Stood on it and danced. Danced hard enough to make the chair spin. His red-and-green hat with silver bells jingled merrily.

Sometimes Jocko typed with his feet. Long ugly toes. Ugly but flexible and limber. Good toes for typing.

His fingers were ugly, too. Everything about his body was ugly. Even his bizarre tongue with its three hairs.

Jocko was a tumor.

Well, he *started out* as a tumorlike lump in the biologically chaotic flesh of one of Victor's New Race in New Orleans. Then he became self-aware. A tumor with attitude. Hopes and dreams. And he grew fast. Later he burst out of that host body. Became something more than a tumor. Something better.

He became a monster. Some people screamed when they saw Jocko. Others fainted. Birds dive-bombed him. Cats hissed and rats fled squeaking. Jocko was a very effective monster. Misshapen skull. Pale warty skin. Lipless slit of a mouth. Eerie yellow eyes, both too large for his head, one larger than the other.

A monster was a more respectable thing to be than a mere tumor. *Nobody* liked a tumor. What was to like? But they wrote books about monsters. Made movies about them, too. People liked some monsters as much as they feared them.

When you started out as a tumor with a brain, you had nowhere to go but up. Jocko was passionate about self-improvement. Although he had become a monster and harbored even greater aspirations, Jocko nevertheless remained humble. He never forgot where he came from. Once a tumor, always a tumor.

Somewhat taller than a dwarf, Jocko secretly wished he were six foot two. And handsome. With hair on his head instead of on his tongue. In some dreams, Jocko was not himself. In dreams, he was a movie star. Often George Clooney. Sometimes Ashton Kutcher. Once he was Dakota Fanning and knew what it must be like to be loved by everyone. He wished that he really could be a handsome male movie star. He didn't care which one, except not Johnny Depp. Johnny Depp scared Jocko.

The thought of Johnny Depp made Jocko's hands shake badly. Ugly fingers stuttered across the keys, and gibberish appeared on the screen. He took his hands off the keyboard. Slow deep breaths. Easy. Calm. Johnny Depp was at least a thousand miles away from Rainbow Falls.

Jocko wasn't just typing on the computer. Wasn't playing games. Wasn't working on Excel spreadsheets. He was *hacking.* His online path wasn't through a phone or a cable company, but through the satellite dish on the roof. Jocko was a total firewall-busting, code-breaking, backdoor-building Internet wildcatter who could drill out more data than Exxon drilled oil.

That was why he wore the red-and-green hat with silver bells. His hacking hat. He had thirteen other hats. Hats for different occasions. Jocko loved hats.

Deucalion—*monster of monsters, Victor's first-made, mentor and maven, legend!*—had entrusted Jocko with an important task. Hack into the department of motor vehicles' secured files. Find out who owned a blue-and-white truck with a certain license-plate number.

Jocko was part of the team. Needed. Maybe a hero.

In the past, Jocko had sometimes been a screwup. Washout. Flop. Failure. Fool. Moron, idiot, ninnyhammer, dumb-bunny.

But all that was behind him. Now he was going to make his mother proud of him.

Erika wasn't his biological mother. Former tumors didn't have real moms. She adopted him unofficially.

They didn't take mother-child trips to the

park. Or go into town for an ice-cream soda. On the rare occasions when people saw Jocko, they wanted right away to beat him with sticks. Sticks, umbrellas, canes, buckets, anything handy. So far, Jocko didn't seem to be one of those monsters that most people feared but also liked. For his safety, Jocko was limited to this house and the forty acres that came with it.

Erika Five, who lived now as Erika Swedenborg, was the fifth of five identical wives that Victor had grown in his creation tanks in New Orleans. The first four displeased him. They were terminated. Victor didn't believe in divorce. Erika Five also displeased him. But she escaped on the night that Victor's evil empire in Louisiana collapsed. Took a bunch of his money, too. She was the only member of his New Race to survive that catastrophe.

Suddenly Jocko peeled the final DMV passcode out of its security skin as easily as stripping a banana, and he was *in.*

"Banzai!" he cried.

He entered the truck's license-plate number. Requested the owner's ID. The information appeared on the screen.

"Huzza! Hoorah! Hooray!"

The truck was owned by a nonprofit corporation, Progress for Perfect Peace. That sounded nice. Warm and cuddly. Progress was a good thing. Perfect peace was a good thing. Even a monster with lemon-yellow eyes and virtually no proper moral upbringing could see what good things they were.

Progress for Perfect Peace had an address. In Rainbow Falls. Jocko printed it.

After he backed out of the DMV, he looked for a Progress for Perfect Peace website. Wasn't one. That seemed peculiar. Suspicious. A charity ought to have a website. Everyone had a website.

Even Jocko had a website: www.jocko thinksaboutlife.com. When he had an important insight about life, he posted it there. Maybe his thoughts could help other people. Just a few days ago he had posted: *All muffins are tasty, but some are tastier than others—which isn't an insult to the lesser muffins, it's just the way life is. I like mine with jelly.*

Jocko checked public records for Montana corporations. No need to hack them. Progress for Perfect Peace, Inc., had an address. It matched the one from the DMV.

The CEO was Victor Leben. The name was no coincidence. Victor Frankenstein. Then Victor Helios. Now Victor Leben. *Victor.*

"Holy moly!"

On the screen, the *o* in *Victor* seemed to be an eye. Watching Jocko. Victor would know Jocko found him. Victor knew everything.

Jocko was wearing a T-shirt bearing the image of Buster Steelhammer, the greatest star in the history of World Wrestling Entertainment. The shirt usually made him feel brave. Not now.

The *o* in *Victor.* Watching. Impossible. But Victor could do anything. Victor was omniscient.

Bad. Very bad. Terrible. *Catastrophe!* Jocko suddenly became supercharged with negative energy. Nerves wound tight. Heart swelling with fear. Work it off, work it off. *Dance! Dance!* Jocko sprang to his feet on the chair. He danced desperately. The chair spun. Victor watched through the *o* in his name, somehow, some way, watched.

Dancing, spinning, watched by Victor, Jocko was as good as dead. Jocko was a dead monster dancing.

chapter 7

Behind the wheel of his Land Rover, Dagget followed a serpentine course through Rainbow Falls, hoping his lawman's intuition inspired the many turns he made. He suspected that he was probably guided by nothing more than whim.

In the passenger seat, Frost studied his laptop. On the screen, a blinking red dot on a partial map of the town revealed the current location of the patrol car driven by Rafael Jarmillo, the chief of police. The day before, they had secretly affixed a transponder to Jarmillo's vehicle, and thereafter they had monitored his movements.

Since the previous morning, the chief had visited a lot of places around town, only one of them with any apparent law-enforcement connection.

"Yeah," Frost said, "he's not just paused at Montana Power and Light. It's a full stop."

The Land Rover was fitted out with a police scanner, but Dagget and Frost no longer bothered to listen to it. More than twelve hours earlier, Chief Jarmillo and his men stopped using a common ten-code that any cop anywhere might understand, and began to use a code of their own creation. Frost had tried to crack it with his computer, but he had failed. The portions of the police transmissions that weren't in this code were crisp statements, revelatory of nothing.

"You want to go to the power company?" Frost asked. "See what's happening?"

"What I'm thinking is, while the chief is out and about, maybe we stop by his house, have a little chat with his wife."

Dagget and Frost, who had been in town three days, were agents with a unit of the FBI so secret that it was unknown even to the director of the bureau. They believed something was badly wrong in

Rainbow Falls, but they didn't have any clue what it might be. The whistle-blower who had alerted them to the situation knew only that during the past couple of years, enormous money had gone into some operation in this burg, channeled to a nonprofit named Progress for Perfect Peace. The sum was so huge—the funds laundered through so many accounts before arriving here—that it suggested a criminal enterprise of extraordinary proportions.

And this past afternoon, from their unit boss, Maurice Moomaw in D.C., they had learned that the Moneyman, source of those funds, was scheduled to arrive somewhere in the Rainbow Falls area the following day. Weather permitting, he would come in by helicopter from Billings. The Moneyman was a high-profile individual. If he was making a personal appearance, the conspiracy—whatever the hell it might entail—must be approaching one critical point or another.

"Talk to Jarmillo's wife?" Frost didn't like the idea. "I'm not ready yet to drop our cover."

"I didn't say we'd flash bureau ID. We snow her with some story just to see what she might say, just to get a look in the house."

Frost shook his head. "I'm not a good bullshit artist."

"You've seen me in action. I can produce more than a herd. You just stand there smiling and nodding, leave the rest to me."

Frost considered the blinking light on the laptop map and then gazed through the windshield at the falling snow. All day, the atmosphere in Rainbow Falls had been strange, disquieting. He could not say why. The behavior of the police suggested they were engaged in some secret and perhaps illegal activity, but that alone wasn't what made him so deeply uneasy. For the past several hours, he had sensed that the apparent normalcy of Rainbow Falls was a deception, as though the quaint and pretty town were only a hyper-realistic painting on a stage curtain, which at any moment would be swept aside to reveal a different municipality of strange and hideous structures in a state of advanced decay, narrow twisted streets, and in every shadow some creeping feral thing without a name.

Now, as the town succumbed to the bleaching snow, it seemed not to be vanishing beneath a shroud that would later be drawn aside by the restorative sun, but seemed instead to be fading entirely from the world. As if, when the snow eventually melted away, Rainbow Falls would be gone as though it had never existed.

Frost was not a man who spooked easily. Until now, he'd never had the kind of imagination that made hobgoblins out of shadows and sensed boogeymen around every corner. The problem wasn't him. The problem was Rainbow Falls. Something was very wrong with this place.

"All right," he said. "Let's go have a chat with Jarmillo's wife."

chapter 8

In addition to the guy in the Stetson and the greatcoat, two other men materialized out of the night and snow. They were also armed with shotguns.

Carson and Michael had their Urban Snipers as well as pistols, but seated in the Grand Cherokee, they were not in a position to survive an exchange of fire.

To Michael, she said, "I could shift gears, tramp the gas."

"Bad idea. I didn't take my invincibility pill this morning."

"Then what do we do?"

"Whatever they want us to do," Michael said.

"That's pussy talk. We're not pussies."

He said, "Sometimes you're too macho for your own good."

The guy with the walrus mustache rapped on her window again with his gun barrel. He looked as if he had been constipated since birth. When she smiled at him, his scowl curdled into a glower.

Carson thought of Scout, her baby, not seven months old, back in San Francisco, in the expert care of Mary Margaret Dolan, housekeeper and nanny. Her little daughter had a smile that could melt glaciers. With Scout in her mind's eye, Carson was overcome by a dread that she would never see the girl again.

Switching off the engine, she said, "They'll make a mistake. We'll get an opening."

"'All is for the best in this best of all possible worlds.'"

"Who said that?"

"I don't know. One of the Muppets. Maybe Kermit."

They opened their doors and got out

of the SUV, raising their hands to show that they were not armed.

The cowboy with the walrus mustache warily stepped back from Carson, as if she were the biggest and meanest piece of work that he had ever seen. His face suggested fearlessness, but his quick shallow inhalations, revealed by rapid frosty exhalations, further belied his fierce expression. He directed her toward the front of the Grand Cherokee.

One of the other gunmen shepherded Michael from the passenger door and told him to stand beside Carson. This one wore a Stetson, too, and a leather coat with sheepskin collar. The cold air revealed his breathing to be less agitated than that of the other man. But his restless eyes, shifting from Carson to Michael and to various points in the night, revealed the fear that he was striving not to disclose.

These were not Victor's creations. They were real men with some reason to know that horrific events were occurring behind the scenes in this apparently peaceful Montana night.

The third man, who quickly searched the SUV, appeared with both his shotgun and one of the Urban Snipers. "They have another of this here. Never seen its like before. Pistol grip. And it seems to be loaded with big slugs, not buckshot. They have two pistols and a satchel full of spare magazines and shotgun ammo."

The second cowboy looked to the one with the mustache. "What you want to do, Teague?"

Teague indicated the Urban Sniper and said to Michael, "You want to explain that cannon Arvid is holding?"

"It's police-issue. Not available to just anyone."

"You're police?"

"We used to be."

"Not around here."

"New Orleans," Michael said.

"Used to be—but you still have a police-only gun."

"We're sentimental," Michael said.

Teague said, "Ma'am, you handle a weapon that powerful?"

"I can handle it," Carson said. "I can handle you."

"What kind of police were you?"

"The best. Detectives. Homicide."

"You come right at folks, don't you?"

"Fewer misunderstandings that way," Carson said.

Teague said, "I have a wife like you."

"Get on your knees and thank God for that lady every night."

Most people weren't as bold at eye-to-eye contact as Teague. His stare was scalpel-sharp. Carson could almost hear her stare ringing off his with a steely sound.

"What're you doing, anyway, riding around all gunned up?" Arvid asked.

Carson glanced at Michael, he raised his eyebrows, and she decided to go with a little bit of the truth, to see how it played. "We're on a monster hunt."

The three cowboys were quiet, weighing her words, glancing at one another. The soft silent snow coming down, breath smoking in the cold air, the great dark trees slowly fading to white all along the street . . . Their quiet reaction to her strange statement suggested they had experienced something that made a monster hunt seem as reasonable as any other activity.

"What have you seen?" she asked.

To his pals, the nameless cowboy said, "They have guns. That means they must be like us. They need guns."

"Clint's right," Arvid said. "Those killing machines don't need guns. We saw what they can do without guns."

Michael said, "Machines?"

Unlike Arvid and Clint, Teague hadn't lowered his shotgun. "They looked like real people, but they weren't. There was a Terminator feel to them but even weirder."

"Space aliens," Arvid declared.

"Worse than that," Carson said.

"Don't see what could be worse."

Teague said, "Ma'am, are you telling us you know what they are?"

"We should get off the street to discuss it," Carson suggested. "We don't know what might come along at any time. Clint's right—you and us, we're on the same side."

"Probably," Teague said.

She indicated the house set deep in the trees and all the parked cars in the driveway, their headlights aimed in different directions. "Seems you expect to have to defend the place. The wife you mentioned—is she over there?"

"She is."

"What's her name?"

"Calista."

"I bet Calista would make up her mind

about Michael and me five times faster than you. She must want to kick your butt sometimes, how long you take to make up your mind."

"I'm deliberate. She likes that."

"She'd have to."

They engaged in another staring contest, and after a half smile jacked up one corner of his mouth, Teague lowered his shotgun. "Okay, arm yourselves. Come with me, let's swap information, see if we can all come out of this thing alive."

Arvid returned the Urban Sniper.

Michael settled into the passenger seat of the Grand Cherokee as Carson climbed behind the steering wheel again. By the time she switched on the headlights, Arvid and Clint had returned to their sentry posts, vanishing into the snow and shrubbery.

She drove forward along the shoulder of the road and turned right into the driveway, following Teague, who had already walked halfway to the house.

As she parked behind the last SUV in the caravan, Carson realized there were more vehicles ahead of her than she had first thought, at least a dozen. The property was bigger than it appeared from the street. The single lane of blacktop curved past the house to a low building, perhaps a combination garage and workshop.

When she got out of the Jeep, she heard the engines of some of the other vehicles idling, those that brightened the snowy night with their headlights. Here and there, in the shadows between the cars, men stood in pairs, quiet and vigilant.

Crossing the yard to the front porch, Carson said to Teague, "Are these people your neighbors?"

"No, ma'am," Teague said. "We belong to the same church. We were at our family social, which we hold once a month out at the roadhouse Mayor Potter owns, when these aliens—or whatever they are— attacked us. We lost three good people. No kids, though, thank the Lord."

"What church?" Michael asked.

"Riders in the Sky Church," Teague said as they reached the porch steps. "Our folks who died earlier—we reckon they all rode heavenly horses through the gates of Paradise tonight, but that's not as fully consoling as it ought to be."

chapter 9

Nancy Potter, wife of the mayor of Rainbow Falls, was at first displeased by the arrangement of twenty-six porcelain figurines that stood on three shelves in a glass display case in the Potter living room. Over the period of an hour, her displeasure became annoyance, which grew into anger, which escalated into rage. If the porcelain figurines had been real people, she would have killed them all; she would have gutted them and torn their heads off and set their remains on fire.

If the real Nancy Potter had not been dead, *this* Nancy Potter would have beaten

her to death just for having bought the figurines in the first place. Three shelves with
twenty-six porcelains simply could not be
balanced and pleasing to the eye. For one
thing, the closest she could come to having the same number on each shelf was
nine, nine, eight. For another thing, the
ideal number per shelf, to ensure that the
display case would look neither too empty
nor too crowded, was twelve. She could
make it look acceptable with eleven per
shelf, but that still left her seven figurines
short. The real Nancy Potter clearly had
no awareness of the necessity for symmetry in all things, for order and balance.

Every Communitarian understood that
perfect symmetry, absolute order, balance,
and conformity were important principles.
There were numerous important principles,
none more important than the others: unde-
viating focus, efficiency, unconditional equal-
ity, uniformity, obedience to the Community's
Creator, the embrace of cold reason and the
rejection of sentimentality. . . .

The real Nancy Potter had been a typical human being, poorly focused, inefficient. And talk about sentimental! These
twenty-six porcelain figurines were angels.

During the hour that the replicant Nancy spent striving to bring symmetry to the display, she had become increasingly disgusted not only with the disorder, but also with all these mawkish, maudlin, insipid, inane angels in their infuriatingly stupid poses of stupid simpering adoration and stupid self-righteous piety. They were an affront to reason, an insult to intelligence, and an offense against efficiency. If the real Nancy Potter had been here, Communitarian Nancy would have beaten her to death but not until she crammed every one of these stupid porcelain angels down the stupid woman's throat or in some other stupid orifice.

Exasperated, she dropped two of the angels on the floor and stomped on them until they were worthless debris. This left twenty-four figurines, eight per shelf: balance. They were still angels, however, and the shelves looked too empty to please the eye. She plucked two more porcelains from the display and threw them on the floor and stomped on them, stomped, and then two more, and yet two more. Destroying these schmaltzy gimcracks gave her intellectual satisfaction, *immense* satisfaction, smashing such crass symbols of blithering ignorance. She despised them, these loathsome little winged totems, she hated them, and she hated the foolish human being who had collected them. They needed to die, every last clueless human being needed to be exterminated, because with them would die their idiot fantasies, their moronic, witless, irrational, dull, obtuse, foolish, imbecilic, puerile beliefs and ideas and hopes. Every last preening, self-deluded man, woman, and child needed to die—especially the children, they were the worst, those filthy excretions of an unthinkably messy biological process—they all needed to be stomped, stomped, *smashed, pulverized, GROUND INTO MEAT PASTE!*

From the archway between the living room and the downstairs hall, Ariel Potter said, "You aren't obsessing, are you?"

This was not the real Ariel, who had been fourteen years old. That Ariel was dead. This Ariel was blond and blue-eyed like the other; but she had been programmed and extruded little more than nine days earlier.

"Because if you're obsessing, I have to report you to our Creator. He'll have to recall you."

Members of the Community were as efficient and as focused as machines. Efficiency equaled morality; inefficiency was the only sin their kind could commit. The sole thing that could render one of them inefficient was obsession, to which a few of their kind were prone. Not many. The tendency to obsession was easily recognized by Hive technicians within three days of a Communitarian's extrusion. The techs identified 99.9 percent of these flawed specimens and dissolved them back into the mother mass from which all of their kind were created. After each crop of Communitarians was tested, the chances of an obsessive making it out of the Hive were virtually nil.

Nevertheless, a single such individual, operating in the world beyond the Hive, might malfunction to such an extent that it would not pass for human. Therefore, each undetected obsessive might expose the existence of the Communitarian race and might alert humanity to the secret war being waged against them.

"I'm not obsessing," Nancy said.

Ariel regarded her with a bland, nonjudgmental expression, for they were absolute equals. "Then what are you doing?"

"I'm eliminating clutter and bringing order to this hideously disordered house."

Ariel surveyed the shattered porcelains littering the floor. "This doesn't look like order to me. Where am I mistaken?"

With a sweeping gesture, Nancy indicated the remaining angels on the shelves, and then her open hand became a tightly clenched fist that she shook at them. "First I have to destroy these stupid icons. That's only logical. They're insipid symbols of unreason and disorder. After I utterly and finally and forever destroy these repulsive, despicable, detestable icons, I will of course sweep up every shard, scrap, splinter, every trace of dust, and the living room will then be ordered, serene, immaculate."

Ariel studied Nancy in silence for half a minute and then said, "Isn't using excessive adjectives and adverbs an indication of an obsession disorder?"

Nancy mulled over the question. Intellectual vigor and honesty were expected of Communitarians in relationships with one another. Smashing the angels had made her feel quite vigorous. "In this case it's only an indication of the intensity of my focus on the task. I am totally focused more sharply than an astronomical telescope, than a laser."

After a moment of consideration, Ariel said, "I've eaten almost everything in the refrigerator and half of what's in the pantry. I'm still hungry. I think the problem is that I'm *hungry to begin.* I want to go out to the barn and become what I am."

"But you're phase two," Nancy said. "You aren't scheduled to begin your work until Saturday, when all the humans in town are dead and we have full, unchallenged control."

Ariel nodded. "But I think I'm like you. I'm so focused like a laser, so dedicated to the mission, so eager to proceed efficiently, that it makes no sense to wait. Logic tells me to act with reason, reason tells me to proceed only with good cause, and I've got a good cause, which is that I can't wait any longer, I just can't, I can't, it's sheer torture to wait, excruciating, I've got to do it, got to become what I am meant to be, tonight, now, *right now*!"

For twelve seconds, Nancy deliberated over Ariel's presentation of her case. Like all Communitarians, a thousand-year calendar and clock were part of her program, and she always knew the precise time to the second, without need of a wristwatch.

Nancy said, "Timeliness is part of efficiency. If you're able to perform your duties earlier than scheduled, that just means you're even more efficient than you were designed to be."

"My readiness, ahead of schedule," Ariel said, "is proof of our Creator's genius."

"He is the greatest genius who ever lived. And my inability to tolerate these stupid, stupid, stupid freaking angels is proof of my commitment to the Community."

"For the Community," Ariel said.

Nancy replied, "For the Community."

"Will you come with me to the barn now?"

"Let me smash the rest of these first."

"All right, if you have to."

"I have to. I really need this. Then I'll assist you with your becoming."

"Just hurry," Ariel said. "I have my needs, too. I need to be in the barn, becoming. I need it so bad I feel like I'll explode if I don't get it really soon."

The Communitarians were produced asexually, manufactured rather than conceived. They had no sexual capacity or desire. But Nancy was pretty sure that what she was feeling now must be similar to what great sex was like for human beings: a powerful tidal rush of energy that shuddered through her entire body, and with the energy came a pure black hatred of all humanity and of all living things not made in the Hive, a hatred so intense and so hot that she half thought she would burst into a pillar of fire, and with the energy and the hatred came a beautiful vision of a dead world that was scourged and silent and stripped of meaning.

Nancy swept the remaining porcelain figurines from the glass display shelves. She stomped on them, one after the other, stomped and ground them under her heels and kicked at the fragments. She snatched up an angel head and threw it across the room with such force that a sharp piece of the broken neck lodged in the Sheetrock. The glazed and haloed head, big as a plum, stared down at her as if with astonishment, like the head of a trophy deer mounted on a hunter's wall. Stomping, grinding, kicking, Nancy suddenly became aware that she was shrieking with a kind of furious delight, her shrill cries echoing off the living-room walls, and the wild sound empowered her, thrilled her.

Ariel must have been thrilled, too, because she took a single step past the archway, into the room, and stood shrieking along with Nancy. She raised her fists and shook them, and she threw her head back and forth, whipping her shoulders with her long blond hair. Her eyes were bright with intelligence and reason. Her voice was strong and clear with intelligence and reason. She wasn't usurping Nancy's moment, but rather encouraging her; this was a you-go-girl shriek.

chapter 10

Mr. Lyss parked at the curb and switched off the headlights, and all the bright tumbling snowflakes came down dimmer in the dark, as if the light that was turned off had been in each of them.

"You positive this is Bozeman's house?"

Nummy said, "Yes, sir. This here's just one block over from Grandmama's place, where I lived before the Martians come."

The cozy brick house was one story with white shutters at the windows. The front porch had a white painted-iron railing and white iron corner posts and what they called a baked-aluminum roof. Nummy always wondered where they found an oven to bake something as big as that roof.

"You sure he lives alone, Peaches?"

"Kiku she's dead and the kids was never born."

"How long ago did Kiku buy the farm?"

"She didn't buy no farm, it was a grave plot."

"I guess I misunderstood. How long's she been dead?"

"It might be like two years. Longer than Grandmama."

"Maybe Bozeman doesn't live alone."

"Who would he live with?" Nummy wondered.

"A girlfriend, a boyfriend, one of each, his grandmama, a damn pet alligator. How the hell should I know? The sonofabitch could live with anybody. If you used what brain you have, boy, you wouldn't ask so many dumb questions."

"The Boze lives alone. I'm pretty sure. Anyway, there's no lights on in there, so nobody's home."

"Alligators can see in the dark," Mr. Lyss said. "But come on, let's go. I want that snowmobile, and I want out of this village of the damned."

The house next door was dark, too, and there were no streetlamps. The blacktop and the lawns were covered with snow, but although that white blanket seemed like it was giving off light, it really didn't. And the falling flakes were so thick they were almost like a fog, so you couldn't see far. Even if someone might be looking out a window somewhere, he wouldn't be able to see that Mr. Lyss carried a long gun held down at his right side.

Mr. Lyss had two pistols and all kinds of extra bullets in the pockets of his big coat. He found the guns in the preacher's house that they burned down because it was full of the giant cocoons growing monsters inside. Mr. Lyss said he was going to pay for the guns with his lottery winnings—he had a ticket in his wallet with what he knew would be the right number—but Nummy had the bad feeling that Mr. Lyss really just stole them. Mr. Lyss seemed like his folks had never churched him when he was growing up.

The snow made a soft crunching sound under their feet as they walked around the house to the back porch, where they couldn't be seen from the street. Mr. Lyss didn't need his set of lock picks, because when he tried the kitchen door, it opened inward, hinges creaking.

Suddenly Nummy didn't want to go into Officer Barry Bozeman's house, not because it was wrong to go into a house when you weren't invited, but because something bad waited for them in there. He didn't know how he knew, but he knew. A sick, sliding feeling in his stomach. A tightness in his chest that prevented him from drawing deep breaths.

"Let's leave now," Nummy whispered.

"Nowhere to go," said Mr. Lyss. "And not enough time to go there."

The old man crossed the threshold, slid one hand along the wall beside the door, and switched on the lights.

When Nummy reluctantly followed Mr. Lyss, he saw the Boze in his underwear and open bathrobe, sitting in a chair at the kitchen table. The Boze's head was tipped back, his mouth hanging open, his eyes rolled back in their sockets.

"Dead," said Mr. Lyss.

Nummy knew dead when he saw it.

Even though Officer Bozeman was dead, Nummy was uncomfortable, seeing him in his underwear. He was also uncomfortable because it seemed wrong to stare at a dead person when he didn't know you were there and he couldn't tell you to get out or even make himself more presentable.

You couldn't look away from a dead person, either. Then it would seem you were *embarrassed* for him, as though it must be his fault he died.

When the dead person was someone you knew, like the Boze—or like Grandmama—you felt a little like you wanted to die yourself. But you just had to look at him anyway, because this was the last time you would see him except in photos, and photos were just photos, they weren't the person.

A silver bead glistened on the Boze's left temple, just like the beads on the faces of those zombie people in the jail cells.

All the people in jail had waited like good dogs told "Stay." And then the handsome young man had arrived and turned into an angel, but then not an angel, and then he had torn them all apart and had taken them into himself.

Nummy hoped the handsome young man didn't show up here anytime soon.

Mr. Lyss closed the back door and crossed the room, leaving clumps of snow on the vinyl floor. He peered closely at the corpse but didn't touch it.

"He's been dead awhile. At least eight or ten hours, probably longer. Probably it happened before dawn."

Nummy didn't have any idea how you could know when a person must have died, and he didn't want to learn. To learn such a thing, you'd have to see a lot of dead people and most likely examine them close, but what Nummy wanted most was *never* to see another dead person as long as he lived.

From the table, Mr. Lyss picked up a sort of gun made of shiny metal. He turned it this way and that, studying it.

On the table stood a bowl of fresh fruit: a few bananas, a pear, a couple of big apples that didn't look quite ripe. Mr. Lyss pointed the strange-looking gun at an apple and pulled the trigger. *Thhuuup!* Suddenly on the apple appeared a gleaming silvery bead just like the one on Officer Bozeman's face.

Mr. Lyss pulled the trigger again, but nothing happened. When he fired the gun a third time—*Thhuuup!*—the second apple now had a silver bead, too. The fourth time, nothing happened again.

"A two-cycle mechanism. What's it do on the second cycle?" Mr. Lyss asked.

There wasn't any kind of cycle in the kitchen, not a bicycle or a tricycle, or a motorcycle. Nummy didn't know how to answer the old man's question, and he didn't want to be snarled at again and told that he was dumb. They both knew he was dumb, he always had been, so neither of them needed to be reminded of it all the time. Nummy kept silent.

As Mr. Lyss returned the silver-bead gun to the table where he'd found it, piano music rose from the living room. The Boze had a piano. He called it an upright, so Nummy figured it originally must have been in a church or somewhere clean and holy like that, not in some barroom. Kiku played the upright, and she taught the Boze to play it, but neither of them could be playing it now, both being dead.

"Let's get out of here," Nummy said.

"No. We're in it now, boy." The old man raised his long gun. "Cowardice is often a fine thing, but there's times when it can get you killed."

Mr. Lyss went to the hallway door, which stood open. He found the light switch, and the dark hall brightened.

As Mr. Lyss stepped out of the kitchen, Nummy decided it was scarier to be alone with a dead person than it was to go see who was at the piano. He followed the old man.

The music was pretty but sad.

At the end of the hall, the living room remained dark. Nummy wondered how anyone could play a piano so well in total darkness.

chapter 11

Sammy Chakrabarty never stood around waiting for someone else to get things done. He was always moving, doing, thinking, dealing with the task of the moment but simultaneously planning ahead. He stood five ten, weighed only 130 pounds, ate enough for two men, but couldn't gain an ounce because he was so active and his metabolism was always revving.

He had been helping to adapt the current broadcast to the failure of all phone service and Internet access, which seemed to be a crisis when it happened in the middle of a talk show. Now it wasn't a crisis anymore, wasn't even a problem, considering that two men had just been killed, men or something passing for men, and KBOW had plunged into the Twilight Zone.

Sammy ran from the engineer's control room to the kitchenette, which featured a refrigerator, microwave oven, ice-maker, and coffee machine. Sammy yanked open the cabinet drawer that contained flatware and various utensils, including a few knives, and he selected the biggest and sharpest blade.

At twenty-three, Sammy was already the radio station's program director, promotion director, and community-affairs director. He lived in an inexpensive two-room apartment, drove an ancient Honda, and invested half his after-tax income, doing his own online stock trading with considerable success. His plan was to become general manager by the age of twenty-six, purchase KBOW by the time he was twenty-nine, and use it as a platform to develop groundbreaking programming that might have enough appeal to be syndicated across the country.

The extraordinary events of the past few minutes might have ramifications that would set back his plan as much as a year, perhaps even eighteen months. But Sammy Chakrabarty could not conceive of any circumstances that might delay him longer than that or thwart him altogether.

Carrying the knife, he hurried back through the building toward the engineer's nest, where the station personnel and the giant with the half-smashed face, who called himself Deucalion, stood over the bodies that looked like Warren and Andy Snyder but perhaps were not.

Ralph Nettles, their engineer, was a rock-solid guy, known for his reliability, truthfulness, and common sense. So it must be true that Warren and Andy had tried to kill him, that this tattooed stranger saved his life and was their ally, and that pale blue vapor gushed from Warren's nostrils during his death throes, as though he might be less a man than a machine in which some reservoir of coolant had been ruptured. It must be true, but everyone preferred to have a bit more confirming evidence.

In the control room, in addition to Ralph

and the giant, there were Burt Cogborn, the station's advertising salesman and ad-copy writer, and Mason Morrell, their weekday-evening talk-show host, who had switched from live chatter to a prerecorded segment that he kept on hand for emergencies like this. Well, not *exactly* like this. The kind of emergency Mason had in mind was an unexpected attack of on-air diarrhea. Everyone but the stranger looked anxious and confused.

In Sammy's absence, the body of Warren Snyder had been stripped to the waist, and his pants had been pulled down far enough to reveal his entire abdomen, sternum to groin.

"I don't know exactly what you'll see," Deucalion said, "but I'm confident it will be enough to prove this wasn't the real Warren Snyder."

The giant knelt beside the corpse and plunged the knife into it, just below the breastbone.

Mason Morrell gasped, probably not because the mutilation of the corpse shocked or dismayed him, but only for effect, to suggest that he, an on-air talent, was by nature more sensitive than those who labored behind the scenes of his show. Sammy liked Mason, though the guy was always per- forming to one degree or another, whether at the microphone or not, and he was some- times exhausting.

A thin serpent of blood slithered from the haft of the buried knife and along the pale abdomen, and for a moment the ca- daver seemed human, after all. But then Deucalion slashed to the navel and be- yond, and the illusion of humanity was cut away. The lips of the wound sagged apart, and the blood—if it was blood— proved to be confined to the surface tis- sues.

Deeper, all was strange, not the viscera of a human body. Some of the organs were the color of milk glass, others were white tinted unevenly with faint streaks of gray like the flesh of certain fish, and a smaller number were white with the mer- est suggestion of green, some smooth and slick, others textured like curds of cot- tage cheese, all of them bizarre in shape and asymmetrical. A double helix of opal- escent tubes twined through the body trunk, and a creamy fluid leaked from those that had been nicked or severed.

Throughout the body cavity lay a fine web of luminous filaments that seemed less biological than electronic, and they glowed softly even though this replicant of Warren Snyder was surely as dead as the real man that he had replaced.

Leaving the knife protruding from the body, Deucalion rose to his full height.

With a quiver of revulsion and with fear in his voice that dismayed him, Sammy Chakrabarty asked, "What is that thing?"

"It was made in a laboratory," the giant said. "Hundreds or even thousands of them are in the process of taking control of this town."

"What laboratory?" Ralph Nettles wondered. He shook his head in disbelief. "Our science isn't far enough advanced to do this."

"The proof is before your eyes," Deucalion reminded him.

Burt Cogborn stared not at the cadaver but at his wristwatch, as if his world of radio-spot sales allowed no room for a development of this magnitude, as if he might announce that he had a deadline looming and needed to return to his office to write ad copy.

"Maybe a laboratory," Ralph acceded. "But not on this planet."

"On this planet, in this state, this county," Deucalion assured them with unsettling certainty. "Who I am, who made these creatures, I'll explain soon. But first, you've got to prepare to defend the station, and warn others, both in Rainbow Falls and beyond, what's happening here."

"Defend it with what?" Mason Morrell asked. "A couple of kitchen knives? Against hundreds—maybe thousands—of these . . . these things? And they're stronger than us? Man, this isn't a movie, there's no big-screen superstar to make everything right in the third act. I can't save the world. I can't save anything but my own ass, split this place, get out of town, way out, leave it to the army."

"You won't get out," Deucalion said. "They've taken over the police, all authorities. Roads are blocked at both ends of town. They're seizing key utilities—telephones, the power company. The weather helps them because people will tend to stay at home, where their replicants can more easily find them."

"Without phones or any text-messaging

devices," Sammy said, "without the Internet, KBOW is the only efficient way to warn a lot of people."

Ralph Nettles said, "I've got guns. I . . . collect."

Sammy had always thought that the even-tempered, responsible, detail-obsessed engineer probably had a plan for every contingency from falling in love to Armageddon. Although he'd never heard Ralph say a word to suggest that he collected guns, he wasn't surprised by this disclosure, and he suspected that the collection would prove to be extensive, though just short of a quantity that would justify the use of the word *paranoid.*

"I have enough to defend this place," Ralph said. "My house is less than a mile away. I could be back here with arms and ammo to spare in . . . twenty minutes or so."

Deucalion said, "I'll go with you, and we'll be much quicker than twenty."

The front-door buzzer sounded. KBOW was locked to visitors after the reception lounge closed at five-thirty.

"That'll be Transport Number One," Deucalion said. "They think they have four zombies to collect. Wait here. I'll deal with them."

Sammy could never have imagined that the stunning revelation of the existence of the replicants and the sight of their alien innards would prove to be less startling than Deucalion's departure from the room. He, Ralph, Mason, and even half-catatonic Burt all cried out in surprise, however, when Deucalion, turning away from them, did not merely walk out of the room but *vanished* from it.

chapter 12

Two extra cushions had been added
to one of the kitchen chairs to elevate five-
year-old Chrissy Benedetto, who otherwise would have been barely chin-even
with the top of the table.

The girl needed both hands to lift her
mug of hot chocolate, and each time that
she drank, her eyes widened as if with delight at the taste.

"You make it different," she said.

"I use almond milk," said Erika, who sat
across the table from the child.

"Almond like that nut almond?"

"Yes. Exactly."

"You must squeeze real hard to get milk out of one."

"Other people do the squeezing. I just buy it at the store."

"Can you get milk out of a peanut, too?"

"I don't think so."

"Can you get milk out of a ka-chew?"

"A cashew? No, I don't think so."

"You're very pretty," Chrissy said.

"Thank you, sweetie. You're very pretty, too."

"I was the Little Mermaid at preschool. You know, last time it was Halloween."

"I'll bet you charmed all the boys."

Chrissy grimaced. "Boys. They all wanted to be scary. They were like *ick.*"

"Pretty is better than scary. Boys always figure that out, but it takes them a long time."

"I'm gonna be a princess this year. Or maybe a pig like Olivia in those books."

"I'd go with princess if I were you."

"Well, Olivia is a *pretty* pig. And really funny. Anyway, Daddy says what you look like on the outside don't matter. What matters is what you're like inside. You make good different cookies, too."

"I add pecans and coconut to the chocolate chips."

"Can you teach my mommy?"

"Sure. And I could teach you, too."

The last quality that Erika Five—now Swedenborg—should have discovered in herself was a talent for relating to and nurturing the young. Having been grown in a creation tank in the Hands of Mercy, in faraway New Orleans, having gained consciousness as an adult, she had neither parents from whom she might have learned tenderness nor a childhood during which she might have been the object of the gentle concern of others. She was created to serve Victor, to submit to him without protest, and was programmed to hate humanity, especially the young. Even then, Victor envisioned a world that would one day have no children in it, a future in which sex had no purpose other than the relief of tension, a time when the very concept of the family would have been eradicated, when the members of the posthuman New Race owed allegiance not to one another, not to any country or to God, but only to Victor.

"Mommy's in the city buying me new teddy bears," Chrissy said.

That was what Michael told her. In fact, her mother was dead.

"That stupid pretend mommy tore up my teddy bears."

The pretend mommy was the Communitarian that replaced the real Denise Benedetto. Michael had rescued Chrissy, and Carson had but moments later killed the replicant.

"Where did that pretend mommy come from, anyway?" Chrissy asked.

She seemed as fragile as a Lladró porcelain. The girl's trusting nature and her vulnerable heart brought Erika close to tears, but she repressed them.

"Well, honey, maybe it's like bad witches sometimes in fairy tales. You know, sometimes with just a spell, they make themselves look like other people."

"Pretend mommy was a bad witch?"

"Maybe. But pretend mommy is gone now and never coming back."

"Where did she go?"

"I hear they threw her in a cauldron of poison that she herself was brewing to use on other people."

Chrissy's eyes widened without benefit of hot chocolate. "That's so cool."

"She tried to turn herself into a flock of bats and fly out of the cauldron to freedom," Erika said, "but all the bats were still covered in the poison, and they just— *poof!*—turned into a cloud of mist and vanished forever."

"That's what *should* happen to bad witches."

"And that's what *did* happen. *Poof!*"

From the study, along the hallway and into the kitchen, came again the voice of Jocko in the throes of hacker excitement: *"Boom, voom, zoom! Got me the puddin', now bring me the pie!"*

Putting down her cookie, Chrissy said, "Your little boy don't sound like any little boy I ever heard."

"No, he doesn't. He's very special."

"Another plum, another plum, another plum for me! Jocko shakes the cyber tree! Ah ha-ha-ha, Ah ha-ha-ha-ha!"

"Can I meet him?"

"In just a little while, sweetheart. He's doing his homework right now."

"Boogers! Boogers! Boogers! BOOGERS! Okay, okay. Sooo . . . clip

it, flip it, jip it, nip it, rip it, tip it, whip it, aaaannnd ZIP IT! Jocko is king of the world!"

Erika said, "You remember what you told me your daddy said about the outside and inside of a person?"

"Sure."

"Well, Jocko is very pretty inside."

"I hope he likes me."

"Jocko likes everybody."

Chrissy said, "Does he like to play teatime?"

"I'm sure he'd love to play teatime."

"Boys usually don't."

"Jocko always wants to please. Honey, have you ever been afraid of something, then you discovered there was no reason to be afraid?"

Chrissy frowned, considering the question, then abruptly beamed. "Like dogs."

"Were you afraid of dogs?"

"The big ones with big teeth. Big old Doofuss next door."

"But then you got to know Doofuss better, huh?"

"He's really all sweet inside."

"And I'll bet he doesn't look scary anymore outside, either."

"He's cute now." Her right arm shot up, and she waved her hand as if she were in a schoolroom and seeking the attention of the teacher.

"What is it, sweetheart?"

"The duke. I first saw the duke, he scared me." The duke was what she called Deucalion. "But then he picked me up and he held me like you hold a baby and said close my eyes tight, and he magicked us from there to here, and he don't scare me anymore."

"You're a good girl, Chrissy. And brave. Girls can be just as brave as boys. I'm proud of you."

Along the hallway, from the study, came Jocko's voice as he continued hacking: *"Jocko spies the cake! Gonna cut him a slice! Then cut a slice twice! They bake, Jocko takes! Delicious digital data! Go, Jocko! Go, Jocko! Go, go, go, GO!"*

chapter 13

Rafael Jesus Jarmillo, chief of police, lived in a two-story American Victorian on Bruin Drive. The house featured ginger-bread moldings along the eaves of the main roof and the porch roof, as well as around the windows and the doors. It was the kind of modest but well-detailed house that, back in the day, Hollywood routinely portrayed as the home of any reputable middle-class family like Andy Hardy and his dad the judge, before moviemakers decided that the middle class was nothing but a dangerous conspiracy of dim-witted, grasping, bigoted know-nothings whose

residences in films should reveal their stu-
pidity, ignorance, boring conformity, greed,
racism, and fundamental festering evil.

Frost really liked the place.

He and Dagget had driven past the house
hours earlier, in daylight. They knew that it
was painted pale yellow with robin's-egg-
blue gingerbread, but at night, with no landscape lights, it appeared as colorless as the
snow-covered ground on which it stood.

As he parked at the curb, Dagget said,
"Wife, mother-in-law, and two kids. That
right?"

"That's what the background sheet said.
No dog. No cat. A canary named Tweetie."

Seen through the bare limbs of a tree, the
second floor lay in darkness, but lamplight
brightened every downstairs room. An oval
of leaded and beveled glass in the front
door sparkled like an immense jewel.

Frost didn't usually find Victorian houses
charming. Following Dagget along the
walkway to the porch, through the snow,
he decided this residence struck him as
inviting primarily because it looked *warm.*

If there was such a thing as reincarnation, then in a previous life, Frost must have
been a member of some loincloth-wearing

tribe in a sultry equatorial jungle—or maybe a desert iguana that spent his days on sun-baked rocks. Deep in his bones and marrow, he seemed to carry a past-life memory of extreme heat that left him not merely especially vulnerable to this Montana chill but also aggrieved by it, offended, abused.

The irony of being born into the Frost family with an intense aversion to cold was not lost on him. The mysterious power who remained hidden behind the machinery of nature expressed His sense of humor in an infinite number of ways, and Frost found the world wonderfully amusing even when he was the butt of the joke.

Dagget rang the doorbell, and they could hear the chimes inside. When no one answered, he rang again.

The draperies were not closed over the windows, and Frost moved along the porch, checking out those rooms flush with warm light. He saw no one, but in the living room, evidence of recent violence caught his attention: an overturned needlepoint chair, a figured-bronze lamp that had been knocked off an end table, a ginger-jar lamp on which the pleated-silk shade had been knocked askew, and a cracked mirror above the fireplace.

After he called Dagget's attention to these signs of a struggle, they went around to the back door, which featured four panes in the top, only half-covered by sheer curtains. On the kitchen floor lay scattered knives, a meat cleaver, a few pots and pans, and shattered dishes.

The door was locked. Dagget unzipped his ski jacket, drew his pistol, tapped the barrel hard against the glass, broke a pane, and reached inside to disengage the deadbolt.

The blanketed night and the thick falling snow muffled sound so much that Frost doubted a neighbor would have been alerted by the cracking of glass. He drew his pistol and followed Dagget into the kitchen, closing the door behind them.

The house was as silent as a dream of deafness.

Bracketing doorways, taking turns crossing thresholds, they searched the ground floor. By the time they arrived at last in the living room, they had found no one.

A cascade of sweet clear notes put an end to the creepy silence as Tweetie, in his cage, greeted them. In spite of the circumstances, Frost found the birdsong cheerful and even calming, perhaps because he was reminded of the parrots and other feathered denizens of the equatorial jungle in his past life.

"What neighborhood of Hell is this?" Dagget muttered.

Frost's attention dropped from the bright yellow bird to a furry blue bedroom slipper lying beside the overturned needlepoint chair. He required a moment to realize that the footwear was not what had inspired Dagget's question. Beyond the slipper lay a bare foot with toenails painted candy-apple red. A woman's slender foot with well-formed toes and a delicate arch. Severed at the ankle.

Severed was not the right word because it implied a blade. The flesh and bone were neither clean-cut, as they might have been if the dismembering weapon were a razor-edged sword, nor ragged and splintered, as any kind of saw would have left them. The stump looked both glazed and finely pitted, as if dissolved but simultaneously cauterized by an acid.

Dagget settled on one knee beside that grisly object, to examine it closely. He spoke in a murmur: "It's damn pale, isn't it? Skin as white as plaster. No visible surface veins or arteries. The exposed flesh . . . it's as pale as halibut. As if all the blood was sucked out of it."

Not a drop of gore marred the carpet around the foot.

Leaning closer, Dagget said, "The flesh isn't pitted exactly. It looks . . . as if it's been chewed on by a million tiny teeth."

"Don't touch it," Frost whispered.

"I don't intend to," Dagget assured him. "It's evidence."

Frost's admonition had nothing to do with a concern about contaminating evidence. The foot looked so strange that he wondered if they could be contaminated *by* it.

Although Tweetie had most likely continued to sing, for a while Frost had not been aware of the canary. The trilling notes reclaimed his attention, but instead of being cheerful, as before, they sounded thin and shrill and bleak.

"What now?" Frost wondered.

"Upstairs."

Leaving the living room through an archway, entering the foyer, they discovered part of a hand.

chapter 14

As Teague took them on a quick tour of the house—the residence of Hank and Dolly Samples—he brought them up to speed regarding what happened at the country-music nightclub earlier in the evening. Considering his certainty about the extraterrestrial identity of their adversaries, Carson wondered how she and Michael would be able to convince these people that their interpretation of events was incorrect.

The men of the Riders in the Sky Church were distributing guns and supplies of ammunition at key defense points throughout the house, fortifying and barring most windows with spaced two-by-fours that were screwed to the interior casings, allocating compact fire extinguishers that they routinely carried in their pickups and SUVs, and taking every precaution they could think of to make the house as much of a fortress as possible.

Meanwhile, the womenfolk were in the kitchen and dining room with the younger children, turning mountains of groceries, brought from other less defendable houses, into pasta salads, potato salads, and casseroles. These could be stored in both the kitchen and garage refrigerators, ready to feed on demand everyone here gathered.

Three portable generators, fueled with gasoline, were being tied into the house's electrical system to ensure refrigeration and microwave-oven availability if Rainbow Falls lost its power supply. Because the heating-oil tank had been filled only two days earlier, they could keep the furnace going for at least a month.

No one expected this war of the worlds to last anywhere near a month. Either the Lord would support humanity in the quick and utter defeat of these obviously godless invaders from a far world ruled by Satan, or this must be Armageddon. If this was in fact the final conflict, it would surely be swift because ultimate Good and ultimate Evil were clashing head-on, at last, and the latter could not endure more than a single pitched battle with the former.

After Teague delivered them to the spacious and busy kitchen to meet Dolly Samples, he went away to rejoin the guards patrolling the perimeter of the property. Although Dolly was industriously rolling out one disc of dough after another, making pumpkin pies—"End Times or not End Times, a well-made pumpkin pie lifts the heart and gives us fortitude"—she insisted on getting mugs of coffee and homemade sugar cookies for them.

Carson noticed that to one side of Dolly's pie fixings lay a .38 Colt revolver. The other women working in the kitchen were talking with one another about the recent events at the roadhouse but also sharing such mundane things as fine details of recipes and their children's latest escapades. They also had serious weapons near at hand: a SIG P245, a Smith & Wesson Model 1076, a Smith & Wesson 640

.38 Special pocket revolver, a Super Carry Pro .45 ACP from Kimber Custom Shop. . . .

They exhibited determination but no desperation, concern and diligence but no obvious fear. There were preparations to be made, work to be done, and busy hands meant busy minds that had no time for dread or despair.

The coffee tasted fabulous. The sugar cookies were divine.

"There were two kinds of these hateful creatures," Dolly explained as she returned to her pie dough. "The first looked like people we knew, and you would think they would be the worst because they're *deceivers* among us, children of the Father of Lies. But when they revealed their true nature by their actions, we could deal with them. They tried to shoot some of us, but we were faster on the draw, and they could be killed. It takes some real good shooting. One well-placed bullet, even point-blank, won't do it."

As she picked up a disc of dough and conformed it to a pie pan, Dolly glanced at a framed painting on the wall above the dinette table: Jesus in white robes and cowboy boots, riding a horse that was rearing dramatically on its hind legs. Instead of a cowboy hat, the Son of God wore a halo.

"The Lord was surely with us at Pickin' and Grinnin', or we'd all be dead now. We can't claim it was our shooting skills alone that saved us."

"But God helps those who help themselves," Michael said. "And the right gun can provide a lot of self-help."

Carson noticed with some relief that in the painting Jesus wasn't packing a pistol.

Dolly said, "The second kind of monster looks like people, too, but not ordinary people. They're as beautiful as angels. They look as good as Donny and Marie Osmond back when they were young and you just couldn't take your eyes off them."

Loreen Rudolph, to whom Carson and Michael had been introduced, was making potato salad on the kitchen island. She said, "Not that Donny and Marie have lost their looks."

Another woman, stirring a pot of boiling pasta on the stove, said, "Even when Marie got fat there for a while, she looked on her worst day five times as good as I look on my best."

"Cindy Sue, don't you go putting yourself down," Loreen said. "There's a world full of women who would give up all their teeth to look as good as you."

"All their teeth and a leg," Dolly agreed.

Michael said, "All their teeth, a leg, and an ear."

Cindy Sue blushed and said, "Oh, Mr. Maddison, you're just a terrible flattermouth."

Frowning at Michael, Dolly said, "I hope it was flattermouth and not mockery."

"It was kind of mockery," Carson said. "But that's how Michael lets people know he likes them."

"Even you, dear?"

"Especially me."

"You must love him very much, although I'd think it's still a burden."

"He's my cross to bear," Carson said.

"I've got my cross, too," Michael said.

"Sweetheart," Carson said, "your cross is you."

"Zinger!" said Loreen, and the church-women all laughed.

"Anyway," Dolly said, "Marie Osmond was more plump than fat, and now she's thin again and gorgeous. So these three angels come on the stage at the road-house, and we expect they're a music act, but then they change shape, and these silvery swarms come out of them and eat people."

Dolly's description didn't help Carson visualize the enemy.

Seeing her confusion, Farley Samples, one of Dolly's teenage sons who had been listening while he peeled carrots, stepped forward and said, "What it was—these aliens have advanced nanotechnology. The three that looked like angels, they might have been machines but they just as easy could have been animals. Say they're animals that were engineered to kill, okay? Then what they probably are . . . see, they're each like a colony of billions of tiny nanoanimals no bigger than viruses, pro-grammed to do different tasks. You follow? So they can come together and operate as one creature, each doing its own part, but they can also become a swarm of individu-als. Each tiny nanoanimal has rudimentary intelligence, a little bit of memory. But when they all come together, they pool their intel-ligence, and so when they're united, they're smarter than even a smart human being."

Beaming at Farley, his mother said, "He's always done well in science. I expect he'll be the next Bill Gates."

"Bill Gates isn't a scientist, Mom."

"Well, he's a billionaire, which is just as good."

"He didn't even graduate from college," Farley said.

"When would he have had the time?"

"Who I want to be," Farley said, "is the next Robert Heinlein. He wrote the best science fiction ever."

Recognizing Farley Samples as the instrument by which she might convince these people that the threat wasn't extraterrestrial, Carson said, "Son, nanotechnology isn't just science fiction, is it?"

"No, ma'am. It's going to be the next big thing. They're making advances every day. But our nanotechnology isn't so far along as what these ETs can do."

"Maybe it is," Carson said. "Maybe there's a secret underground lab out there somewhere along what you folks around here call the End Times Highway. Maybe I know who runs the place, and maybe Michael and I are part of a team trying to shut it down. What would you say about that?"

Farley said, "Holy—"

"Bite your tongue, boy," his mother warned.

"—macaroni," Farley finished.

Calling to a couple of the women at work in the adjacent dining room, Dolly said, "Shanona, Vera—the best way for Carson and Michael to understand what we're up against is to show them your video."

Shanona Fallon and Vera Gibson came into the kitchen with their cell phones, with which they had been taking video of the stunningly beautiful young woman at Pickin' and Grinnin' when suddenly she had turned into a death machine that bored through Johnny Tankredo's face and then seemed to dissolve and absorb him entirely.

Michael, being Michael, said, "Holy macaroni."

Carson said nothing, because if she had put her thoughts into words, she could only have said, *We're dead.*

chapter 15

Mr. Lyss switched on the living-room lights, and Nummy saw the Boze sitting at the upright piano, playing sad music.

The real Officer Barry Bozeman was dead in the kitchen in his underwear and bathrobe. If Mr. Lyss was right, this was like a Martian Xerox of the Boze.

The Xerox didn't react to the lights coming on. He just kept making music.

Holding his long gun out in front of him, Mr. Lyss crept closer to the piano player, but not dangerously close. Mr. Lyss was bold but he wasn't dumb.

Nummy stayed farther back and ready

to run. He was dumb, all right, but not dumb enough to think he might not have to run.

"You," Mr. Lyss said sharply. When the Xerox didn't respond to him, the old man said, "Hey, you sonofabitch Martian ass-wipe, what're you doing?"

The music was so sad it made Nummy want to cry. It was that kind of music in movies when a young mother is dying of cancer and they bring her little children one at a time to her bed for good-byes, and the kids' daddy is coming home from war but might not get there in time for his good-bye, and you want so bad to switch to Animal Planet or the Food Network or even Spike TV, anything but this. You can't remember why you started watching this, but now you can't look away, you have to know will the daddy get there in time. He always gets there in time, but the mother always dies, and then you're just a *mess* for the next day or two, you go through *boxes* of Kleenex, and you'll never know what happened to the little kids with no mother. That kind of music.

When the Xerox still didn't speak, Mr. Lyss said, "You too good to have a conver-sation with me? Don't you dare snub me, you murderous Martian filth. You snub me, I'll cut off your stuck-up nose, put it in a blender with ice cream, make a meat shake, and drink it up. I've done it before, a hundred times."

The thought of a nose-flavored milk shake made Nummy gag and gag again, but he felt pretty sure he wasn't going to puke up his dinner.

"I'm giving you one more chance, you stinking outer-space pile of crap. What're you doing here?"

The Xerox didn't look up. He watched his hands, the keys. He said, "What I'm doing here is playing the piano," and he sounded exactly like the Boze.

"I've got eyes. Don't tell me what I can see already. *Why* are you playing the piano?"

"When I downloaded his memories, I learned how to play. He could play pretty well, and now so do I."

"What—am I supposed to applaud?" Mr. Lyss asked, his anger growing ever brighter, as it usually did when he got it lit. "Should I go out and buy a dozen roses and wait at the damned stage door for your sorry Martian ass? You never did a minute's practice, so don't expect any standing ovation from Conway Lyss. Why're you screwing around with the piano instead of taking over the world like the rest of your pestilent kind?"

"I sat down here before dawn, and I've been playing straight through since then," the Xerox said.

Nummy was impressed, and he wanted to ask the Martian how long he could go without peeing, but he figured then he would become the target of Mr. Lyss's anger. He liked not being the target.

"You're trying my patience, Darth Vader. You're no more to me than a smear of cockroach vomit, so don't try my patience. I didn't ask you how long, I asked you *why*?"

For some reason he didn't know, Nummy was half hypnotized by the hands of the Martian Boze, how they seemed to float across the keyboard, barely touching the black notes and the white, in fact seeming not to touch them at all, seeming instead to draw the music out of the piano with magic.

The Xerox said, "This morning . . . in the kitchen . . . during memory transference, as his life experience was being transmit-

ted to me . . . he died of a brain hemor-
rhage."

"I *know* he's dead," Mr. Lyss said, and
spat on the floor. "That copper is as dead
as Wyatt Earp, deader than a freaking
rock. What the hell is wrong with you? All
you do is tell me what I already know, not
what I want to know."

The hands floated across the keys like
they were searching for something. To the
left together, then apart, then together in
the middle, then both to the right, like they
lost something important, they were trying
to find it, and the music was just something that happened during the search, the
way music just happened in movies when
the actors needed it. Whatever the hands
were searching for, they were sad because
they couldn't find it, and that was why the
music was sad.

The Xerox Boze still didn't look up from
the keyboard. He said, "When he died, our
minds were twined. I saw exactly what he
saw in the moment."

"In the moment?" Mr. Lyss asked impa-
tiently. "In the moment? *What* moment?"

"In the moment between."

"Damn it all and damn it twice!" Mr.

Lyss exploded. "Are you a Martian *dummy*? Do I have two dummies to contend with, neither of you able to speak so that more than other half-wits can understand you? The moment between what and what?"

"Between life and death," the Xerox said. "Except it wasn't death."

"More double-talk! I could just pull this trigger and blow your head clean off your body, and maybe that would kill you or maybe it wouldn't, but it would for sure at least be a big inconvenience for a while."

Usually music itself couldn't make Nummy cry, it needed to be music in a certain kind of movie, but this music was getting sadder and sadder, and he was worried that he was going to cry. He knew—he just *knew*—that if he cried, Mr. Lyss would make fun of him and say really mean things, call him "sissy boy" and worse.

"The moment between life and life," the Xerox said.

Now his hands looked as sad as the music sounded, but beautiful, too, beautiful sad hands floating back and forth on the music.

The Xerox piano player said, "For just a moment, as he slipped away, I saw the world beyond the world, where he was going, where my kind can never go."

Mr. Lyss was silent. Watching Mr. Lyss be silent was almost as hypnotizing as the hands floating on the music. He was silent for a long time, too, longer than seemed possible in a situation like this.

Finally the old man said, "Your kind. What kind are you? Not a Martian, I know."

"A Communitarian."

"And what might that be?"

"Not born of man and woman," said the piano player, and now the soft notes came as sad as drizzling rain in a graveside-funeral scene in a movie where good people die in spite of being good.

"If not from man and woman," the old man said, "then from what?"

"From laboratory and computer, from genetically engineered flesh combined with silicon nerve paths, from inert materials programmed with something that pretends to be life, and then programmed further with something that resembles consciousness, something that imitates free will but is in fact obedient slavery. From nothing into the pretense of something and from there . . . . eventually to nothing again."

Those words were to Nummy what his conversation sometimes was to Mr. Lyss: gibberish. Yet his heart must have understood part of what was said even if his brain couldn't make sense of it, because a big feeling came into him, a feeling so enormous that he seemed to swell with it. Nummy couldn't give a name to the feeling, but it was like sometimes when he was walking through a meadow with trees along one side, and suddenly there was a break in the trees so he could see the mountains in the distance, mountains so big and yet he had forgotten they were there, mountains so big that the tops of them poked through a layer of clouds and reappeared above, mountains so high and beautiful and strange that for a moment he couldn't get his breath. This feeling was like that but many times more powerful.

Mr. Lyss was silent again, as if he was remembering mountains of his own.

The sad music played into the silence, and after a while, the Xerox Boze said, "Kill me."

Mr. Lyss said nothing.

"Be merciful and kill me."

Mr. Lyss said, "I've never been a man

known for his mercy. If you want to be dead, be merciful to yourself."

"I'm what I am, and have no mercy in me. But you're human, so you possess the capacity."

After another silence, Mr. Lyss said, "Whose laboratory?"

"Victor's."

"Victor who?"

"He calls himself Victor Leben. And Victor Immaculate. But his real name, of which he's proud, is Frankenstein."

Nummy knew that name. He shivered. Those were the kind of movies he never watched. He'd seen part of one some years earlier, turned it on not knowing what trouble he was getting into, and it so upset him that Grandmama came in the room to see what was wrong, and she turned it off. She hugged him, kissed him, made him his favorite dinner, and told him over and over that none of that stuff was real, it was just a *story,* the same way that a nice and happy story like *Charlotte's Web* was just a story, what Grandmama called fiction, and no fiction story could ever be real.

If the Xerox Boze wasn't lying, Grandmama was wrong. She had never been wrong about anything before. Not any blessed thing. The possibility that Grand-mama could have been wrong about even one thing was so disturbing that Nummy decided never to think about it again.

"Frankenstein? You think I'm a fool?" Mr. Lyss asked, but he didn't sound angry, just curious.

"No. You asked. I told you. It's the truth."

"You said you're an obedient slave. You were made that way. Why would you be-tray him?"

"I'm broken now," said the Xerox Boze. "When I saw what Bozeman saw in the mo-ment between, something broke in me. I'm like a car and the engine runs all right but the gears won't shift anymore. Please kill me. Please do it."

The piano player still didn't lift his gaze from the keys, and Mr. Lyss watched those floating hands as if they fascinated him as much as they hypnotized Nummy.

The tune sort of slipped into a new tune, which was even sadder than the first. Grand-mama said great composers could build mansions with music, mansions so real that you could see the rooms in your mind. Nummy could see the room that was this one song. It was a big empty space without furniture, and the walls were dull gray, and the windows were gray because they looked out on nothing.

"Frankenstein," Mr. Lyss said. "If men from outer space, then why not this. But I won't kill you. I don't know why. It just doesn't feel right."

Surprisingly, the old man lowered the long gun.

Nummy worriedly reminded him, "Sir, he killed the Boze. He'll kill us. He's a monster."

"He was," Mr. Lyss said. "Now he's just what he is. He saw too much through Bozeman's eyes, too much . . . beyond. It finished him. I'm just damn glad I didn't see it. At least he's got the piano. If I'd have seen it, whatever it was, I'd probably be lying on the floor, just talking baby talk and sucking on my toes. Come on, Peaches, let's find that snowmobile."

The old man turned away from the piano and crossed the room toward the hallway.

Nummy backed out of the room, keeping his eyes on the Xerox.

chapter 16

Mason Morrell's evening talk show centered around advice about relationships between husbands and wives, between parents and their children, between spouses and their in-laws, between siblings, between young romantics seeking their ideal mates. . . . He was not married, had no children, had no brothers or sisters, and had burned through six women in the past eighteen months. But he was a successful talk-show host because he had extraordinary confidence in his opinions, could subtly browbeat his callers while seeming to be their best friend, was able to fake compassion exceptionally well, was a fearless host who would not shy from any topic no matter how outrageous, and had a baritone voice that was both masculine and silky.

Mason was a fraud, but a likable and amusing fraud now carried on five other stations in Montana and Wyoming, and he might prove to be one of those talents whom Sammy Chakrabarty could build into a nationally syndicated money machine. Therefore, the talk-show host's reaction to the gutted replicant on the floor and to Deucalion's disappearance was deeply dismaying to Sammy not only because their survival might depend on a united front against an imminent assault on the building but also because losing Mason might have a negative impact on his plan to own KBOW by the age of twenty-nine.

The moment the tattooed giant vanished to deal with whatever contingent of lab-born monsters was pressing the door buzzer, Mason lost all of his trademark confidence and fearlessness. In a voice that soared two octaves, he said, "I'm not dying like a cornered rat in a crappy, tank-town, AM noise shop."

The first step he took put his foot in some of the pale spilled guts of the thing that had looked like Warren Snyder, which inspired an almost girlish shriek of horror. Scrubbing his shoe on the carpet in disgust, Mason shuffled across the room, went through the open door to the hallway, and turned left, away from the broadcast booth.

Ralph Nettles said, "He's going to unlock the front door. He could get us all killed," and Burt Cogborn, whose usual ad-salesman glibness had deserted him, said, "Uh."

Sammy Chakrabarty began to move on the word *front.* He entered the hall in time to see Mason pull open the door to the reception lounge. He cried out, "Mason, don't!" but the talk-show host kept going.

At the front door, Sammy caught up with his quarry as Mason twisted the thumbturn on the deadbolt. Sammy grabbed him by the belt and tried to pull him backward, off his feet. But Sammy stood five ten and weighed 130, Mason stood six two and weighed 200, and even the most desperate effort of a determined radio entrepreneur could not compensate for the talk-show

host's advantage of size. With Sammy trying to climb his back, Mason flung open the
door and plunged into the snowy night.

Sammy had dreamed of becoming a
radio-made multimillionaire for as long as
he could remember. He never wanted to
be a rodeo cowboy, but a little experience
in that field might have helped as now he
clung to his star talker's broad back like a
buckaroo riding a bull. Mason snorted in
rage and panic, shrugged his big shoulders, heaved hard and twisted.

In the light of the parking-lot lamps, from
his continuously pitching and spinning
perspective, Sammy glimpsed a large
white panel truck with a dark blue cab. He
saw an apparently dead man sprawled on
the snow-covered pavement, which was
probably not really a man but instead a
replicant like the Warren Snyder duplicate
with the abdomen full of something like
fish parts in alfredo sauce. He saw Deucalion lifting another man off the ground,
above his head, which seemed an impossible feat, something that even the great
Buster Steelhammer, superstar wrestler,
wouldn't dare pretend to be able to do
even in an extravagantly choreographed

performance. But then Sammy briefly lost sight of the giant, and when next he could see him, the tattooed wonder slammed the second replicant down on the radiator cap of the truck, surely shattering the creature's spine.

Mason's shirt tore. Sammy flew off his mount, landed facedown, slid through the snow, came to a halt against a lumpy something, and found himself face-to-face with one of the dead replicants. From the nostrils of the thing streamed a noxious blue gas that plumed into Sammy's mouth.

Spitting in revulsion, rolling away from the fiendish creature and onto his knees, Sammy wondered for the first time in his life if his mom and dad had been wise to emigrate from New Delhi. Maybe contemporary America was too wild for anyone to ride, not just an angry bull of a country but a *crazy* bull of a country, all hooves and horns and bucking muscle.

Sammy's doubt lasted only as long as he took to get to his feet. Mason was climbing behind the wheel of his Toyota Sequoia, which was the last in the line of parked vehicles, and Sammy was the only alternative for the on-air voice that would warn Rainbow Falls and the county at large about the invasion (or whatever it was) of the Stepford people (or whatever they were). An hour from now poor Burt Cogborn would probably still be able to say nothing but "Uh, uh, uh," and though Ralph Nettles was a good man, a solid man, he was far from a silver-tongued orator. Sammy didn't sound like a geek or a snark or a weasel, but he didn't have a trained voice. He wasn't radio talent, he was radio executive. He wouldn't be half as convincing as Mason. Suddenly Sammy was energized once more by his particular American dream.

Not only for the people of Rainbow Falls (who were evidently being slaughtered), and not only for the future of humanity (which might hang in the balance), but also for Chakrabarty Syndication (which had not yet been incorporated but which would one day *dominate* the AM landscape), Sammy staggered toward the Sequoia. He intended to drag Mason Morrell out of the SUV or be clubbed senseless in the attempt.

Fortunately, Deucalion got to the Sequoia not only first but in time. The doors of the SUV were locked, but before Mason could start the engine, the giant thrust both big hands under the flank of the vehicle, gripped the frame, and with an effort that made him roar in agony or rage, or both, he lifted the passenger side off the ground. Deucalion heaved, heaved again, and he rolled the Sequoia onto its roof.

chapter 17

In the foyer of Chief Rafael Jarmillo's house, the portion of the hand on the floor consisted of the thumb, the forefinger, the connecting span that was called the anatomical snuffbox, and a piece of the fleshy thenar eminence. The tips of the thumb and finger were pressed together as if in the OK sign.

Frost had no way of knowing if someone had arranged the digits in that fashion or if instead the macabre gesture occurred by chance. In either case, he was not amused.

Most cops lacked a sharp sense of

black humor when they entered law enforcement, but they quickly developed one as a psychological-defense mechanism. Nevertheless, Frost suspected that nothing he encountered in this house would tickle the dark side of his funnybone.

The eaten edges of the flesh had the same appearance as the stump of the foot in the living room. Bloodless. Glazed but pitted. And the flesh was unnaturally pale.

Dagget flicked a switch, and the open staircase brightened. In a hunt, stairs were always bad, either going up or coming down. You were vulnerable from above and below, with nothing to duck behind, with nowhere to go other than straight into the line of fire, because turning your back and running was even more surely a ticket to the morgue.

Cautiously but quickly, they ascended. Dagget took the lead, back to the curved wall, attention on the head of the stairs. Frost followed six steps behind, focused on the foyer below; although they had cleared the ground floor, there might be a way someone could get behind them.

They didn't even whisper to each other anymore. They had nothing to say. From here on, what needed to be done would be clear as events unfolded.

They didn't find any additional scraps until they reached the upper hall, where a bloodless ear, as white as a seashell, lay on the carpet. Judging by the size and the delicacy, it must have been the ear of a young child.

Chief Jarmillo had two children.

Of all crimes, those involving violence against children most infuriated Frost. He didn't believe in life sentences for child murderers. He believed in any kind of slow execution.

Jarmillo's behavior on duty the previous twelve hours argued strongly for his corruption. If the chief was part of some bizarre conspiracy, then it seemed to follow that he, rather than a serial killer chancing upon them, must have murdered his wife, mother-in-law, and kids. Murdered and dismembered.

But Frost couldn't make sense of what they had found thus far. The huge sums funneled into this town through Progress for Perfect Peace suggested a criminal enterprise vast in scale. In fact the laundered funds were so enormous that the possibility of a terrorist plot of historic dimensions could not be dismissed. A cop on the take, getting immensely rich for helping the bad guys conceal their activities, wasn't likely to derail the money train by chopping up his family over a disagreement with the wife.

Four bedrooms, a master-suite sitting room, various closets, and two of three bathrooms offered them only two more grisly pieces of evidence. Both were in the master bedroom.

On the floor near the dresser lay a fragment of a jawbone from which protruded two molars, two bicuspids, and a single canine tooth. Something green trailed from between the molars, perhaps a sliver of skin from a bell pepper or a jalapeño. The facets of the bone that should have been shattered, where they had broken away from the rest of the jaw, instead looked . . . melted.

Because it was not just another bit of biological debris but an impossible construct out of a surrealist's fantasy, the second find in the master bedroom proved more unsettling than anything they had discovered thus far. It lay at one corner of the neatly made bed, near the footboard, not as if carefully presented but as if tossed aside—or as if spat out. The thick tongue, curved and with the tip raised as though licking something, would have been repulsive and alarming if it had been nothing more than that, but instead it was like an image by Salvador Dalí inspired by H. P. Lovecraft. In the center of the fat tongue, not balanced upon it but snugly embedded in its tissue, actually growing from it, was a brown and lidless human eye.

Frost saw the monstrosity first. In the instant of discovery, he was overcome by a sensation about which he'd often read but of which he had no previous experience. The skin on the back of his neck went cold and seemed to be crawling with something as real as centipedes or spiders.

As an agent of the FBI assigned to the equivalent of a black-ops division, he had seen horrors enough and had known fear in a variety of textures and intensities. But nothing until this had touched that most deeply buried nerve, which was not a physical nerve at all, but an intuitive sensitivity to the uncanny, whether of a supernatural or merely a preternatural kind. Neither all of his education nor his vivid imagination could explain the existence of this abomination. As he stared at it, the crawling sensation burrowed deeper, from the back of his neck into his spine, and a chill scurried down his laddered vertebrae.

He gestured for Dagget to join him. Frost didn't need to look up to gauge his partner's reaction to the loathsome object. The sudden intake of breath and a wordless expression of revulsion in the back of his throat conveyed Dagget's disgust and dread.

For a moment, Frost anticipated that the eye might turn in its fleshy socket, focusing on him, or that the tongue might flex and curl in an obscene quest. But that expectation was imagination run wild. The tongue and the eye on the bed were dead tissue, no more capable of movement than the teeth in the jawbone fragment would be able to chew the carpet under them.

A mere pistol and two spare magazines seemed to be inadequate armament against whatever enemy they faced. The explanation behind events in Rainbow Falls was neither ordinary criminal activity nor terrorism of a kind before seen.

As though he had been cast back to childhood, to the confusions and anxieties of a preschooler, Frost looked down at his feet, inches from the hem of the quilted bedspread, and he wondered if something hostile might be hiding under the bed. Where in the past there had never been a boogeyman or a troll, or any kind of witch's familiar, might there now be something more mysterious and yet more real than any of those fairy-tale threats?

The spell of childish timidity held him in thrall only for a moment and was broken by the announcement of a real threat. From the darkness in the adjoining bathroom, through the half-open door, into the stillness of the master bedroom came a sound like scores of urgent whispering voices.

chapter 18

The front passenger-side window dissolved as Deucalion rolled the Toyota Sequoia onto its roof. When Mason Morrell refused to abandon the overturned SUV, the giant expressed the intention of smashing the windshield, as well, and hauling the reluctant warrior from the vehicle whether he wanted to come out or not.

Sammy Chakrabarty prevailed upon Deucalion to let him negotiate with the on-air talent. He reached through the broken window, pulled up the lock stem, and dragged open the passenger door. After using the side of his foot as a broom,

sweeping away the broken glass that sparkled in the snow, he got on his hands and
knees, and he crawled into the Sequoia.

On all fours on the ceiling of the overturned SUV, he faced Mason at a curious
angle. The talk-show host hung upside-
down in the driver's seat. Actually, he wasn't
hanging because he hadn't taken the time
to put on his safety harness, so eager had
he been to start the engine and split the
scene. He maintained his position by holding tightly to the steering wheel and by
hooking the heels of his shoes under the
seat as best he could. Of the two men,
Mason was the one whose head was
nearer the ceiling. Sammy found himself
peering down into his friend's face when
the orientation of the SUV suggested that
he should be looking up into it.

The only light, the bluish glow of the
parking-lot lamps, seeped through the low
windows of the inverted vehicle. The air was
cold and smelled of new-car leather and of
Mason's spicy aftershave. Besides their
breathing, the only sounds were the clicks
and tinks and pings of the Sequoia adjusting to its new, unconventional relationship
to the pavement.

"I'm so sorry this had to happen," Sammy said.

Mason sounded more resigned than aggrieved. "It didn't have to."

"Maybe it didn't, but it has. The station will pay for repairs."

"That's the way you are, but it's not the way Warren is. Warren pinches pennies."

"Remember," Sammy said, "Warren Snyder is dead. And the thing that looked like Warren is dead, too, its weird guts all over the floor in there. So I'm in charge now."

Refusing to look at Sammy, Mason declared solemnly, "We're all going to die."

"That's not what I believe," Sammy said.

"Well, it's what I believe."

"I haven't told you this," Sammy said, "but I have big plans for you and your show."

"It's the end of the world. There won't be any radio after the end of the world."

"It's not the end of the world. It's a national crisis, that's all. If we pull together, if we defend the station and get the word out about what's happening here, we can turn this around in no time. I've always been an optimist, you know, and my optimism has always proved to be justified."

"You're not just an optimist. You're insane."

"I'm not insane," Sammy said. "I'm an American. Hey, you're an American, too. Where's your can-do spirit? Listen, I have plans to expand the format of your show, make it emotionally deeper, really let you spread your wings. I want to advertise it more widely, too. With your talent and my dogged determination, we can take this show to regional syndication, then national, not just five other stations but hundreds. You could be the male Dr. Laura. You could be a more human Dr. Phil."

"I'm not a doctor."

"You are if I say you are. That's how radio works."

A few flakes of snow spiraled through the broken-out window and danced on the frosty plumes of their breath.

Sammy was cold. And the thinly padded ceiling was hard under his bony knees. The weird angle made him feel like he was in one of those topsy-turvy dreams in the movie *Inception.* But he smiled and patted Mason on the arm, in a most friendly way, as if to say *I'm here for you.*

Tipping his head forward, rolling his

eyes down and sideways to get a better look at his program director, Mason said, "Because I'm tall and built like a football star, people think I'm tough. I'm not tough, Sammy. I don't think I'm tough enough to stand the pressures of national syndication."

"I'm tough enough for both of us," Sammy assured him. "And did you just listen to your voice? The timbre, the natural reverb, the exquisite diction—it's a gift, Mason. You can't throw away a gift like that."

"I don't know," Mason said doubtfully. "Sometimes I kinda sound squeaky to myself."

"Trust me, big guy. Listen, if you were doing one of those shows about flying saucers and parallel worlds and secret civilizations under the sea—well, then you'd be all wrong for what we've got to do tonight. Everyone would think it was just the usual shtick. But your show is intimate, people let you into their lives, all the way in, they trust you, they take your advice, they admire you. They *love* you, Mason. You're a friend to your listeners. They think of you as *family*. If you tell your listeners that monsters made in some laboratory, capable of passing for human, are taking over Rainbow Falls, they'll believe you. They wouldn't believe my voice. I sound like a skinny kid."

The talk-show host closed his eyes and hung—or clung—upside down in silence for a long moment, like a big frightened bat. Then he said, "They love me?"

"They *adore* you."

"I try to do my best. I really try to help them."

"That's why they adore you."

"It's a terrible responsibility, giving advice."

"It is. I know. I think it would be exhausting. But you're a very giving man."

"I'm always afraid one of them will take something I say the wrong way."

"They won't, Mason. You express yourself with great clarity."

"I'm afraid some wife will like, you know, misunderstand my advice and go shoot her husband."

"That only almost happened once," Sammy counseled. "And *almost* happened. It didn't really happen."

Eyes still closed, Mason chewed on his

lower lip. Finally he said, "Orson Welles sold that crazy Jules Verne thing, back in the 1930s. He had half the country believing it was true when it was just a stupid sci-fi story."

"*The War of the Worlds,*" Sammy said, and didn't correct Jules Verne to H. G. Wells.

"He got famous from that. It was just a silly sci-fi thing, but he got famous. This is *real.*"

Sammy smiled and nodded even though Mason's eyes were closed. "By the time this is over, you'll be huge. An international star. Not just a star, Mason. Not just a star—a hero."

Mason shook his head. "I'm not hero material. I'm not a hero just because you say I am, like you can make me a doctor."

Sammy was freezing, so cold that his voice trembled in time to his shivering. He wanted to grab the talk-show host by the ears and shake a sense of urgency into him, but he remained calm.

"Yes, you are a hero, Mason. It's even easier to make you a hero than to make you a doctor. Some people might want to see a college degree to prove you're a doctor, and we'd have to go to the trouble of buying you a PhD from some online university. But if we say you not only saved the world but at the same time you fought off a horde of violent clones trying to seize KBOW—remember, we already have the bodies of four—who's to say you're not what we claim you are."

"Burt and Ralph. They'd know."

"Burt and Ralph become part of the Mason Morrell team. Their careers soar with yours. They'll play along."

"I don't think they will."

"They will."

"I don't think so."

"THEY WILL!" Sammy shouted, and immediately added, "Sorry. I just get frustrated that you keep underestimating yourself. You're always so confident on the air."

"That's on the air. This is life." At last he opened his eyes. "But I guess I'll do it, what you want."

"You won't try to run away again?"

"No. I can't run away from this. There's nowhere to run. I see that now."

Sammy said, "My hero."

"I think this door might be buckled. If

you back out, I'll crawl over the console and come through the passenger door."

Grinning, Sammy said, "Let's do radio."

"Yeah. Let's do great radio."

"Immortal radio!" Sammy declared.

Mason hanging upside down, Sammy kneeling on the ceiling, they tried to high-five each other, but the weird perspective defeated them. Mason boxed Sammy's left ear, and Sammy blew the Sequoia's horn.

chapter 19

Pistols ready, flanking the partially open door to the master bathroom, Frost and Dagget listened to the voices whispering in the darkness beyond the threshold. They sounded conspiratorial and eager and sinister, but if anything being said had a scintilla of meaning, the conspirators were speaking in a foreign tongue. Frost couldn't understand a word.

This sounded like a language entirely of sibilants, hissing and sissing and snuffling and fizzing, which seemed highly unlikely. Then, after a moment, the whispering no longer struck him as being conspiratorial, but instead restless and agitated. When he began to think of it that way, he realized he wasn't listening to whispering voices, after all, but to friction of some kind. One thing sliding against another. Or a horde of small things swarming over one another, all their carapaces and quivering antennas and brittle legs rubbing together.

The door was hinged on the left, and Frost stood to the right. He reached around the jamb with his left hand, found the switch in there, and flipped light into the bathroom. Dagget moved even as the doorway brightened, crossed the threshold, said a word that Frost had never heard him—or any other Mormon—say before, and backed into the bedroom so fast that Frost hadn't yet moved in behind him.

The large bathroom featured white ceramic tile with blue tile accents, a pair of sinks in a long counter, a shower stall directly ahead, and to the left a soaking tub spacious enough to accommodate husband and wife at the same time. Over the bathtub, depending partway into it, hanging from the ceiling on a thick and lumpy organic rope that looked like the umbilical cord of the Antichrist, was a greasy-looking

sack larger than a man, glistening in a variety of shades of silver and gray.

The teardrop shape suggested preg-
nancy. The slithering noise that arose from
the sack—the whispering he'd heard
through the open doorway—perhaps indicated a restless fetus of an unthinkable
nature. And the overall impression was of
a cocoon. The movement within that ominous incubator did not distort it; the surface neither bulged nor rippled.

Farther from the doorway, beyond the
tub, in the shower stall, behind a glass
door hung another cocoon. It virtually filled
that space.

Foreboding had gripped Frost upon the
discovery of the eye in the severed tongue.
Now that feeling ripened fully into dread.
He tried to reassure himself that these
things were *preter*natural, beyond the ordinary course of nature, strange and inexplicable, yes, but only because this was
an expression of nature never seen before. An extraterrestrial life form. Natural to
the universe, just not to this world. Or the
consequence of some mutation of an
earthly animal. Intuitive knowledge, however, trumped what he had been taught to

know. He could not reason himself out of the recognition that behind this scene, at the bottom of this situation, a *super*natural force was at work.

Adjusting to the shock of his first sight of the cocoons, Dagget entered the bathroom again. Frost stepped onto the threshold behind his partner. They had never before fled from any threat, not because they were fearless but because once they took the coward's way out, they would take it again, and again, until they would be forever incapable of fulfilling their duties.

With evident uneasiness, Dagget approached the cocoon that hung over the bathtub, and Frost cautioned him, and Dagget said, "There's something strange about the surface of this thing."

"Not just the surface," Frost said.

The continuous slithering noise didn't grow louder, but Frost found it increasingly sinister. He thought of snakes, but he knew that it wouldn't be snakes, wouldn't be anything he had ever seen before.

Dagget's face was hardly twelve inches from the sack when he said, "It looks greasy or wet, but I don't think it is. It glistens because the surface is in constant motion, crawling with something silvery, like tiny specks of metal, but they can't be metal because they seem . . . alive. Like fleas, only smaller than fleas, so small I can't see what they are, thousands of them, maybe millions, all sort of shivering, ceaselessly dancing across the surface."

Where the umbilical met the ceiling, the gray tissue appeared to have eaten through the plaster in order to anchor the cocoon to a joist.

"This is beyond our pay grade," Frost said.

"Light-years beyond."

"And we need backup."

"Yeah," Dagget said, "like maybe the National Guard."

"Or a Vatican SWAT team."

"Be ready to shoot the sonofabitch if it does anything," Dagget said as he holstered his pistol in the rig under his ski jacket.

Although he knew his partner to be prudent, Frost's dread was now sharpened with alarm. "What're you doing?"

Snaring a hand towel from a wall rack and folding it into a thick pad, Dagget said, "When we call Moomaw about this, we

better have all the details we can gather."
Maurice Moomaw, their boss, had the
glower of a carved-stone god. "I'm not saying Moomaw is scarier than this thing. But
when we're three sentences into a report,
if we aren't convincing, he's going to punch
the speaker-phone button and start filling
out a psychiatric-evaluation order for both
of us."

Frost took a two-hand grip on his pistol
as Dagget wiped the folded towel down
the side of the glistening sack.

Holding up the towel so Frost could see
it, Dagget said, "It's clean. All those tiny little things crawling over the surface—why
didn't some of them wipe off on the towel?"

He stroked the cocoon again, and as
before, the cloth remained clean.

"I just realized," Frost said. "Bacteria.
Extraterrestrial viruses. We could be contaminated, infected."

"Microbes are the last thing I'm worried
about."

"What's the first thing you're worried
about?"

"Is the thing that spun this cocoon now
curled up inside it?" Dagget wondered.
"Or did it plant something in this, like in-

side a spider's egg case, and then crawl away? And if maybe it crawled away, where is it?"

"Not in the house. We searched the house."

"We didn't search the attic."

Frost glanced at the ceiling. He imagined some immense insect queen in the raftered space above them, attracted by their voices and homing in on them. He focused on the cocoon again, and it didn't seem as ominous as it had a moment ago, considering other possible threats.

Dagget shook out the folded hand towel. With only one thickness of the cloth between his hand and the sack, he pressed his palm against the glistening surface.

Frost watched the front sight of his pistol jittering on the target. He took a slow deep breath, exhaled even more slowly than he had inhaled, imagined his hands perfectly still—and his tremors faded.

"Interesting," Dagget said, towel-protected hand flat against the sack.

"What?" Frost asked.

"It's very warm, even hot. The heat comes right through the towel, and yet I don't feel any heat escaping from it into the air, none at all."

Ever more disturbed by the slithering noise, Frost said, "Can you feel movement in it?"

Dagget shook his head. "Nothing moving. But do you smell that?"

"No. Nothing."

"Very faint. . . ."

"What?" Frost asked.

"Sort of like burning insulation on a shorting electrical cord."

"I don't smell anything."

Leaning closer to the sack and sniffing, Dagget said, "Yes, like burning insulation."

"Maybe it's the hand towel scorching."

"No." Dagget's face was six inches from the glistening cocoon. "Not the hand towel. It's hot but not that hot. Oh . . ."

"Oh, what?"

"The smell just changed. It's like roses now."

"From burning electrical cord to roses?"

"And I think . . ."

"What?" Frost asked.

"I'm not sure, but I think I just felt something moving in there."

With a sound that was like two lengths

of Velcro detaching from each other but also like the bloated belly of a cadaver parting wetly under the scalpel of an autopsist, the sack split.

chapter **20**

After pausing in the mud room to take off their snow-caked boots, the male parishioners of Riders in the Sky Church came to the kitchen in groups of four or five to listen to Carson and Michael sell them the alternative to the space-alien explanation. They knew their wives had already been persuaded, and they put a lot of store in their opinions. The Riderettes, as they were sometimes called, were women that the world could never confuse or make weary; they firmly held the reins of their lives and kept their feet in the stirrups.

Neither Carson nor Michael mentioned

the name Frankenstein. Dolly and Hank Samples and their friends were remarkably open-minded. They had proved they could cope with developments that in an instant turned their world upside down. But Carson and Michael were outsiders in this community, and even the most welcoming and trusting and swayable of the Riders would at some point hit a wall of disbelief.

Nanotechnology, people-eating machine-animals, replicants, a scheme to kill all of humanity: The current situation was already over-the-top fantastical. Adding to it the revelation that at the root of this chaos was a 240-year-old scientist much farther off his nut than Colin Clive had played him in the movie and a 200-year-old monster who had made himself into a good man, even a hero . . . This was sensible rural Montana; this was not a place where people were conditioned to believe anything they were told.

Carson claimed she and Michael had been working on an industrial-espionage case that led them to the discovery of the replicants—and now the people-eating nanomachine-animals—and to the belief that these things were being produced in a federal facility buried deep along the End Times Highway. A thousand movies and books prepared the Riders to believe in evil extraterrestrials, but *their daily lives* prepared them to embrace the idea that their own government might want to replace them with obedient engineered citizens.

As Carson expected, fifteen-year-old Farley Samples proved to be a great help convincing the Riders that their enemies didn't have to be from another planet, that nanotechnology was a real and rapidly advancing field on *this* world. His enthusiasm for science and for science fiction proved contagious, his deferential nature allowed adults to learn from him without feeling belittled, and he had absorbed a thing or two about effective storytelling from those novels of Robert Heinlein that he loved so much.

More than Carson's and Michael's private-investigator licenses, more than their expired photo IDs from the homicide division of the New Orleans Police Department, what gave them street cred were their weapons. The Riders revered guns nearly as much as they loved Jesus. They were impressed with Carson's and Michael's SIG Sauer P226 X-Sixes with 19-round magazines but especially with the Urban Sniper slug-firing shotguns.

Even though Carson proved, at the kitchen table, that she could hold her own in arm wrestling with men half again her weight, some were dubious that she could fire that hard-core shotgun without being knocked flat by the recoil. None of the doubters among the Riders were women.

When Carson stood up from the table after an intense battle-to-a-draw with a man named Glenn Botine, a full-time car mechanic and part-time quarter-horse breeder, he said, "Thank you, ma'am, for a lesson in humility. Now as ex-police, what do you and your husband think we should be doing here that we're not doing?"

"Instead of just preparing to defend this place, we need to go door-to-door in the neighborhood," Michael said, "alert as many people as possible. You've got the cell-phone videos. You're locals. They'll believe you. Make the entire square block a garrison and defend it, falling back to individual houses only if the larger perimeter can't be held."

Carson thought of her brother, Arnie, and little Scout in San Francisco, safe for now if perhaps not for long, and she asked, "How many children do you have here?"

The women conferred and quickly agreed that there were seven teenagers and twelve younger children among the forty-four Riders at the Samples house. Eighty-some other Riders had either gone to their individual homes from the roadhouse or, like these folks, were gathered at one or two other more defendable locations elsewhere in Rainbow Falls.

"Making a garrison of the entire block, with fallback positions—that's a good idea," Carson said. "But I think we also need to get the twelve younger kids out of town, to a safe house, just in case everything goes badly here."

The sudden anxiety among the Riders was palpable. They knew what she suggested was the right thing to do, but they were loath to be separated from their young ones.

Glenn Botine said, "But how? Both highways out of town are roadblocked. Maybe we could get hold of some snowmobiles. But one adult could only drive out with one kid at a time. That'll either take all night or a caravan so big it'll draw attention we don't want."

Carson said, "There may be a way."

chapter 21

In the basement of Memorial Hospital, the replicant of John Martz, a Rainbow Falls policeman and the husband of a member of the local Red Hat Society, was greatly enjoying the slaughter. He had witnessed the killing and processing of scores of people, but he was not in the least bored. In fact, he delighted in each new murder more than the one before it.

Communitarians were granted no free will. They possessed no capacity for any kind of sexual activity. They were engineered to have no appreciation for music and the arts because such interests were an impediment to efficient function. But in the interest of motivating them to carry out their mission with enthusiasm, they were programmed to take great pleasure in the destruction of each despicable, world-polluting, self-important, grubbing, grasping human being.

In John Martz's case, pleasure had grown into something like delight, and each killing that he witnessed gratified him more than the one before it. Genocide proved to be addictive.

Four more patients had been brought to this unfurnished basement room under the pretense that they needed to give blood samples to be sure they had not been contaminated by an unspecified toxic material supposedly released by accident in the building. The four were in wheelchairs, three women and one man, but only two of the women were actually too incapacitated to walk.

The replicant of Nurse Ginger Newbury was present to assist John Martz with the management of the patients. Managing these people was enormous fun.

A number of hospital visitors had been dispatched, as well. They couldn't be permitted to leave after they arrived and discovered that friends and loved ones were missing from their rooms. Because the visitors were not ill, they were more difficult to manage than the patients, which was why John had a nightstick and why Nurse Newbury kept a Taser clipped to her uniform belt, under a white cardigan sweater.

Three Builders were busy here on the basement level, first reducing their victims to various component molecules and then using those resources to create another generation of gestating Builders in the suspended cocoons. Builders produced only others of their kind; Communitarians were extruded and programmed only in the labs of the Hive.

Several rooms were now filled with cocoons that hung from the ceiling, which was a sight that profoundly pleased John Martz. Gestation required not fewer than twelve hours but not more than thirty-six. As new Builders emerged, fed on more useless human beings, and created ever more of their industrious kind, their numbers would increase geometrically. Within a week, they would be traveling to other towns with support teams of Communitarians, and by then they would be an unstoppable force, a rapidly growing army of exquisitely lethal biological machines, a nanotide of death.

The pajama-clad patients in the wheelchairs expressed their worries and confusions in that whiny way that was a hallmark of humanity, but Nurse Newbury coddled them with what seemed to be genuine sympathy until the Builder arrived. This one was a young woman designed to the highest standards of human beauty. Whether a Builder looked like a man or woman, it was always crafted to be so striking in appearance that the people who were its potential victims would be at first sight enchanted by it.

Beauty disarms. Beauty lures.

All of the patients, regardless of gender, were riveted by this blond and blue-eyed vision who wore ordinary hospital greens, as if she were an intern or an orderly. She stood in front of them, their wheelchairs arranged in a semicircle of which she was now the focal point.

"I am your Builder," she told them, her voice seductively musical and smoky.

She first approached the male patient, who smiled at her and no doubt entertained the last lascivious thoughts that he would ever have. She reached toward him, right palm turned up, and he seemed as charmed as he was confused by her apparent invitation. He reached out and put his hand in hers.

In the instant, the details of her hand—skin, fingernails, knuckles—seemed to dissolve up to the wrist. The shape of a hand remained, but her flesh appeared to have magically transformed into countless millions of extremely tiny insects with iridescent wings, swarming among one another while maintaining the basic shape of a hand.

The patient cried out in surprise, tried to snatch his hand back, but could not break free of her grip. Her hand, the teeming horde that it had become, bloodlessly consumed his flesh and bones to his forearm and then, in a mere two seconds, all the way to his shoulder.

Terror broke the hold of paralytic shock, and the patient began to scream, but she silenced him. Her generous mouth widened until it became grotesque, and she vomited another silver swarm into his face, which collapsed inward. The nanoanimals invaded his skull, consumed it from within, and surged downward through his neck stump into his body, continuously feeding the essence of him back along the stream into the Builder's mouth in a kind of reverse regurgitation.

The only ambulatory patient among the three women bolted up from her wheelchair, but Nurse Newbury Tasered her into submission. The twitching woman fell at the feet of the Builder.

The other women were screaming, too, while the hollowed-out body of the male patient withered inward, as though he were a deflating balloon, and disappeared altogether. These women were old and sick, but nevertheless they wanted to live. John Martz loathed them. They were avaricious for life even in their decrepitude, because the cancer that was humanity would accept no restraints on its greed.

The Builder had become weirdly misshapen from the incorporation of the man's body mass. As she redirected her attention to one of the wheelchair-bound prey, her clothes seemed to effervesce into a mist that she absorbed into herself, for they had never been clothes but instead an aspect of her amorphous body. In her nakedness, she was no longer beautiful by any human standard, and abruptly she ceased to be human in any aspect of her appearance. She became a furious fluid mass of mottled gray-and-silver matter, ribboned through with ugly streaks of red that rapidly darkened to fungal gray, a churning storm of living tissue that seemed to revel in chaos and required no structured organs or skeletal system to function.

From out of this seething mass came a thick silvery corkscrew composed of perhaps billions of nanoanimals, which bored into the chest of one of the women in the wheelchairs, at once silencing her. The turning motion of the corkscrew changed direction and appeared to draw the reducted substance of the dissolving patient into the Builder, which throbbed and swelled further, blistered and cankered and healed.

The other nonambulatory patient tried to turn her wheelchair around, intent on getting to the door, but John sprang into action, clubbing her hands with his nightstick. He pulled her to her feet, thrust her toward the now immense and looming Builder, and with savage glee cried, "Use her, use her, *use her*!"

The Builder took the weeping woman even more violently than it had taken the other patients and then rendered the Tasered woman on the floor with such brutality that John's delight escalated into a kind of rapture. The nature of a Communitarian's program made it impossible for him to know any joy other than the joy of efficient destruction. And so he gave himself completely to the experience and was transported as were certain members of some Pentecostal sects during worship, though the reasons for his vigorous jubilation were far different from theirs. He beat his chest with his fists, pulled at his hair, writhed, thrashed, and spoke in tongues, meaningless words gushing from him until he gagged himself by biting on his fisted right hand.

John became aware of Nurse Newbury watching him with what might have been disapproval, but he didn't care. This was a joy that he was permitted, and he needed it, *needed* it. He felt justified in

giving himself to it because the four patients were killed and processed, and
there was no one for him to manage at
the moment, in this brief point of stillness
between the Builder's destruction and its
acts of creation.

Now a toothless, lipless orifice formed
on the amorphous mass of the Builder,
and from it spewed a stream of gray goo
that struck the ceiling, penetrated the
plaster, and at once firmed into a thick and
gnarled rope. At the end of this anchor
line, a cocoon spun into existence as billions of nanoanimals with various tasks,
working in concert, formed the womb from
which another processor of human debris
would eventually emerge, and flooded it
full of themselves and the reduced substance of the four patients, which was the
raw material they would use to build another Builder.

As the current Builder began to hang
another cocoon, John Martz's rapture
peaked and declined to a much quieter but
delicious gladness. He stood motionless,
overcome by awe, still biting on his fist, because biting better expressed his deepest
desire more than did any of his previous

frenetic motions or speaking in tongues. If he could have any wish fulfilled, he would wish to be a Builder, to bite into human flesh as if with a thousand chain saws, devour them, and transform their hateful kind into a killing machine that would destroy even more of them.

He wanted to eat people alive.

He realized that he should not express this desire to Nurse Newbury or to anyone else. Such a longing was an affront to Victor, who had made him what he was and to whom he must always be obedient and grateful. Besides, one of the principles of the Communitarian culture was that every one of them was absolutely equal to all the others, that no one was smarter or stronger or better in any way. That he could even dream of being a Builder, which was an infinitely more deadly and efficient killing machine than any Communitarian, meant that he aspired to being more than what he was and, therefore, must think that he had the capacity to be superior to others in the Community.

He wanted to eat people alive. Lots of them.

But that was okay as long as he didn't

think about it too much. If he allowed himself to dwell obsessively on what it might
be like to be a Builder and process human
flesh into human-killing machines, he
could not be an efficient Communitarian.
Inefficiency was the only sin.

When the current Builder finished the
second cocoon, it returned to the form of a
beautiful young woman, clothed once more,
and walked out of the room. After glancing
at John in what he believed to be disapproval, Nurse Newbury departed, too.

John remained there for a moment, ad-
miring the pair of cocoons. As he was
about to leave, he noticed something lying
on the floor, under one of the wheelchairs,
half hidden by the chair's footplates. He
rolled the chair aside, dropped to one knee,
and saw a human ear lying concave-side-
down on the vinyl tile. The convex back of
the ear was smooth, with no torn tissue, as
if it had never been attached to a head and
therefore had never been cut off, though
this peculiar detail didn't mean much to
him at first.

During all other jobs of rendering and
processing to which he had been witness,
John had not seen a Builder overlook even

a tiny scrap of human tissue. To leave a portion of a body unused must surely qualify as inefficiency.

When he turned the ear over in his hand, he saw that it proved something worse than inefficiency. In the folds and curling down into the exterior auditory canal were human teeth, not loose but embedded, growing from the ear. This shell of flesh and cartilage was not a scrap of any of the four patients; it could only be a created object, manufactured by the Builder during the rendering and processing and then . . . spat out. Most likely the toothy ear had been created without conscious intent, just as the human urinary tract didn't think about making a kidney stone before producing one. This was proof that the Builder was malfunctioning.

The only sin was inefficiency, and the ultimate inefficiency was malfunction. By comparison, John's yearning to be a Builder and to eat lots of people seemed insignificant. After all, his desire could never be fulfilled. He was what he was and could be nothing else. He therefore could not malfunction by realizing his desire. But this Builder had badly malfunctioned by creating this macabre ear and spitting it out instead of using the tissue in its assigned work.

John felt better about himself.

He probably should report the transgressive Builder. But there was no rule requiring him to do so, most likely because Victor did not believe Builders could malfunction.

Throughout development, only the Communitarians had sometimes gone wrong by acquiring obsessions. And even that, too, had been resolved by identifying the potential obsessives and eliminating them before they left the Hive.

If John reported the Builder, Nurse Newbury would also be asked to provide a report. She might then make note of John's rapturous reaction to the Builder's work, whereupon he would be asked to explain his actions.

He turned the ear over and over in his hand. He ran his thumb along the curve of teeth within that fleshy shell.

He decided that he had better not report the Builder.

Before moving on to his next assignment, he bit off the lobe of the ear and chewed it. An interesting taste.

chapter 22

In the KBOW parking lot, after Sammy Chakrabarty coaxed Mason out of the overturned Sequoia, and as they and Burt returned to the station, Deucalion asked Ralph Nettles which of the other vehicles belonged to him.

Still unsettled by the tattooed giant's magical disappearance from the engineer's nest and by the way he had almost effortlessly overturned Mason's Toyota SUV, Ralph hesitated before indicating a three-year-old black Cadillac Escalade.

"We'll go to your place and get the guns

and ammunition you mentioned," Deucalion said. "Give me the key."

Producing the key, Ralph hesitated to surrender it. "Uh, well, it's my car, so I should drive."

"You can't drive like I do," the giant said. "You saw how I took one step from your room back there and into this parking lot? I had no need to walk it, no need to use doors. I can drive the same way. I understand the structure of reality, truths of quantum mechanics that even physicists don't understand."

"Good for you," Ralph said. "But I love that Escalade. It's my big-wheeled baby."

Deucalion took the keys from his hand. Having seen how the giant killed four of those things called replicants, Ralph decided against an argument.

The snow came down hard, obscuring everything like static in a lousy TV image. In fact, Ralph half felt as if he had stepped out of reality into some television fantasy program in which all the laws of nature that he knew well as an engineer were laws that Deucalion—and perhaps others—could break with impunity. He liked stability, continuity, things that were true in all times and all places, but he figured he'd better brace himself for turbulence.

He got in the front passenger seat of the Escalade as Deucalion climbed behind the wheel. Ralph wasn't a small man, but he felt like a child next to his driver, whose head touched the ceiling of the SUV.

Starting the engine, Deucalion said, "Your place—is it a house or an apartment?"

"House." Ralph told him the address.

Deucalion said, "Yes, I know where it is. Earlier I memorized a map of the town laid out in fractional seconds of latitude and longitude."

"Makes as much sense as anything else," Ralph said.

Light pulsed through the giant's eyes, and Ralph decided to look away from them.

As Deucalion popped the brake and put the Cadillac in drive, he said, "Do you live alone?"

"My wife died eight years ago. She was perfection. I'm not a big enough fool to think it can happen twice."

Deucalion began a wide U-turn in the

parking lot. "You never know. Miracles do happen."

During the turn, for an instant, there was no falling snow and every source of brightness in the storm clicked off—the parking-lot lamps, station lights, headlights—and the night was more deeply dark than any night had ever been. Then snow again. And lights. But though they should have swung around toward the exit to the street, they had turned directly into Ralph's driveway, five long blocks from KBOW.

chapter 23

As the sack split, Dagget staggered backward into the counter that contained the bathroom sinks.

Pistol in both hands, covering the cocoon, Frost almost squeezed off a shot. He resisted the urge to fire when he saw what began to emerge.

Even in childhood Frost hadn't been given to picturing monsters in his closet, but he had never before encountered a cocoon as big as a grown man, either. Now his pent-up imagination suddenly abandoned the usual mundane trail and galloped into grotesque territory. He expected something insectile to spring out of the splitting sack, nothing half as attractive as a Monarch butterfly, some strange hybrid cockroach with three heads or a spider with the face of an evil pig, or a ball of snakes because of all the slithering noise.

Instead, from the sack came a breathtakingly gorgeous, nude young woman, such a perfection of face and body as Frost had never seen before, such a flawless brunette that she seemed to have been airbrushed and photoshopped. Her complexion was not marred by even the smallest blemish. Her smooth and supple skin seemed to glow with good health. If she had not been so provocative in her nudity, even an atheist might have entertained the thought that an angel had appeared before him.

This lovely apparition, gliding gracefully from the cocoon, stepping out of the big Jacuzzi tub and onto the bathroom floor, did not seem surprised to discover two strangers in her house. Neither did she appear to be embarrassed by her nudity or concerned about their intentions, or the least bit alarmed by the pistol in Frost's two-hand grip. She had an air of supreme confidence, as if she had been raised to believe that the world had been made just for her and, in the intervening years, never had a single reason to question that belief.

When this exquisite woman emerged from the silvery-gray sack, which now sagged like some immense leather raincoat hung on a hook, Frost wondered if the thing was not a cocoon, after all. Perhaps it might be a new invention, in this age when revolutionary products poured out of the cornucopia of high technology by the thousands every year. Maybe it was a luxury beauty appliance into which a woman could climb in order to be moisturized, depilated, toned, tanned, and oxygenated for better health.

When it was directed at Frost, the woman's smile was spectacular and exhilarating and contagious, but when she smiled at Dagget, Frost filled with a simmering jealousy, which made no sense. He had no claim on this woman, didn't even know who she was.

"Who are you?" Dagget asked. "What were you doing in that thing, what *is* that thing?"

She glanced at the deflated sack and

frowned as if she had seen it now for the first time. She looked at Dagget again, and opened her mouth as if to speak. All her teeth spilled over her lips and rattled like thirty-two dice on the tile floor.

As though puzzled but not alarmed, she surveyed the scattered teeth until they had stopped bouncing. She looked up, exploring her toothless gums with her tongue—and new teeth sprouted in the empty sockets, bright white and as perfect as the rest of her.

Frost saw that Dagget's pistol had gone from the shoulder rig under his jacket into his right hand almost as magically as the new teeth had materialized. He eased along the counter, away from the woman, toward the doorway that Frost occupied.

The teeth on the floor were related some-how to the severed foot in the living room, to the OK thumb and forefinger in the foyer, to the portion of jawbone with teeth on the bedroom floor, and to the tongue from which grew a lidless eye. But Frost couldn't put it all together. *Nobody* could have put it together. It was crazy. This wasn't like any-thing he'd expected to find, not just a crimi-nal enterprise or a terrorist plot.

The woman wasn't just a woman. She was something more, and her singular beauty was perhaps the least astonishing thing about her. But whatever else she might be, she *was* a woman, naked and seemingly defenseless, and he couldn't shoot her just because she could grow teeth in an instant, apparently at will. Never in his career had he shot a woman.

As Dagget arrived at Frost's side, the woman studied herself in the long mirror above the twin sinks. She cocked her head, frowned, and said not to them but to herself, "I think my builder built this builder wrong."

On the floor, the thirty-two teeth abruptly became animated and rattled against the ceramic tiles, returning to the woman as if she produced an irresistible magnetic field. As each tooth drew within an inch or two of her bare feet, it ceased to be a tooth and became a cluster of tiny silvery specks, and all the clusters vanished into her skin as if she were a dry sponge and they were water.

Frost's training had given him tactics and protocols for every situation that he had previously encountered in his career, but not for this. He could see nothing that he and Dagget could do other than wait, observe, and hope for understanding. The woman was more than a woman, and she was strange, and the pieces of bodies strewn here and there were proof that terrible violence had been committed in the house, but there was no proof that she committed it.

Traditional interrogation wouldn't get them anywhere in these extraordinary circumstances. She seemed to be half in a trance, not much interested in them. Although Frost couldn't make sense of what she'd said—*I think my builder built this builder wrong*—he detected in her tone the dismay of someone who had sustained a serious offense, suggesting that she was a victim rather than a victimizer.

As she regarded herself in the mirror again, a fine twinkling cloud of mist came off her skin, and for a moment she seemed to have the radiant aura of a supernatural being. And then the mist coalesced into a blue silk robe that clung to her body.

Dagget said, "Sonofabitch."

"Yeah," Frost agreed.

"Something is going to happen."

"It just did."

"Something worse," Dagget said.

The woman raised her right hand to her face and stared at it in what appeared to be bafflement.

She turned her head to look at Frost and Dagget as if she had just remembered that she was not alone.

She reached out to them with her right hand, and when her arm was fully extended, she revealed to them her palm. In it was a mouth bristling with teeth.

chapter 24

One-eyed, one-eared, with a steel-and-copper mechanical hand at the end of his left arm, Sully York could see and hear as well as anyone, better than some. As well as anyone, he could serve up mixed nuts, three varieties of cheese, three varieties of crackers, thick slices of Armenian sausage, and drinks, a forty-year-old Scotch for him and Bryce Walker, and a Pepsi for the boy, Travis Ahern, who was only about ten, which in Sully's opinion was four years too early either for Scotch or women, or life-and-death exploits.

By the time that Sully had been fourteen,

he had enjoyed a good whiskey now and then and could hold his liquor. But of course he had been six feet three at that age, had looked twenty-one, on his own in the world and ready for adventure. Back then, he hadn't lost the eye yet or the ear, or the hand, and he hadn't sustained the sabre slash from his right eye to the corner of his mouth that left him with a livid scar in which he took much delight. In fact, at fourteen he hadn't known much fun at all but was determined to have some, which he damn well did over the decades. Back then, all of his teeth had been real, whereas they were all gold these forty-seven years later, and he had cracked and broken off and simply lost each of them in a thrilling and memorable fashion.

They settled in Sully's den, which was his favorite room in the house. Over the stone fireplace hung a fierce boar's head, the tusks as pointed as ice picks, and with it the knife that Sully wielded to kill the beast. One wall and his desktop offered framed photographs of him and his buddies in exotic locales, from jungles to deserts, from mountain passes to ships sailing on strange tides, and in every case he and those good old boys—all dead now, each killed as colorfully as he had lived—had been in the service of their country, though never once in uniform. The kind of work they did was so deep cover that it made the CIA seem by comparison as open as a community-outreach organization. Their group had no name, only a number, but they had called themselves the Crazy Bastards.

On shelves and tables were souvenirs: a perfectly preserved six-inch-long hissing cockroach from Madagascar; an ornately carved wooden leg once worn by a dwarf Soviet assassin; a dirk and a dagger and a kris, all of which had cut him and all of which he had taken away from the cutters, who were rotting in Hell; the knobkerrie that had knocked out his left eye and with which he had dealt immediate vengeance to the one who had half blinded him; a blowgun, a scimitar, a pike, a tomahawk, a yataghan, intricately worked iron handcuffs, and many more items of sentimental value.

They settled in big leather armchairs around the coffee table where all the food was laid out, while Bryce and Travis recounted events they had witnessed—and escaped—at Memorial Hospital. Of the two, Bryce did most of the talking and most of the eating, as the boy slumped in a bleak mood that damn well did not become him. Sully had no patience for sulkers or whiners or negativists in general. He would have given Travis some sharp advice about the necessity to have a positive and high-spirited response to everything in life, from a certain glorious young woman in Singapore to a knobkerrie in the eye, but he restrained himself because he suspected that in spite of the boy's current annoying mood, he had the right stuff. Sully York had a nose for people with the right stuff, which was one of the reasons he was the only surviving Crazy Bastard.

The story Bryce told—of patients being killed at the hospital, of some kind of mass-murder conspiracy that Travis insisted had to be the work of extraterrestrials—was so screwball and wild-assed that Sully quickly recognized it as the dead-serious truth. Besides, Bryce had as much of the right stuff as anyone Sully York had ever known. Bryce hadn't spent his life cutting the throats of slick villains who needed their throats cut; he hadn't pushed off cliffs the people who, in being pushed off, gave noble meaning to those cliffs. Instead, Bryce had written Western novels, damn good ones, full of heroism, in which he portrayed *exactly* how true evil operated and how good people sometimes had to deal hard with the bad ones if civilization was to survive.

When Bryce finished, Sully looked at the boy, who sat holding a cube of cheese at which he had fitfully nibbled. "Son, I really believe you've got moxie in your veins and steel in your spine. I have a nose for people with the right stuff, and you smell to high heaven of it. But there you sit as spiritless as that damn chunk of cheese. Hell, the cheese looks more capable of being ornery than you do. If half of what Bryce has told me is true—and I think it's full true, front to back—then we have a hard job of work ahead of us, and we have to go at it with spunk and spirit and absolute confidence that we're going to storm the hill and plant the flag. If we're to be on the same team, I have to know why you're moping like this and that you have the guts and the love of glory to get up out of your funk and fight to *win*."

Bryce said, "Sully, his mother has gone missing. Travis doesn't know for sure, can't know, but he thinks they got her. He thinks she must be dead."

Thrusting up from his armchair, making a fist of his mechanical hand, Sully said, "Maybe she's dead? Is that all? Hell, no, she's not dead. Nobody's dead until you see the stinking body. I won't damn well believe that *I'm* dead until I can look down on my corpse and see for sure there aren't any vital signs. I've known people who were surely dead—he was flung out the door of a chopper at two thousand feet without a parachute, another supposedly took three rounds in the back and fell into an ice crevasse—but a year or two passes and one night in a dark alley or in a crowded bazaar in Morocco, here he is coming at you with a meat ax or pushing you face-first into a huge old basket full of cobras! Dead, my ass. You haven't seen your mother dead, have you? If you haven't seen her dead, she's not dead, and we're going to go out there and find her. So eat the rest of that cheese and prepare yourself. You understand me, short stuff?"

The flat dull look in Travis Ahern's eyes had given way to a lively light.

"Better," Sully York said.

chapter 25

Carson would have preferred to stay at the Samples house with the Riders and Riderettes, having all those well-intentioned, well-armed, tough, and savvy people covering her back. Not to mention the excellent coffee and the pumpkin pies in the oven. But considering their numbers, the percentage of them who had been in the military and therefore knew something about strategy and tactics, and the cell-phone videos of the horror at the roadhouse, they didn't need Carson and Michael to recruit their neighbors and turn their block into a garrison.

The most urgent task at hand was locating Deucalion. With his singular gifts, only he would be able to drive the children out of Rainbow Falls, past the roadblocks, to the comparative safety of Erika's house four miles west of town. With no telephone service of any kind, they would need to track him down somehow, which at first seemed to be an almost impossible mission in a town of nearly fifteen thousand.

As Carson piloted the Grand Cherokee through a sea of snow, tides washing across the windshield and foaming at the wheels, heading toward the center of Rainbow Falls, Michael said, "I've got an idea."

"You always have an idea. You always have a dozen ideas. That's why I married you. Just to see what ideas you'll come up with today."

"I thought you married me for my looks, my sensitivity, and my fabulous bedroom stamina."

Carson said, "Lucky for you, beauty is in the eye of the beholder. But I will acknowledge you really do an exhaustive job cleaning the bedroom."

"Here's an idea. Why do I have to do

any housecleaning? We have a full-time housekeeper. Why doesn't she do it?"

"Mary Margaret is a great cook and a nanny. She does only light housekeeping. Keeping a spotless house requires someone with muscle, determination, and fortitude."

"Sounds like you."

Carson said, "Do you want me to clean, and from now on you do all the stuff I do, like fix plumbing and electrical problems, keep the cars fine-tuned, do the accounting and taxes?"

"No. I'd wind up electrocuted trying to replace a valve in the toilet just before the IRS seized the house. But back to my idea—we know Deucalion intends to take out the crews of as many of those blue-and-white trucks as he can. So if we can locate one that's still operating and we tail it, maybe we'll find Deucalion when he finds the truck."

"That's pretty much a lame idea."

"Well, I don't hear any dazzling suggestions from our plumber-electrician-mechanic-accountant."

They rode in silence for a couple of minutes.

Then she said, "I've got a bad, bad feeling about this, Tonto."

"The way I see it, kemo sabe, we can't fail. When Deucalion received his gifts on the lightning, they had to have come from a higher power."

"The Riders call Him the Trail Boss in the Sky."

"I didn't know that."

"Loreen Rudolph told me. You were at the other end of the kitchen, checking out the contents of all those cookie jars faster than the kids could."

"Have *you* ever known anyone with five cookie jars? Anyway, for over two hundred years, Deucalion has been on Victor's trail, and he won the round in New Orleans. I think he'll win this round, too, the entire fight. He's on a divine mission. It's his destiny to stop Victor and undo everything Victor does, so this is going to turn out okay."

No snowplows were on the streets. The replicants of the city employees were engaged in other activities, mostly murder.

Carson drove past a park where walkway lampposts dwindled along a serpentine path, the snow like white-hot sparks immediately around each lamp but like

pale gray falling ashes in the gloom between them, and past the last post lay a
black nothingness that felt as vast as the
ominous dark of an ocean on a moonless
night.

"The thing is," she said, "this is Deucalion's mission. We're supporting players.
We don't have to live for him to fulfill his
destiny."

"Well," Michael said, "I'm putting my
trust in the Trail Boss."

Only a few pedestrians were on the sidewalks, heads bent into the endless skeins
of snow, and Carson looked them over as
she passed them, wondering if they were
ordinary men and women or instead might
be dark beasts slouching into the world
from a subterranean manger where demons were born.

When Carson turned left off Cody onto
Russell Street, she saw one of the blue-
and-white trucks parked at the curb, engine running, crystallized exhaust smoking
from the tailpipe. She coasted past it.

Michael confirmed what she thought
she had seen: "No one in the cab. Go
around the block."

She went around to Cody, turned onto

Russell again, parked fifty feet behind the truck, and doused the headlights. They watched the vehicle for a few minutes. The pale exhaust feathered up into the night like a procession of spirits answering some celestial trumpet that only they could hear.

"Why would they leave the truck unattended?" she wondered.

"And they wouldn't herd their silver-beaded zombies into it in such a public place. Alleyways, back entrances . . . that's where they'd want to load up."

"Check it?"

"Let's check it."

No businesses remained open in this block. Traffic was even lighter than it had been before they stopped at the Samples house. Russell Street looked as lonely as a trail through some arctic wasteland, so they boldly carried the Urban Snipers.

The night had grown colder, the snowflakes icier.

The cab of the truck was still unoccupied, but two dead men were sprawled in the cargo hold. Not men. Replicants. This was clearly Deucalion's work.

Closing the cargo-space door, Michael said, "I already have another idea."

"Your last one didn't get us killed, so let's hear this one."

"Instead of us trying to find a truck to follow until Deucalion attacks it, we switch our gear from the Jeep to this and cruise until our monster buddy comes to kill the crew."

"Let's hope he recognizes us *before* he breaks our necks."

chapter 26

The sad piano music followed them through the house and all the way into Officer Bozeman's two-car garage. The garage contained no cars, but there were a Ford Expedition, a motorcycle, and in front of the cycle a snowmobile on an open trailer, just as Nummy O'Bannon had told Mr. Lyss there would be.

"Peaches, every time I think you're as useless as a two-legged cat, you come through for us. You're all right."

This praise greatly pleased Nummy until he realized they were stealing another vehicle, just one without wheels this time.

He was being praised for helping Mr. Lyss to steal.

"Sir, when that there lottery ticket in your wallet wins big, it'll be good if you pay for the Boze's snowmobile then."

"Hell and all, who would I pay? Bozeman is dead in the kitchen. His wife is dead and buried. They never had kids. I'm damn well not going to pay his monster look-alike so it can make the next mortgage payment and just sit on its ass playing morbid piano." He poked Nummy in the chest with one finger. "You've got this fixation about always paying for things." He poked Nummy again. "It's not just because you're a moron. It's psychological." He poked Nummy a third time. "It's neurotic is what it is. Sick. It's deeply sick. Sick and damn annoying. Nobody pays for everything. I guess I should pay for the air I breathe! For the sounds I hear! For all the things I can see because I've got eyes! Who do I write those checks to, hmmmmm? Who?"

Nummy was pleased that Mr. Lyss had begun to understand. He said, "You want to tithe? Grandmama she always tithed to St. John's over on Bear Claw Lane, so if you want to tithe where she did, then that would be good."

Mr. Lyss just stared at Nummy while the piano got even sadder. Then he threw his hands in the air as if shouting *hallelujah* and tossing away all his cares. "I give up. How can I expect you to learn some street smarts when you don't have any other smarts of any damn kind? Can a donkey waltz? Can a monkey sing opera? Can a cow *jump over the freaking moon*?"

Nummy didn't know what to say because he didn't understand any of those questions. They didn't make sense to him.

Fortunately, Mr. Lyss didn't try to shake answers out of Nummy, like he sometimes did. Instead, the old man climbed into the open roofless trailer with the snowmobile and began examining the controls, all the while muttering to himself.

Nummy shuffled around the garage, looking at the tools hanging on the walls, the workbench with all its little drawers, several gasoline-company signs the Boze collected, and the spiderwebs here and there in corners. He didn't like spiders at all. Charlotte in *Charlotte's Web* was okay, she was nice, but she wasn't a real spider, she was a story spider with a good heart. He hoped it was too cold for spiders now because real ones didn't have good hearts.

Once, more years back than he could count, he came upon a web where a fly was stuck and a spider was eating it alive. Nummy felt awful for the fly because it didn't know webs were sticky, it just didn't know, it made one mistake, and now it was being eaten. The fly was hardly alive. Nummy was too late to save it. He turned away but couldn't stop feeling awful for the fly. He felt awful all that day, way back when. And later that evening, he realized why he was upset about the fly's suffering. The little fly was dumb, and the spider was smart, making its sticky web, and so the dumb fly never had a chance. When he figured that out, Nummy told Grandmama about the fly, and he cried while he told her.

Grandmama listened to every word, she never cut him short, and then she said the fly wouldn't want Nummy to cry for it. She said the fly led a happy life, just as free as any bird, exploring all day and always delighted by what it saw in the world, playing fly games, no need to work because it ate crumbs and other things that were free, and it didn't have to have a house with all the upkeep *that* required. Meanwhile, the spider was always spinning webs, scheming, either working or lying in wait, which was just another kind of work. The spider couldn't fly. It crouched in corners while flies flew. The spider could only watch flying things and envy them. The spider lived in shadows, darkness, but the fly's life was full of light. Because it only ate flies and such, never a cookie crumb or a dropped bit of a candy bar, the spider never tasted anything sweet. The spider was proud about how smart it was, but when you really thought about the situation, the fly had all the fun. And even though the fly came to a terrible end, it didn't know that such a thing could happen to it, and therefore it lived without worry. Because the spider knew what it did to flies, it also knew that some other creature might do the same to it, some toad or frog or bird. So the fly lived without worry and free and flying, while the ever-working spider lived in fear and shadows, crouched and wary or scuttling for cover.

After circling Officer Bozeman's garage,

Nummy saw no spiders in the webs or out of them, but he found the keys to the three vehicles on a Peg-Board by the open door to the kitchen. He knew which one was for the snowmobile because he'd seen the Boze use it. He took the key to Mr. Lyss, who was just climbing over the railing of the open trailer.

Accepting the key, pointing at the snow-mobile, the old man said, "I think I've got this bugger figured out. But before we go scooting off into the storm of the damn century, let's find some gloves and get your feet properly protected."

Mr. Lyss led the way back into the house and into the sad piano music. Nummy reluctantly followed because he didn't want to find a spider when he was alone in the garage.

Searching the bedroom closet, the old man found waterproof boots. Mr. Lyss was already wearing good boots, but Nummy had only shoes. Mr Lyss stuffed some of Officer Bozeman's socks in the toes of the boots, and then they fit Nummy's feet well enough.

"I won't take these here boots," Nummy said. "I'll only borrow them."

There were a few pairs of gloves. For both of them, Mr. Lyss chose two pairs with what he called wrist and gauntlet straps. He could pull the straps to make the gloves fit nice and tight.

"I'll only borrow these, too," Nummy said.

"Me too," Mr. Lyss said. "I'll just borrow these gloves for the rest of my life, and when I'm dead like Bozeman, I'll give them back to him."

Because the Boze had only one snow-mobiler helmet, which Mr. Lyss would need because he was driving, Nummy had to settle for a toboggan cap. He could pull it down over his ears once they were moving fast and making cold wind.

"But don't you go thinking that cap is yours now," Mr. Lyss said. "It's only yours on loan."

"I know," Nummy assured him.

Mr. Lyss found a red-and-gray wool scarf for Nummy to wrap around his face later, when they were speeding through the snow. "You understand this is only on loan, too?"

"That's right."

"You lose it, I'll make you pay for it, even

if you have to work the rest of your life to earn the money."

"I won't lose it," Nummy said.

From the Boze's bedroom, Mr. Lyss went to stand in the living-room archway. He watched the Xerox Boze playing the piano.

At last the old man said, "I don't know why it doesn't feel right, but it doesn't. I just can't kill him."

"Maybe you're not a killer."

"Oh, I'm a killer sure enough. I've killed more men than you've ever met in your whole life. I'd as soon kill most people as look at them. I've killed some people just because they smiled and said hello to me."

Nummy shook his head. "I'm not sure you really did."

"You better not be calling me a liar. Somebody calls me a liar, I cut him open, rearrange his innards, sew him up, and for the rest of his life he has to pee out of his left ear."

"What you said before is you cut out his tongue and fried it with onions for breakfast."

"That's right. I do that sometimes, and sometimes I make him pee out of his ear.

Depends on my mood. So you better not be calling me a liar."

"I'm not. That wouldn't be nice. People they should always be nice to each other."

In the garage again, the old man pushed a button to put up the big door. A little wind had come up, and snow blew in from the night.

Putting his long gun on the workbench, he said, "I can't see any way to take this. It won't fit in the saddlebags. We'll have to hope the pistols are enough."

The smaller guns were in the deep pockets of his long coat, and there were lots of bullets in other pockets, all borrowed from the preacher's house that they burned down.

Nummy had been with Mr. Lyss not even a day yet, but it seemed like a life's worth of stuff had happened. You didn't have time to be bored around Mr. Lyss.

"We'll pull the trailer into the driveway and drop the ramp in the snow," the old man said. "But wait. Just let me put on this damn thing."

The damn thing was the helmet. It was silver and black with a clear window across the face.

A circle of little holes in the helmet, in front of Mr. Lyss's mouth, let out his voice. "How do I look?"

"Like a spaceman."

"Scary-looking, am I?"

"No. You look funny."

"You know what I've done to any snarky bastard who says I look funny?"

"Nothing nice," Nummy said.

chapter 27

The instant he saw it, Frost knew the mouth in the palm of her hand was real, but nevertheless he tried to tell himself that it was just an unusually dimensional tattoo or a joke decal, because if it was real, none of his training or experience would be worth spit in this situation. If it was real, this town didn't need undercover FBI agents; it needed exorcists, a platoon of them.

When the tongue licked out of the mouth, fondling the teeth and fluttering obscenely, Frost looked to the woman's eyes. Previously they were glazed, as if she were half in a trance, but they changed now. Her stare became bold and sharp, her eyes as fierce as the eyes of any bird of prey, although no bird's gaze ever burned with the scorching hatred that informed this creature's eyes.

The blue-silk robe that had materialized around her became mist again, like the smoke that rises off dry ice, and the mist appeared to be absorbed into her skin. From her toes to the top of her head, she rippled like a heat mirage, and the ultimate-Playmate proportions of her body melted away as her flesh and bones flowed like soft wax. Some of the substance of her torso poured into her outstretched right arm, which swelled, the skin stretching like sausage casing being pumped full of liquified meat. Her hand thickened, and the tongue in the mouth of that hand unraveled toward them, now silvery-gray, as flat as a tapeworm, undulating through the air, the tip of it flaring like the hood of a cobra.

Dagget let out a cry of revulsion and terror that startled Frost but also prepared him for the deafening boom of his partner's pistol, six quick shots that echoed off the tile floor and walls, off the glass shower door, off the mirror, like flying through the heart of storm clouds when thunder broke the sky. The range was point-blank and Dagget was a master marksman and Frost saw the bullets tear into the naked body, which was now as weird as someone reflected in one of those distorting mirrors in a carnival funhouse.

But no blood spilled, no wounds bloomed raw and red. The beast didn't drop or reel backward from the impact of the high-power rounds, but instead absorbed them as a pond would absorb a dropped stone. The flesh didn't even dimple with concentric ripples as water would have done. The tissue received the bullets and at once closed around them, smooth and unscarred.

Dagget's next four shots had no greater effect than the first six, except that the undulating gray tongue abruptly grew thicker and shot at him with the lightning speed of a striking snake. It wasn't a tongue anymore, it was an auger, and it bored into Dagget's face. In an instant it was not a drill anymore, either, and it seemed to have become the hose of a vacuum cleaner, sucking out the contents of his head, his skull imploding like a papery husk, head gone in a blink.

Backing out of the bathroom doorway, Frost stumbled, almost fell, got his balance.

In the bathroom, beyond the open door, Dagget's pistol clattered against the floor tiles, but his headless body didn't collapse. The ravenous gray tentacle now seemed to be composed of a swarming mass of small somethings, millions of tiny silvery piranhas, and all of them schooled down through his neck, into his dead body, apparently holding him erect, his legs jittering and his feet seeming to dance on the bathroom floor. Looming beyond the headless marionette, the thing that had been a beautiful woman was now nothing that had a name, a mottled gray-and-silver mass, clotted with red that quickly darkened to veins of charcoal-gray, larger than it had been. It surged even larger as the substance of the corpse was drawn out like soda through a straw, until there were only empty clothes flapping in the air like a scarecrow's costume, but then the clothes wadded up and were sucked away into the vacuuming tentacle.

Dagget had been killed and devoured in five seconds.

Frost ran.

chapter 28

Sammy Chakrabarty always thought the old building that housed KBOW was an ugly pile, but the features that made it off-putting in the past were virtues in the current crisis.

Built in the 1870s by the local arm of the Patrons of Husbandry, otherwise known as the Grange, it served as the Grange Hall, offices and meeting rooms and a big space for community dinners and dances. The Granger movement was an organiza- tion of farmers who, in those days, wanted the government to confiscate and operate the railroads and the grain elevators as a public service, thus shifting some of the farmers' costs from them to the taxpayers.

For most people in the Grange, the motivation was self-interest, but as in any such political organization, a minority of the members were also paranoids. When you were lobbying to have the government seize some people's property for your benefit, it wasn't paranoid to think those on the losing end of that deal might take decisive action to halt your activities, might even come around one night with the intention of using more than words to persuade you to rethink your position. But the truest apostles of the paranoid faith spread wild stories, fevered fantasies of bloodbaths in distant states, fierce armies of railroad goons and brutal mercenaries in the employ of grain-elevator barons, entire units of the Grange shot in cold blood, hundreds of people at a time, shot and beaten and stabbed and set on fire and then shot again and then hung and then rehung, and subjected to verbal abuse, their farm animals sold into slavery, their dogs forced to wear humiliating costumes, their barns burned, their land salted and paprikaed.

As Sammy quickly walked the rooms and the hallways of KBOW, assessing the strengths and weaknesses of this fort, he figured that the head of the building committee for the Rainbow Falls Grange had been one of the squirreliest of the group, forcing a design that assumed any Grange supper-and-dance night could become a battleground and the building put under siege. The exterior walls, alternating layers of concrete and brick, were eighteen inches thick. The double-hung windows were kept to a minimum number, narrow and protected by decorative bronze grids that were essentially attractive prison bars. In respect of the building's historical status, the decorative bronze doors remained, as well, one on each side of the structure, but they were so heavy that they had been retrofitted with concealed ball-bearing hinges to make them easier to use.

By design, nothing in the construction materials was flammable. Yet the contents of the place would have made it a firetrap without the sprinkler system that had been added decades ago to meet the building-code requirements for KBOW to occupy the premises.

The parapeted, nearly flat roof featured glazed-brick paving sloped just enough to the perimeter scuppers to let rain drain off quickly. In snow season, maintenance men regularly shoveled the roof. But tonight would be the first time—at least in recent history—that a gunman would be stationed up there to defend the building.

Ralph Nettles and Deucalion were gone less than ten minutes, and they returned with enough firearms to delight the paranoid head of the Grange building committee if he had still been alive to see them. Six pistols, four assault rifles, three pistol-grip shotguns. They also brought several metal ammunition boxes with strap handles, packed with boxed ammo and with preloaded spare magazines for the various weapons.

In the conference room, which they had chosen to designate the armory, Sammy said to Ralph, "I know you're not a gun nut in the negative sense."

"How do you know?" Ralph asked, sweeping his arms wide to indicate the array of firearms on the conference table. "This is like one-fifth of my collection—and none are antiques."

"You're not any kind of nut. You're steady. So you have some good reason to gun-up like this."

Ralph hesitated. He wasn't a guy who talked much about himself. "I used to have only a single pistol for the nightstand drawer. Eight years ago this past September, I started the collection."

Eight years earlier, Sammy had been just fifteen, a high-school student in Corona del Mar, California, where his parents lived.

Deucalion said to Ralph, "Your wife died eight years ago."

Sammy knew this but hadn't made the connection.

"Jenny couldn't die that young. She was so good. So very alive. It was the most impossible thing that could ever, ever happen. But it happened. So I knew then everything else that seemed impossible might happen, too. All my life, I've been practical, prudent, prepared. The three P's—that's what my mother called them. There was no way I could have been prepared for Jenny dying, but the day I buried her, I swore to myself I'd be ready for every other impossible thing that could happen next. So maybe I am a nut, after all."

Sammy glanced at Deucalion, saw pulses of strange light throb through the giant's eyes, and looked at Ralph again. "Evidently not."

chapter **29**

Suddenly an ardent believer in everything that he previously disbelieved, from extraterrestrials to Satan, Frost sprinted across the room, past the eye-in-the-tongue still lying on the bed, and into the upstairs hallway. His heart galloped and he heard himself gasping for breath. He *knew* that he was sprinting as fast as he ever had, ever could, but he *felt* that he moved in slow motion, through air as resistant as water, his legs as leaden as those of a deep-sea diver in a pressure suit and a massive helmet, trudging across the ocean floor.

Even above the desperate bellows of

his ragged breathing and the slamming of his feet, Frost heard his pursuer, a buzzing-hissing-sizzling-zippering that was all those things and yet none of them, nothing like the sly slithering noise that had come from the cocoon, a never-before-heard sibilation, now a wet and clearly biological sound but *now* as dry as windblown sand.

At the midpoint of the hallway, he turned right toward the open staircase, and as he changed directions, he glanced back. The thing wasn't giving chase in either its womanly form or as the amorphous mass of seething tissue that it had been when it sucked in the last of Dagget. Now it manifested as an airborne silvery-gray mass, as dense as smoke, a teeming and twinkling swarm that might have been insects so tiny that the eye could not discern any details of them, billions upon billions. But he knew in fact they were together the body of the woman who came from the cocoon, nothing as ordinary as insects, but the substance of the woman now a racing cloud of gray that, falling upon him, would render him as rapidly as Dagget had been rendered.

Pistol in hand but under no delusion that it would be effective, Frost plunged down the stairs. The swarm passed overhead, perhaps intending to swoop around and into his face and dissolve the eyes out of his skull as they entered and possessed him. In passing, however, they encountered the chandelier above, a many-armed brass affair with amber-glass cups containing flame-shaped bulbs. They sizzled through it, dissolving the chain from which it was suspended and the cord from which it drew power, leaving the foyer lit only by the staircase lights and a soffit light above the door.

The extinguished chandelier fell but only half as fast as gravity demanded, borne by the boiling cloud of ravenous microscopic mites, descending toward the ground floor like a ship slowly sinking through the fathoms, diminishing as it went because it was being consumed in its fall. What reached the foyer below was in the end only the cloud, the swarm, no twist of metal or shard of glass remaining of the chandelier.

Just past the landing, on the lower of the two curving flights of stairs, Frost halted. Death waited below him. The swarm appeared less bright now, less silvery, darker shades of gray . . . and clotted. It looked more like dirty water than like smoke, slopping around in the foyer, lapping at the walls, seeming to build a tide toward the lower hallway that led back into the house, but then rolling toward the front door.

In spite of its watery appearance, the swarm didn't make liquid sounds, still buzzed and hissed and sizzled, but the tone had become lower, less the furious *zeeeeee* of angry wasps, more the grumbling drone of bumblebees. Through the spiraling currents of this pool, which included numerous whorls that intersected and spun off new coils and curls, there bobbled what appeared to be lumpy forms more coherent than the rest, though they seemed to dissolve as new lumps formed elsewhere.

Frost might have fled back to the second floor, to leave the house by an upper window and a porch roof, if instinct had not said *Wait.* Weak-kneed and shaking on the stairs, he slipped his pistol in the shoulder rig under his jacket. He gripped the railing with his left hand to steady himself, leaned against it. With his right sleeve, he wiped at the cold sweat that stippled his brow.

In the foyer below him, under a mirror, stood a narrow side table holding three ceramic vases of different sizes. The gray tide washed under it, around its legs. For a moment the table seemed to be of no interest to that voracious multitude, but then the slender legs began to dissolve. The table tipped forward, and the vases slid off. They didn't shatter as they fell into the pool, but bobbled briefly before apparently dissolving. The table came apart and the pieces were briefly flotsam before deliquescing out of sight into the spiral currents.

Intuition needed a while to be heard through the roar of Frost's terror, but finally he began to suspect that the swarm had lost track of him. There was something aimless in its motion as it swashed back and forth in the foyer, as though it had forgotten its purpose and quested this way and that, in search of some reminder of what it had been pursuing.

Frost suspected that if he moved or in

any way drew attention to himself, he might inspire an attack. He leaned against the railing and quieted his breathing.

Dagget was dead. They had been not just partners but also best friends. Frost wanted revenge. But he knew there would be none. The best he could hope for was to survive. And with his sanity.

chapter 30

After Nancy Potter, replicant of the
mayor's wife, threw down the last of the
angels and crushed them underfoot,
shrieking with delight, she eventually grew
somewhat calmer. But she was not able to
keep her promise to hurry at once with
Ariel to the barn to assist the girl in becoming what she was meant to be. All of
the shattered figurines had left a mess on
the living-room floor, and Nancy could not
merely walk away from such appalling disorder. She was alarmed that by eliminating the porcelain icons, which in themselves
were symbols of unreason and disorder,

she had created this *other* chaos herself, and she was unable to remember the chain of reason by which she had justified such behavior. In a disordered environment, the highest efficiency could not be achieved, and she must at all times be efficient. She must vacuum the living room and restore order before going to the barn.

Ariel was not a replicant. She was a Builder, although a much different kind of Builder from those at work elsewhere in Rainbow Falls. As a Builder, she lived by the same principles that were programmed in the replicants. Indeed, Builders had an appreciation for order and efficiency even greater than that of the replicants. Each replicant was a single organism, but each Builder was a colony of billions of nano-animals *each of which* was mandated to destroy only for the purpose of efficiently constructing other things—new Builders—that were more finely ordered than those beings that they *de*constructed. When the colony acted as one, either as a swarm or in the form of a single creature, the imperative to order things around them according to their programmed directives was an irresistible motivating force.

Consequently, Ariel fretted about the delay but didn't protest much when Nancy wanted to clean the living room and put things right once more. She dusted diligently while Nancy gathered the larger fragments of the figurines, and she vacuumed while Nancy polished the glass shelves in the display case with Windex. When Nancy became disturbed about a few scratches in the shelves, realized she could not make them look perfect, and smashed them, Ariel picked up the bigger shards of glass and disposed of them. She also vacuumed again while Nancy went to the kitchen and for a while sat at the dinette table with her eyes closed and her hands limp in her lap.

Replicant Nancy's thoughts were as jumbled as laundry tumbling in a dryer. The real Nancy had not kept the most spotless possible house, but she'd been a demon about laundry. Therefore, because the replicant had downloaded the woman's memories, the laundry metaphor occurred to her, and it served her well. One by one, she took her tumbling thoughts from the dryer, ironed them, folded them, and put them away.

When Ariel finished bringing order to the living room, she came into the kitchen and said, "Can we go to the barn now?"

Eyes still closed, Nancy said, "I need a couple minutes more."

After nine minutes and twenty-six seconds, Ariel said, "I really need to become what I'm meant to be. I really do."

"Just a minute," Nancy said.

Four minutes and nine seconds later, Ariel said, *"Please."*

At last Nancy opened her eyes. She felt much better. Her mind was ordered. Efficiency was again possible.

Oblivious of the weather, Nancy and Ariel crossed the yard from the house to the barn.

Most of the building's sixteen hundred square feet were in the main room, with a small tack room at the back. The walls were well insulated, and there was an oil furnace.

Along the south wall, horses watched the women from three stalls. Queenie and Valentine, the mares. Commander, the sorrel stallion.

The interior of the stalls in which the mares stood had earlier in the day been fortified with eighth-inch-thick steel plating. All of the windows had been filled with insulation and covered with inch-thick squares of sound board.

When the work began, the mares, in terror, were likely to try to kick out the walls and doors of their stalls when they saw what happened to the stallion.

Victor's plan was more ambitious than merely the elimination of humanity to the last pathetic individual. He intended also that every thinking creature in nature should be chased down in every field and forest, and deconstructed by Ariel's variety of Builder. Victor's definition of *thinking* included any life form with even minimal self-awareness. Any animal that took joy in life, that exhibited even the least curiosity about the world, that had the slightest capacity for wonder, must be hunted to extinction. The substance of those creatures would be used to make more Builders that could mimic all the myriad species, to mingle with their herds and run with their packs and fly with their flocks, and ruthlessly eliminate them. In the seas, too, were beings with capacity for joy and wonder—dolphins, whales, and others—

that must eventually be extinguished to the last specimen by aquatic Builders in the event that the seas proved too vast and self-cleaning to be effectively poisoned.

With a triumphant smile that Nancy understood, Ariel walked to Commander's stall. The girl had no apple for him, but she let the stallion snuffle and work his soft lips over her hand.

When in time nothing lived upon the planet other than Builders, replicants, insects, and plants, the two kinds of Communitarians would die at Victor's satellite-broadcast command. Only he would remain for a short while to witness a world without performers or audience, without anyone but him to remember its history, with no one to seek a future or even to want one. In the beginning had been the Word, but in the end *no* word would ever be spoken again, from pole to pole. Victor's rebellion had begun more than two hundred years earlier, and it had not ended with his death in Louisiana, for it continued here under the management of his clone, Victor Immaculate. This rebellion would be the greatest in history, not only in the history of the earth but also in the history of all that is, for Victor Immaculate would in the end kill himself, the last self-aware creature on Earth, and thereby signify that his maker, the New Orleans Victor, and his maker's maker were as meaningless as history, which had led to this nothing, these unpopulated landscapes in which no eye delighted.

The triumph that Ariel anticipated as she moved to the mares in response to their nickering, the triumph that tasted sweet to Nancy, as well, was the eventual obliteration of everything of which they could not be a part, which happened to be everything, whereafter even the Community, having fulfilled its purpose, could cease to exist.

They had been made to unmake and ultimately to be unmade. An exquisite efficiency.

In time, the insects whose existence depended on animals would perish, and the insects who fed on those insects would perish next, and the plants whose roots were aerated by *those* insects would die off. On it would go, until the world in every corner remained irreparably barren and silent and still.

Returning to the center of the barn, Ariel said, "Help me to become what I am meant to be."

Surveying the scattered stalks of hay that littered the floor, Nancy grimaced and said, "Just give me a few minutes to sweep this floor. You can't create in all this disorder. Just because it's a barn, there's no excuse for this mess, no excuse at all, this just makes me *livid*."

chapter 31

From the arsenal on the big conference-room table, Mason Morrell chose only a pistol, and from the cache of ammunition, he selected one spare magazine, which he loaded.

"I'll be locked in the broadcast booth," he told Sammy. "If they get as far as breaking down that door, the rest of you are dead and I won't have any hope of holding out against them. I'll want to kill a couple, just for the principle of it, but then I won't need anything but one round for myself."

He went away with Deucalion, who needed to coach him a few more minutes about what he should say when he pulled the current recorded program and went live.

More familiar with all of these weapons than the average radio ad salesman might have been in, say, Connecticut, Burt Cogborn took some time deciding what he might need. He chose a pistol, an assault rifle, and a pistol-grip shotgun, plus spare magazines for the first two and a box of shells for the 12-gauge.

"I know there isn't time," Burt said, "but I sure wish I could go home and get Bobby, bring him back here."

Bobby was his Labrador retriever. He always took Bobby with him on sales calls and usually brought the pooch to the station, as well. Mason Morrell called them the Cogborn twins, Burt and Bobby. For some reason, Burt had left the dog at home this time.

"I don't know what I'll do if anything happens to Bobby."

"Nothing's going to happen to Bobby," Sammy assured him. "He's smart and tough."

"If something happens to me," Burt said, "will you take in Bobby and treat him like your own, like you'd had him since a puppy? I'd trust you to be good to him."

Sammy was touched, though he figured that if Burt died defending KBOW, they would all be overwhelmed and killed. "I will, sure. I'll take him in."

"He really likes those Royal Canin treats." Burt spelled the brand name. "They're made with fruit and vegetables, so they're good for him. Little brown cookies with ridges in them."

"Royal Canin treats," Sammy said.

"His favorite toy is the bunny. Not the fully stuffed one, the floppy one. Not just the one with floppy ears but the one that the whole thing is floppy. And not the white floppy one, but the light-green one."

"Light-green fully floppy bunny," Sammy said. "I've got it."

Burt was not by nature an emotionally demonstrative person, but with tears standing in his eyes, he hugged Sammy. "You're a good friend, Sammy. You're the best."

Burt took his guns to the reception lounge to set up a defense position near the front door.

Ralph Nettles had already armed himself, which left only Sammy to choose from the dazzling variety of weapons that remained.

Because his roots went back to the land of Mahatma Gandhi, some people assumed that Sammy must be an ardent advocate of nonviolence, but that was an erroneous assumption. His family had long included Hindu apostates who had numerous reasons to be unmoved by Gandhi, and many who were Americophiles. Sammy's grandfather had been a fan of the hard-boiled novels of Mickey Spillane, and his father thrived on Spillane and the thrillers of John D. MacDonald. Sammy had read everything by both those authors, adored the work of Stephen Hunter and Vince Flynn, and couldn't resist learning to use the guns in the stories that he had been reading since he was ten. Besides, this was not gun-fearing San Francisco or Malibu, this was Montana, and Sammy wanted to fit in with the locals, unlike most Californians who fled their state and moved here and then wanted to make Montana into a version of what they left behind.

As the program director, promotion director, and community-affairs director of KBOW, Sammy was the most senior company officer on the scene. With Warren Snyder dead—dead twice if you counted his replicant—Sammy was certain to remain the big bear as long as this crisis continued. By his standards, this required that he take for himself the most difficult role in the station's defense: rooftop sniper and guardian of the broadcast tower.

At 130 pounds, he would find many shotguns difficult to control, but he could handle the low-recoil Beretta Xtrema2 12-gauge, which some well-trained shotgunners could even fire with a one-hand grip. He also—and primarily—wanted the Bushmaster Adaptive Combat Rifle, which was a gas-operated semiauto with a thirty-round magazine with Trijicon optics.

He didn't think he would need a pistol, but he took one anyway.

Ralph Nettles had brought three spare loaded magazines for the Bushmaster. Sammy filled a waterproof ammo bag for the other guns, collected additional gear that he needed, and piled everything in the break room, off the kitchenette, where a set of spiral stairs in one corner led up to the roof door.

The areas of the studio directly associated with the broadcast were kept cooler than other rooms, and Sammy tended to chill easily. He had come to work wearing insulated longjohns, blue jeans, and a wool sweater, so he wasn't underdressed for rooftop work.

When he went into his office to snatch his ski jacket from the hook on the back of the door, Sammy realized that the station feed coming through the wall speaker was no longer the recorded material that had been running. Mason had gone live again, although not with advice to the lovelorn and dysfunctional families. Sammy turned up the volume.

". . . this town that I love, the wonderful people of both this town and the county beyond, and perhaps the people of Montana and of the entire United States are in grave peril tonight. Many who are listening might have turned on their radios to find out why they have no telephone or Internet service. Others may have tuned in to KBOW because they've seen something strange or inexplicable, and they're seeking information that might make sense of it to them."

It's begun, Sammy thought, and for the first time he began to feel the true momentous nature of these events. So much had happened so fast, so much of such a fantastical nature, that his ability to absorb it, believe it, and react properly to it had required all of his energy and had prevented him from grasping the more profound implications of events. The danger had initially seemed primarily personal, to himself and his coworkers, to his plans for KBOW. Now he had a chilling sense of the full existential nature of the threat: to the town, the county, the state, and to all of humanity.

"Others of you may be missing family members," Mason continued, "some for a short enough time that you attribute it to bad weather, delays because of road conditions. Others may know people who have been missing for the larger part of the day and are puzzled as to why the police seem to dismiss your concern. Folks, you've been listening to me for two years, you know I tell people truths that they need to hear, no matter how difficult it is for me to say it or for them to hear it. And what I tell you now is truth of a very hard kind, hard both to say and believe: You cannot trust the Rainbow Falls police. They aren't who they appear to be. Your missing friends and family members may be dead. An unknown number of people in this town have been killed. The killing continues as I speak."

Sammy ran to the spiral stairs in the break room. He needed to get to the roof. Mason had blown the lid off the conspiracy, and the blowback would be coming.

chapter 32

On the stairs, leaning against the railing, making not a sound, Frost warily watched the thing in the foyer, seething swarm or Blob like in the movies, machine or animal, terrestrial or alien from a far world, he didn't know which, didn't *care* which, at least not now, not until he got out of this house and away and was somewhere safe, where he could think.

After the table and the three vases were dissolved, the thing became less active. The arches, loops, and whorls formed by apparent currents in its substance were fewer and churning slower than before.

Frost's initial impression was that the beast must be resting, but after a couple of minutes, he decided that it might be thinking. Something about its attitude—if the Blob was capable of having an attitude—suggested deliberation, a pondering of the situation and a consideration of its options.

Options? Based on what he had seen of the thing's capabilities, its options were virtually unlimited. It was a shape-changer, it could fly, bullets had no effect on it, it was fearless and aggressive to an extent that suggested it was invulnerable, and instantaneously it could incorporate into itself people and objects of all kinds. Why would such a creature have any need to brood about its options? It could do anything it wanted, with no mortal consequence to itself but with plenty of mortal consequences for everyone who got in its way.

The idea of this thing meditating, musing, reflecting somberly upon its destiny almost teased a laugh from Frost, but he didn't give in to the impulse because the laugh would have been a dark, despairing giggle.

Besides, he remained convinced that if he made a sound, the creature would be reminded of its pursuit of him and in an instant would be upon him in one hideous form or another. The wisest thing he could do for the time being was remain still, silent, and wait for some development that he might be able to use to his advantage.

He didn't have to wait long before something happened. The thing began to act once more like a pool of thick liquid, washing back and forth in the foyer, its whorling currents returning to their previous level of activity.

Frost tensed. He put a hand under his open jacket, on the grip of the pistol in his shoulder rig, but then withdrew his hand without the weapon. Going for a gun was a reflex action. An agent's reflexes were usually reliable, the result of experience, but in this case reflexive responses would get him killed.

The living pool, whether its life was that of an animal or an intelligent machine, or both, or neither, slopped against the bottom step, lapped at the front door and the walls. The patterns of the currents within it were for the most part as liquid and sinuous as before—but here and there the currents twitched, stuttered briefly, before spiraling smoothly once more.

Suddenly a woman's hand rose out of the pool, a hand in various shades of gray with veins of black, as if carved from stone and yet animated, clutching at the air in search of something to which it could secure itself. After a moment, other hands reached through the surface of the pool, or rather formed from the substance of it. A second female hand, slender and beautifully shaped, had skin like brass, like the shiny brass of the fallen chandelier that had been incorporated into the swarm. A man's hand, then a second, one with skin the color of the glazed vases that had stood upon the foyer table, the other with normal flesh.

All the hands receded, melted into the pool, but then the gray surface glistened like water, and an immense face appeared in it, as if just below the surface, perhaps five feet from the point of the chin to the top of the brow. This countenance was at first as blank as that of a stone-temple god, with pale limestone eyes. But then it swelled from the surface, taking dimension and acquiring the color of skin, and Frost saw that it was becoming Dagget's face. The eyes opened, but they weren't eyes, were instead ovals of what seemed to be amber glass like the cups that contained the flame-shaped bulbs on the chandelier.

Frost waited for the glass eyes to shift toward him, but they did not. The Dagget face dissolved to be at once replaced by another immense countenance, that of the beautiful woman who had emerged from the cocoon in the bathroom. Her eyes looked real but had a fixed gaze like that of a blind person. The enormous face formed more completely than Dagget's had done, and the woman seemed to be struggling against invisible bonds, trying to free herself from the pool. Her mouth went wide, as if in a scream, but no sound escaped her.

Frost remembered what she had said upstairs, after the teeth had fallen out of her mouth and she had grown new ones, as she gazed at herself in the mirror above the bathroom sinks: *I think my builder built this builder wrong.* As he watched the huge face strain to scream and form

further out of the pool, he began to suspect that everything this creature had done
since taking down the chandelier had been
evidence of malfunction.

Abruptly the face disintegrated back into
the pool or the swarm, whichever or whatever it was, and the whole of the abomination became highly agitated, roiling as
though a school of eels thrashed in it, serpentine forms slithering across the surface, wriggling, twisting. From it issued
both the grumbling bumblebee drone and
the *zeeeeee* of angry wasps that Frost had
heard before.

The sounds swelled in volume and
seemed to promise violence greater than
any thus far committed, so that Frost dared
to take a step backward and then another,
even if movement might still make a target
of him. He retreated cautiously to the landing, ready to run but also mesmerized by
the spectacle in the foyer below.

Simultaneously, the pool stopped thrash-
ing and the two insect voices fell silent.
The creature became very still, exhibiting
none of its previous spiraling currents. Its
color began to change. Instead of many
shades of gray from charcoal to mouse-

skin with patches of glittering silver, it grew dull, with no sheen anywhere, and swiftly paled to a uniform concrete-gray.

It looked as dead as any dead thing Frost had ever seen.

Minutes earlier, he had thought that it must be invulnerable and therefore immortal. Now he imagined that if he descended the stairs and stepped on that gray mass, it would prove to have petrified, to have turned to hardest stone underfoot, a strange slab there in the foyer. Perhaps if sliced with a high-powered mason's saw, it would appear to have the grain of granite, allowing no clue that it had ever been anything else, certainly not anything more.

But he did not descend to test the accuracy of his perceptions. He backed quietly off the landing and onto the upper flight of the open staircase, all the while watching the stone-but-not-stone through the railing.

He found a bedroom with a window that opened onto the front-porch roof. He climbed out of the house, crept toward the edge of the snow-covered roof. The slope was gradual, and he did not slip. He jumped to the yard below, tucked and rolled as he landed, and sprang to his feet, covered in snow, turning fearfully in a circle, certain that something must be coming at him.

Nothing pursued him. He was alone. No neighbors seemed to have heard Dagget's ten shots. Maybe no one remained alive to hear them. No traffic passed in the street.

The silence could have been no deeper if he had been sealed in the vacuum of a snow globe.

Behind the wheel of the Land Rover, he realized that Dagget, who had been driving, had the key. The key was not a key anymore. It was whatever Dagget had become, part of the granite-like mass in the foyer.

If it had been an older vehicle, he might have tried to hot-wire it. But it was too new for that, with an electronic ignition.

He got out of the Land Rover and stood in snow that fell so thickly it seemed to be something other than snow. It seemed to be the whole world coming apart around him.

chapter 33

In the offices of the *Rainbow Falls Gazette* on Beartooth Avenue, Addison Hawk, the editor-in-chief and publisher, worked late. He was alone, and aside from the noises he made at his cluttered desk, the only sound was the *tick-tock* of the silver-plated pendulum in the grandfather clock.

Among the original furnishings of these premises, the handsome clock dated back to the late 1800s, when Elsworth Hawk, Addison's great-grandfather, founded the *Gazette.* It had stood in the reception lounge for decades until he moved it into his private office upon ascending to the editorship. Many people these days had no patience for the monotonous counting of such a clock, but to Addison it was lovely background music. He would no more have disposed of it than he would have ripped out the stained-oak beadboard wainscoting and the ornate decorative tin ceiling. He was an advocate for tradition in a world that had gone mad for change, that valued destructive and constructive change equally, and in fact seemed unable to tell the difference between the two.

He generally put in long hours, but it never seemed like work because he treasured this town, its history, its people. Chronicling life in Rainbow Falls was a work of love, and therefore his writing and editorial duties were really play. This evening, he might have left earlier, but he was slowed in his work by the loss of phone service and Internet connection.

And his mind wandered repeatedly to the California detectives, Carson and Michael, who had paid him a visit in the late afternoon. They told him a patently false story about working on an inheritance case, searching for an heir. He had known they were stonewalling him, and they had known that he knew, but he had liked them anyway.

In spite of the couple's personable nature and, at times, even lighthearted demeanor, Addison had been aware that they were tense and worried, even though they were hiding it well. *Worried* might be an inadequate word. His newsman's sixth sense told him that they were scared, which had been most evident when they had talked about the End Times Highway. If something frightened two former homicide detectives who had worked a tough city like New Orleans, perhaps Addison needed to be concerned, too, for the people of this town.

These thoughts kept distracting him—until suddenly he wondered if there might be some connection between the detectives' case and the failure of phone and Internet service. The weather could not be responsible. At most, two inches of snow were on the ground, which most locals would dismiss as flurries. Full-scale blizzards rarely disrupted services because everyone here was prepared for extreme winters.

The *Gazette*'s receptionist, Katie Ormond, kept a radio on her desk. Addison went out there to switch it on and see if KBOW might be reporting anything about the phone problems.

Mason Morrell seemed to have lost his mind. Or not. While the talk-show host's usual material held no interest for Addison, he knew the man was not one of the tinfoil-hat crowd. The media community in Rainbow Falls was arguably the smallest social circle in town; he and Mason often found themselves at the same functions. Never had Mason said a word about alien abductions or black helicopters, or anything else to suggest that for him reality and the Syfy channel were one and the same. He wasn't a conspiracy theorist who thought Osama bin Laden was secretly a Zionist and that the Holocaust was all a lie invented by the same crowd that faked the moon landing.

Besides, Sammy Chakrabarty, who lived for the radio station and would have slept there if permitted, would never allow Mason to rant like this if the talk-show host had come to work stoned. Sammy had big plans and, given his intellect and drive, he had a good shot at fulfilling them. Sammy would pull the plug on Mason rather than let him ruin *both* their careers.

Something else chilled Addison: Mason sounded sober, afraid, and sincere. Indeed, there was almost something Churchillian in the force of his delivery—but no faintest note of hysteria or inebriation.

But mass murder? Brain probes? Replicants? Monsters among us? It defied belief.

". . . collecting people in these big blue-and-white panel trucks and taking them to warehouses where they're killed, having been replaced by their replicants. . . ."

Still listening, Addison put on his Stetson, coat, and neck scarf. He lived near the heart of town and always walked to work. Now he intended to go home, get his SUV, and drive out to KBOW to discover firsthand whether this was some kind of ill-advised stunt to promote the radio station or an inexplicable descent into madness by the talk-show host.

He clicked off the radio, switched off the lights room by room, stepped outside, and locked the front door behind him. As he turned toward the street, before he stepped onto the lamplit sidewalk, he saw an approaching panel truck—blue cab, white cargo section—just as in Mason Morrell's warning.

In the lightless recessed entryway, Addison shrank back against the door. The truck was the sole vehicle on Beartooth, which usually wouldn't be this deserted even in the early stages of a snowstorm. He could discern two people through the windshield, but he doubted that they would spot him in this dark pocket.

Maybe his imagination had been overheated by what he'd heard on the radio, but the night felt *wrong,* the only sound being the engine of the truck, no pedestrians passing even though the hour was not yet late. The street hadn't been plowed or salted, although the town's maintenance department always hit the pavement by the time the first inch was down, to stay ahead of the storm. The wrongness wasn't in those details alone. There was also an eerie atmosphere that Addison felt but could not easily define.

Because he was intensely watching the suspicious truck, he saw the tall hooded figure, immense across the chest and the shoulders, appear out of thin air on the running board on the passenger side of the vehicle.

Magically.

Materializing like an apparition.

Gripping the assist bar at the back of the cab, the giant smashed the side window with his fist and wrenched open the door as the truck braked, skidded slightly in the snow, and came to a halt.

chapter 34

One second Papa Frankenstein's prodigal son wasn't there, the next second he was *very* there, and fragments of the shattered window cascaded in upon Michael without harming him. The door came open, and Michael shouted his name— *"Michael, Michael, me, me, it's me!"*—so that the big guy wouldn't break his neck, although even as he cried out and even as Carson braked, he saw that he had been recognized.

Deucalion dropped off the access step as the truck came to a stop, and Michael clambered out. "Thanks for not killing me."

"Anytime."

Michael didn't know why Deucalion should look even bigger in the falling snow than he had looked in other environments, but he seemed to be a lot bigger. Maybe it was because heavy snow at night created a magical mood in any circumstance, which emphasized Deucalion's nearly supernatural appearance. Maybe it was because this was the start of Armageddon, they were in the quick of it, and Michael was so happy that Deucalion was on their side that he imagined the giant to be even bigger than he was.

"I'm babbling," Michael declared.

Deucalion frowned. "You only said five words."

"In my head. I'm babbling to myself in my head."

Carrying her Urban Sniper, Carson hurried around from the driver's door to the giant. "What have you learned?"

"Does the truck have a radio?" Deucalion asked. "Have you been listening?"

"We haven't really had time to be diggin' any tunes," Michael said.

"I convinced the radio-station staff.

They're warning anyone who might be listening."

"Convinced them how?" Carson wondered.

"Killed the replicant of their general manager, slashed open his gut to show them what was inside."

"Vivid," Michael said.

"I get the feeling this thing is coming down faster than we can form a resistance to it," Carson worried.

"Why do you say that?"

"Listen."

She had switched off the truck engine. The silence of Rainbow Falls was the silence of an arctic outpost a thousand miles from any human habitat.

"Significant but not decisive," Deucalion decided. "The weather keeps some inside. And anyone listening to KBOW will be fortifying their homes to better defend them. We've told them the roads out of town are blockaded, so it would be foolish to try to drive out."

Carson shook her head. "I don't know. I'm no quitter. The way of the world is you kick ass or you die, and I'm always going to kick. But we've got to be real. A lot of people are dead already, and a lot more are going to die. I don't want to see children dying. Not any that we might just save."

Michael thought of Arnie and Scout, back in San Francisco. He wondered if the day would come when he and Carson, if they survived Rainbow Falls, would find themselves on the shore of that western bay, with nowhere left to run, only the sea at their backs and a city full of replicants coming for them.

"We've already got a dozen kids at this house, the Samples place," Carson told Deucalion. "We'll have more soon. Only you can drive them out, with that trick you have, take them to Erika."

Deucalion agreed. "It's strategically smart. The adults will put up a better fight if they don't have their children at hand to worry about."

"You can use this truck to transport them," Michael said, "once we get rid of the dead replicants in the back."

Something drew Deucalion's attention to a nearby building. Carson saw it, too, and leveled the shotgun.

Following their lead, Michael recognized

Addison Hawk as he stepped out of the recessed entryway to the offices of the *Gazette.* More than ever, he looked like a town sheriff in an old Jimmy Stewart Western.

Carson did not lower the shotgun. The publisher had evidently been alone in his office. Maybe the real Addison Hawk was sitting in there in the dark, a bead of silver face jewelry on his left temple.

"I heard the radio," Hawk said, "but I didn't think I could believe it."

"Believe it," Carson said, "and stop right there for a minute."

"I want to help," the publisher said. "What can I do to help? This can't happen, not to this town, not to this town of all towns."

"How can we be sure of him?" Carson asked Deucalion.

"You mean short of opening him up and looking inside? I don't know. But we have to decide quickly. Not just about him. Everyone we encounter from here on."

This night provided Michael's first experience of snow. None in Louisiana, none in San Francisco. He expected it to be beautiful, which it was, but he didn't expect it to be unsettling, which it also was. The millions of flakes whirling, movement everywhere, so much movement that you couldn't trust your peripheral vision or your visual instinct to identify something hostile if it was approaching with any subtlety. In the windless dark, the graceful descent of the flakes, still fluffy although a little icier than before, was as lulling as it was alluring, fading the hard edges of things, by its beauty ceaselessly selling the lie that the world was a gentle place, soft, with no sharp edges.

Michael said, "Carson, you remember those guys who came into the restaurant to get Chrissy Benedetto's mother? How they were?"

Denise Benedetto, muted and brain damaged, a silver bead on her temple, had somehow gotten away from her captors. Two policemen and one man in civilian clothes had come after her, into the restaurant where Carson and Michael were having dinner.

"They were bold," Carson said. "Arrogant. Cold bastards."

"I've lived my whole life here," Addison Hawk said with some distress, "except when I was away in the service. My dad and mom are here. My aunt Brinna, she's all alone now. Uncle Forrest and Aunt Carrie. What're you telling me is going to happen to them? What're you telling me?"

"Arrogant, cold," Michael agreed, "and something almost dead in their eyes."

After a hesitation, Carson lowered the shotgun. "I guess sometimes . . . we'll just have to trust and hope."

chapter 35

At first Ariel seemed all right with Nancy's need to bring some order to the littered floor of the barn. There was a push broom for the purpose of doing exactly that, and Nancy wielded it diligently, starting near the door by which they had entered and working her way back toward the tack room. She had no intention of cleaning out the stalls—*mucking* them out was the correct term—and she felt sure that she could resist that temptation as long as she didn't look inside them.

Horses were engines of disorder, dropping all their road apples, pawing their hooves at the soft covering of their stall floors until little clouds of dust and minced hay and probably feces billowed out from under the doors. They were no messier than other animals, of course. Pigs and cows and chickens and goats, dogs and cats, birds and fish, all of them crapping, on land and in the sea and in the air, pissing and crapping every day, every hour, every minute. All of nature was a filthy, untamed chaos, a riot of plants that cast their seeds and spores everywhere, growing in wild tangles, relinquishing their fruit to rot on the ground, growing until they collapsed and rotted themselves and then grew again out of their own disgusting rot. All of it topsy-turvy, unsymmetrical, pure confusion, muddle, jumble, all living things a bedlam, pandemonium, since time began. Someone had to put an end to it, to the chaos, and the Community was ready for the job.

Nancy was *particularly* ready for the job, sweeping the scattered stalks of hay into little piles, and then sweeping the little piles together into bigger ones. If she could have swept the horses into piles, she would have done that, too, the horses and the mice. No doubt there were dozens of mice quivering in corners all over the barn, quivering and crapping.

Eleven minutes and forty-one seconds after she began to sweep the barn floor, Nancy Potter became aware of Ariel's screaming. She realized that the girl had been shrieking for a while, perhaps for a minute or longer. Initially the sound didn't seem sufficiently important to allow it to distract Nancy from the sweeping, and she didn't register the source; it was just a mildly annoying background noise. Reluctantly, after hesitating another twenty-three seconds, she paused in her sweeping and turned to the girl.

Ariel trembled violently as she screamed. More than merely trembled. Vibrated. She was like a machine with several flywheels coming loose inside all at the same time, connecting rods knocking, cranks rattling against crankshafts, overlapping waves of succussion loosening every weld and rivet and bolt and screw.

The horses were growing agitated. The mares whinnied in fear. The stallion began to kick the barn wall at the back of his stall. His quarters hadn't been fortified with steel plate because he was supposed to be the first to be processed, in which case it would be the mares who, standing witness, might attempt to kick out of their stalls.

"All right, Ariel, all right," Nancy said, "just let me finish sweeping. Then I'll bring Commander out here, I'll prep him, you can tear him down and get started. I need a few minutes to finish the sweeping, to do it exactly right, and then I'll wash out the bristles of the broom. I can't put the broom away when the bristles are full of hay bits and mouse crap."

Ariel's scream escalated for a moment, and then her mouth grew so wide that the corners of her lips extended to her earlobes. She gagged, choked off her scream, and spewed forth a thick stream of silvery nanoanimals, such a violent disgorgement of her essence that she appeared to deflate. She pulled off the seemingly impossible feat of collapsing inward, sort of folding up, and disappearing into the tail end of her spew.

Airborne as a dense cloud of buzzing-hissing nanoanimals, Ariel became frenetic and appeared to ricochet around the room, diving and soaring. She ate a hole through the barn roof and disappeared into the night—only to reappear through another hole, plunge into the dirt floor, and tunnel across the room. The swarm resurfaced under Nancy's left foot, surprising her, consumed her leg to midthigh in an instant, and raced away.

The leg stump was essentially cauterized by the action of the nanoanimals. No vital fluids drizzled out of it. Because Nancy was a Communitarian and not a mere human being, she had no pain. She remained on her feet—foot—because she could use the push broom for a cane.

This development would make sweeping up the last of the hay a more difficult task, and Nancy was not sure how she would be able to proceed in a timely and efficient manner. And now she needed to deal with the additional issue of two holes in the floor and the fifteen-foot-long swale caused when Ariel's tunnel collapsed between her entry and exit points.

Furthermore, Nancy noticed for the first time that where she had already swept the hard-packed earthen floor, the stiff bristles of the broom left shallow brush marks going every which way in the dirt.

She wouldn't feel the job was done until all the brush marks went in the same direction.

The horses were going nuts. Nancy glared at them, but of course they didn't care. They were like so many other animals in the mismade nature of this world: so easily startled, frightened, panicked, stampeded like herds of cattle or packs of lemmings, like frantic flocks of gobbling turkeys and overexcited fans at rock-and-roll concerts trampling one another to get nearer the stage.

Toward the back of the barn, the swarm was behaving strangely, spinning in place like a miniature tornado. Under the buzzing and hissing rose another sound like a starter grinding and a car engine trying to turn over on a bitter-cold morning. The funnel cloud kept trying to form back into the shape of a girl, Ariel, but appeared to be having difficulty making the transition.

Nancy wondered if this Builder had something like indigestion. Ariel was designed to use the flesh, blood, bone, cartilage, and even the waste matter within the horses and eventually other animals to create the specific molecules with which to build more Builders of her variety. She was not supposed to eat sections of barn roofs or nibble on dirt—or, for that matter, on the legs of non-Builder Communitarian associates who were simply trying to make a barn floor neat in an efficient manner.

The funnel cloud of nanoanimals at last coalesced into a kind of Ariel, although this Ariel was short and had two heads. And after a moment, she began vibrating violently.

chapter 36

En route to Meriwether Lewis Elementary School, Sully York drove his black
Hummer not much differently from how he
would have driven a Ferrari Testarossa,
with a love of speed and with great pa-
nache. The snowy streets were of no concern to him, nor were the curbs at corners,
which he sometimes drove over while
making a turn. Every time they passed a
telephone pole to which was stapled a
politician's sign that had not been taken
down after the last election, Sully gestured
rudely at it and declared, *"Bunkum!"*

Bryce Walker, now riding shotgun, had

traded his pajamas and robe and slippers for some of Sully's clothes that fit him well enough. He had been in Memorial Hospital after a heart-attack scare that proved to be *only* a scare, and young Travis Ahern had been there for tests to determine what caused three bad episodes of anaphylactic shock that apparently were triggered by an allergy to something in his drinking water, perhaps even to chlorine. When it became clear that the staff of the hospital weren't who they had once been, that no patient was going to be allowed to leave, and that they were killing patients in the basement, Bryce and Travis had conspired to escape.

Travis's mom, a dietician and chef, worked in the kitchen at Meriwether Lewis. She had not called him all day, nor had she come to visit. She was reliable. She loved him. She would not have failed at least to call, unless something happened to her. After escaping from Memorial, when Bryce and the boy went to the Ahern house in that neighborhood known as the Lowers, they found no one home.

The boy's father had abandoned his wife and son so many years earlier that Travis had no memory of him. The family now was just Grace and Travis, and they were close, the two of them against the world. He adored her.

Bryce knew that if Grace had perished, the loss would not break the boy. Nothing would ever break Travis. He was so young, but Bryce could see the toughness in him. Travis would grieve hard and for a long time, but he would neither bend nor break, because he was a fine boy and he had been raised this far by a woman of strong character.

Bryce prayed that Grace would turn up alive. As a widower, he knew too much about grief. There would be great grief in this town in the days to come, supposing that any of them survived to mourn the dead. If Grace was alive out there somewhere, he would give his life to save her, if it came to such a sacrifice, because he wanted to spare the boy from the long-enduring sorrow of such a loss.

In the backseat, Travis said, "If she's not at the school, where would we look next?"

Sully said, "In an investigation as tricky as this, conducted in the midst of an invasion of hostile moonmen or whatever the hell these critters are, it doesn't pay to get ahead of ourselves. What happens next is surely not going to be like anything we might expect, because they're aliens, after all, meaning they think as different from the way we think as we think different from the way a bunch of pencil-neck Ivy League professors of conflict resolution think. So putting ourselves through the what-if wringer until we're all wrung out—well, that's just a hellacious waste of time and energy. We're going to think positive and make the world be what we want it to be, which is a world where your mom is safe at Meriwether Lewis, where maybe an injury has incapacitated her just a little, but where she's probably only in hiding."

Travis said, "I like the way you talk, sir."

"I like the way I talk, too. You know that question they always ask—if you were stranded on a desert island for a year, what three books would you take? Truth is, I find myself so damn entertaining I wouldn't need any books. I wouldn't even need a short story. If it was just me, my memory, and my mouth on that island, then I might even sign on for a second year."

"Here's the school," Bryce said.

They cruised past, looking over the place.

All the windows on the two-story building were dark.

At the end of the block, Sully turned left and drove to the parking-lot entrance, which was on the cross street.

Bryce noted that no tire tracks marred the mantle of snow on the entrance and exit lanes. Another entrance/exit served the lot from the parallel cross street, at the farther end of the school, but he suspected that the snow over there would also be pristine. Everyone had gone home before the storm began, and no evening maintenance crew had reported to work.

The parking-lot lamps weren't aglow, but Travis said they never were used at night unless there was a school function of some kind. This was his school, he was in fifth grade, so he knew what he was talking about.

Draped in snow, half a dozen school buses stood in one corner of the lot. Sully parked between two of them, where the Hummer couldn't be seen from the street. He switched off the headlights, the engine.

Sully said, "Travis—now there's a name that's always ready. Are you as ready as your name, boy?"

"I'm not afraid," Travis said.

"You better be afraid. Afraid but ready keeps you alive."

"I meant," Travis said, "I'm not afraid of what we'll find. She's going to be in there, and if she isn't, she's going to be some-where else and okay."

"By all that's holy, boy," Sully said, "before this is over, I just might have to make you an honorary member of my old unit, the Crazy Bastards."

The three of them walked through the snow to the back of the school. Sully and Bryce each had a shotgun, and the boy had Sully and Bryce.

Of the several doors they could choose from, Travis led them to a double pair marked KITCHEN DELIVERIES. He had come here a few times at night, with his mother, when she'd needed to do some prep work for the following day's lunch. As he had told them earlier, there was an alarm, but he knew his mother's four-digit code that would disarm the system from the keypad just inside the door.

Their only problem was that he didn't have his mom's door key.

Sully kicked the doors twice, where they

met, hoping to break the lock. Then he said, "One big noise is better than a hundred half-big," and he blew out the lock with his shotgun and pushed open the right-hand door, which wasn't latch-bolted to the sill as the left one was.

"We've got one minute to enter the code before the alarm goes off," Travis said. The boy stepped into the receiving room, to which food and other kitchen supplies were regularly delivered, went to the lighted keypad, and entered 4-4-7-3. The tiny red indicator lamp turned green.

Without the lock or latch to hold it closed, the door was likely to drift open.

As Sully used an eye-and-hook bungee cord to link the door handles together, he said, "We're far away from the nearest house, not much chance anyone could say for sure where that shot seemed to come from. Nevertheless, let's be quick about this."

From the receiving room, guided by three flashlights, they entered the large walk-in refrigerator. Beyond the walk-in lay the kitchen, where everything was weird.

chapter 37

Victor Immaculate's mind races whether he is sitting as still as the heart of a stone or taking random walks through this windowless world of which he is the prince. Cloned from the DNA of the original Victor Frankenstein, he is Victor Purified, Victor Distilled, Victor to the nth degree, and therefore has the most brilliant mind in all of history.

The facility is hardly less immense than a dream labyrinth that the sleeping mind constructs as a metaphor of eternity. Sterile white corridors with polished gray concrete floors branch and branch again.

Spacious rooms open into expansive laboratories, beyond which lay more chambers of daunting scale, some equipped with extrusion machines in the process of making Communitarians, others featuring towering mazes of supercomputers. Each silent stairwell earns the last four letters of its name, far below ground from even its highest level, boring down through the strata of the vast building as if through bedrock toward a perpetually dark subterranean lake.

Considering that civilization is being overthrown and the world is being unmade from this redoubt, there is little noise. Except for the soft treading of Victor's rubber-soled shoes, he usually walks in silence. Constructed to sustain direct nuclear strikes and continue to function, the building is not only buried deep in the earth, under a deflecting steel-and-concrete cowl sixty feet thick, but every wall and every floor is made of massively thick steel-reinforced concrete. Few sounds can penetrate from room to room or from level to level, and Victor seldom hears anything but the voice of his own thoughts in the eleven-dimension nautilus of his intricate mind.

Two hundred twenty-two work here, replicants of the scientists who originally staffed the facility. Needing no sleep, they toil at all hours, every day.

Victor speaks only to a handful, key personnel, and never sees most of the others. Face-to-face encounters are distractions. His mind works most efficiently in solitude, for no one is a fraction as intelligent and insightful as he is, and no one exists who might inspire him to greater brilliance than that with which he already shines. The core computer tracks Victor and everyone else in the Hive, and by direct-to-brain messaging, as he approaches, they are warned to retreat to other rooms until he passes.

Victor is not a replicant, he's a clone, and so he's technically as human as the original Victor. Direct-to-brain messaging is not an option for him. Throughout the facility, at strategic points, hang plasma screens that are part of the communication system, and as he passes one of these, it brightens and sounds a three-note tone to attract his attention.

Across the screen unscrolls a message to the effect that one of the Builders has ceased to transmit its position in Rainbow Falls. It is one of the second generation, made from the rendered bodies of several police officers lured to Chief Rafael Jarmillo's house.

This does not mean that the Builder has been killed. They cannot be killed. They are invulnerable to disease and injury.

Neither does it mean that this Builder is malfunctioning. Victor does not believe the Builders are capable of malfunctioning, for their design is perfect and their construction program without flaw.

He is certain that the fault lies in the mechanics of the equipment that receives the Builders' telemetric signals. The Builder is still functioning efficiently, rendering people and building other Builders, still transmitting its position. But the tracking system is off-the-shelf equipment not of Victor's design, and therefore it is not perfect. This is an annoying but insignificant detail, a gnat crossing the path of the Communitarian war machine.

Continuing his random walk, Victor Immaculate comes upon a small three-legged table that has been set out in anticipation of him. On the table stands a cold bottle of water. Next to the water is a pale blue saucer. In the saucer lies a white capsule. He holds the capsule between his teeth, opens the bottle, tongues the capsule into his mouth, and washes it down with two swallows of water.

He walks and thinks. Through his mind race torrents of ideas, theories, plans, models of complex entities constructed from unique molecules that the universe is incapable of creating but that *he* could create if he wished to do so. Now, as he routinely does, he engages in multitrack cognition, keenly following several completely different lines of thought simultaneously.

As he passes another plasma screen, it brightens, issues the three-note request for attention, and informs him that the first-generation Builder that went into the world as Ariel Potter has ceased to transmit its location. This is of course the same tedious problem, another failure of the tracking system, an argument for never using government-surplus equipment, but after all it is only another gnat.

As he is turning away from the screen, it

issues the three notes once more. This time the scrolling message is in regard to the fleet of trucks efficiently collecting brain-probed people to be taken to extermination centers and rendered there by Builders. Three of the vehicles have fallen behind schedule.

Two of them have stopped at locations not on their manifests and have remained there for extended periods of time. This is certainly a consequence of mechanical failure, because Victor did not design the trucks and have them built at his facility. They, too, are off-the-shelf equipment.

The third truck is on the move again, but it is not proceeding to any of the addresses at which it is expected. One of several possible explanations will account for this, and contingency plans exist for all of them.

"Consult the master strategy-and-tactics program, apply the appropriate remedy, and press forward without delay," he tells the screen.

Feeling the need for a change of atmosphere to refresh his eyes and mind, Victor rides an elevator down many floors and disembarks on one of the levels that he has not needed to occupy for his project. Because the building is hermetically sealed, impervious to water and insects, and receives its microbe-free, ideally humidified air through a filtration system that applies fourteen different processes of purification, these lower corridors and chambers are without dust and shelter not a single silverfish or spider.

The walls here are a pale shade of gray, and the floors are white, the reverse of the color scheme on higher levels. He does not know why, nor does he care to know. He has no interest in those things that are produced by talent: decor, fashion, art, literature, music, dance, craftsmanship. Every kind of talent is a human aptitude. Victor Immaculate despises and scorns humanity, and every gift that men and women possess only reminds him of the one thing that he hates more than them.

On this deeper level, the walls hold no plasma screens to nag him with three-note alerts; the higher floors have been retrofitted with that communication system to facilitate his work. These rooms are not only deserted but also without equipment and furnishings. Thermal sensors detect his presence and switch on the lights overhead as he progresses; therefore, he moves forward always toward a blackness of liquid density that retreats from him as though the very darkness fears him. Here he can walk in true solitude and enjoy without interruption the infinite genius of his ceaselessly laboring mind.

He is not concerned that he will miss being informed of some crisis, for there will be none. Whatever problem might arise in the conquest of Rainbow Falls, it will be but another gnat, and there will be numerous contingency plans to cope with it and ensure the triumph of the Community.

Throughout the centuries, popes have claimed infallibility, only in matters of faith but infallibility nevertheless. Victor Immaculate knows with the certainty of genius that all popes are frauds, but he is not of their ilk. Victor Immaculate, Purified, Distilled, Victor to the nth degree, is infallible in *all* things. The war against this Montana town will inevitably proceed until every last man, woman, and child is slaughtered and processed into an army of new Builders who will be the shock troops of Armageddon.

chapter 38

Nummy thought a snowmobile trip would be fun. He never rode one before, but often he watched other people zoom around on them, and he figured it must be like the best carnival ride ever.

The first thing that went wrong was his seat, not his backside but his seat on the machine. Mr. Lyss drove, so Nummy had to perch behind him and hold on for dear life. Some machines, two people could ride real cozy. But this one had these sad- dlebags that you couldn't take off without tools and time, so Nummy sat part on the seat and more on the saddlebags, which wasn't comfortable, especially when they flew off a little hill and bounced down.

Another thing that went wrong was how cold it was, even colder because of the wind they made, how it stung Nummy's face where the wool scarf didn't cover, how it almost right away began to bite his ears even through the toboggan cap he pulled over them.

This neighborhood was Nummy's, and it was near one edge of town, and he knew the fields all around, where to find the stream and where you would go if you followed it for a while and where you would go if you turned away from it near Bear Rock. Mr. Lyss didn't know the land in these parts. Nummy was supposed to hold tight to the old man's coat—which was really not his coat but stolen—and look around Mr. Lyss to keep an eye on where they were going. Then if Mr. Lyss should bear left, Nummy was supposed to pull on the left side of his coat, on the right side if he was to go right. Mr. Lyss said he would be the pilot, and Nummy would be the navigator, and if they got lost, he would cut off Nummy's peewee with a blunt knife and tie it on the handlebars for decoration.

The thing that was most wrong with the wind they made and with the cold was that Nummy didn't have a helmet like Mr. Lyss did, so the cold wind stung his eyes, made them water. Even with headlights showing the way, Nummy found it hard to tell what was what in all the whiteness and the dark. When his eyes watered too much, getting lost got so easy that even he could do it without trying.

Another thing that went wrong was that Mr. Lyss didn't drive a snowmobile as well as he drove a car. Worse, he must have thought he was a better snow driver than he really was, and he went dangerous fast. Or maybe he was scared that the noise of the machine and the headlights would draw the attention of the monsters, and he wanted to get as far from town as quick as he could. Nummy bounced on those saddlebags so much, he was afraid he might come down just the wrong way so hard that one of the saddlebags would get stuck between his butt cheeks.

So there they were, running flat-out into snow and dark, Nummy pulling hard left when he wasn't even sure left was right, Mr. Lyss shouting curses that Nummy was grateful he could only half hear, and they came to a place where the land changed. The land dropped maybe three feet, and they were flying. The snowmobile wasn't an airplane, so it didn't fly far before it dropped, too, and if Mr. Lyss wasn't giving the machine more gas even while flying, it sure *sounded* like he was. They came down so hard they both fell off, and the snowmobile slid maybe a hundred feet across the field before it came to a stop, all the falling snow sparkling pretty in its headlights.

Nummy was first on his feet, ready to run if Mr. Lyss pulled a blunt knife from a coat pocket.

If the snowmobile was broken, this was maybe even worse than getting lost, but almost at once, an even worse thing happened. Just as Nummy got off the ground, a thing *whooshed* overhead, its tail of flames blue and orange, and a second later the snowmobile went *boom* and for a moment disappeared in a ball of fire.

Even Mr. Lyss was left speechless by this development, and after a few seconds Nummy heard the engine purring overhead. He looked up and saw the pale plane not far above, like a ghost plane, gliding through the storm, big but not as big as the airplanes that people flew in. When it passed over the burning snowmobile, firelight throbbed across its belly, and then it hummed away into the dark.

On his feet near Nummy, looking after the plane that he couldn't see anymore, Mr. Lyss said, "That sonofabitch was like one of those drones, those drones they send off to kill hard-core terrorists in Afghanistan and other hellholes. Predators, they call them. Armed with missiles. Must've been drawn by the engine heat. If we hadn't just fallen off, we'd be charred meat for a bear's dinner. What the Sam Hill is a Predator doing here, blowing up snowmobiles?"

Nummy didn't have an answer, but he didn't think Mr. Lyss would hold that against him. Mr. Lyss knew Nummy wasn't an answer man.

The more the old man thought about his question, the angrier he became. "Nobody has the right to chase us down and try to make toast out of us, just blow a valuable snowmobile to smithereens. Yes, yes, Peaches, I know it's not my machine,

I stole the damn thing from a dead man who might want to ride it to his funeral, and now he can't because of me and my thieving ways. But I've still got a perfect right to be offended by such an arrogant assault. I'm a citizen in good standing of the United States, after all, I've got my rights. I'm no damn terrorist. You're no terrorist. We're just a peaceable hobo and a dummy, trying to save ourselves from monsters, and these bastards blow up our transportation."

The flames were less bright than at first, but all around the broken-apart snowmobile, the falling snow seemed to catch fire, too, a million sparks whirling down. Reflections of firelight spread and fluttered like gold-and-red wings across the white land, as if there were angels in the night.

Mr. Lyss grew so angry he couldn't even finish his sentences. Everything he started to say ended in sputtering and spitting, and one group of words didn't seem to belong with the next group. He did a wild dance of anger in the meadow, around in circles, kicking at the snow, punching the air with his bony old fists, shaking them at the sky.

Nummy was reminded of one of the stories Grandmama read to him a long, long time ago, about a princess who spun straw into gold and a mean little man who taught her how if she would give him her firstborn baby. Nummy couldn't remember the name of the princess, but the little man was Rumpelstiltskin, a name that stuck with you.

At the moment, Mr. Lyss wasn't being mean. He was just being angry, but he sure did look like the man in the story. He said he was so mad he could spit. He said it over and over again, and every time he said it, he *did* spit. Nummy couldn't make sense of any of that, so he just stood and waited until Mr. Lyss at last burned himself out, which took almost as long as the snowmobile.

When the old man stopped muttering, spitting, and kicking, Nummy said, "I really, really don't want to say this, but I got to."

"Say what?" Mr. Lyss asked.

"We're lost. I don't know where this place is, all this white and dark, but it's not my fault because the cold wind it stung my eyes and blurred everything. I don't want my peewee cut off. Anyway there's no handlebars to decorate with it anymore."

"Relax, Peaches. I don't blame you for this."

"You don't?"

"Didn't I just say I don't?"

"I guess you did."

"Besides, we're not lost."

"We're not?"

"You are, as usual, a dazzling conversationalist. No, we aren't lost. We've only come a mile or so, maybe a mile and a half. I have this flashlight that I stole from the dead Bozeman." He switched it on. "We just have to follow the trail the snowmobile left until we get back to his house, where I hope to God that piano-playing monster has got sick of that morbid music and is pounding out some ragtime."

Nummy looked at the beam from the flashlight sliding over the snowmobile tracks, and he said, "Your being smart just saved us."

"Well, *saved* might be too strong a word, considering that we're going nowhere but back into the village of the damned."

They trudged side by side along the tracks the snowmobile had left, and after a while, Nummy said, "I haven't wished I was smart in a long, long time, but now I wish it."

"Don't," Mr. Lyss said. "Being smart isn't all it's cracked up to be. Besides, like I told you before, the world is full of educated smart people who are ten times dumber than you."

Nummy's nose watered from the cold, and the nose water half-froze on his upper lip. He wiped with his coat sleeve, but then he realized that was disgusting, so he just put up with the lip ice.

After another while, he said, "I wonder what it's like to live with palm trees, a place like that."

"It's nice enough. I'll take you some-place like that if we live through this."

"Oh, I don't know. Grandmama she's buried here and all."

"We can dig her up and take her with us, bury her where there's sun and flowers year round."

"I don't know they'd let us do that."

"Anything can be arranged for money."

"I wouldn't know how."

"I would."

"I guess you would."

After another silence, Mr. Lyss said, "Good thing for us there's no wind, or these tracks would smooth right over before we found our way back."

"That's another smart thing to figure out."

"My brain is so big and still growing so fast, every couple years, they have to open my skull and take out a piece of brain so there's room enough in there."

"I don't think that could be true," Nummy said.

"Well, it is true. My medical bills are enormous."

chapter 39

When Carson, Michael, and Addison returned to the Samples house with Deucalion, she knew the Riders and Riderettes were going to need a lot of persuading to turn over their children to a menacing-looking giant with half his face broken and tattooed, even if the other half was rather handsome.

He would need to demonstrate his ability to move any distance that he wished in a single step. He would need to explain that he could take with him anything on which he placed his hands, including other people or—with a slightly different technique—an entire vehicle full of people.

But Carson worried that such a demonstration might have the opposite effect of the one intended. Considering his appearance, the occasional luminous pulses passing through his eyes, his deep voice with its rough timbre, and his strong hands that seemed to be as large as shovels, these people might find him downright demonic and refuse to entrust their precious children to him even if they might be safer out of Rainbow Falls.

Having Addison with them would be helpful. His late uncle Norris and aunt Thelma had been parishioners of the Riders in the Sky. He said that the *Gazette* had a few times reported on the church's annual socials and on their charitable work, always with care not to write anything that might suggest that their faith was more *colorful* than the traditional denominations.

Just as Deucalion, reluctant to risk stretching his credibility to the snapping point, had not spoken the name Frankenstein to the people at KBOW, so Carson had avoided mentioning it to these folks.

With the help of young Farley Samples, she talked them out of the alien-invasion theory and into an acceptance of the nanotechnology explanation, leaving them to imagine that the villains were part of some totalitarian faction of the government. If the Riders and Riderettes could not bring themselves to trust Deucalion, who might seem to have less in common with them than with the killing machines that attacked them in the roadhouse, she would at last have to speak Victor's name and try to bridge their skepticism and guide them to a full understanding of the situation.

As Carson led the way through the front door into the living room, five men were finishing the window fortifications and the weapons preparations on which they had been engaged earlier. Behind Michael and Addison, Deucalion entered last, pushing back the hood of his coat as stepped into the house. The five churchmen looked up—and in every case froze at the sight of this man who, at various times in his long life, had earned a living as a sideshow freak in carnivals.

Although none of the Riders reached for a weapon lying near at hand, Carson felt the tension in the room, as though the barometric pressure had plunged in anticipation of a storm. Some men's eyes widened, others' narrowed, but they all seemed to have made up their minds about Deucalion on sight, as Carson had feared.

"This man is a friend of ours," Carson said. "He's a friend of Addison's, too. He's the key to victory for all of us and the best hope of saving the children."

She was little more than halfway through that introduction when one of the five Riders hurried out of the room and thundered up the stairs toward the second floor, while another disappeared into the dining room.

When Carson began to warn them that their first impression of Deucalion was mistaken, one of the remaining three Riders raised a hand to silence her. "Ma'am, best wait so you won't have to repeat yourself so much."

In their aprons, Dolly Samples leading and drying her hands on a dish towel, the Riderettes came in from the kitchen and the dining room. Numerous thunderous footsteps hurriedly descending the stairs heralded eight or ten men who entered the living room through the hallway arch.

They crowded the farther half of the room, keeping some distance from Deucalion, their expressions somber and their stares as sharp as flensing knives. Loreen Rudolph covered her mouth with one hand, as though stifling a scream, and another woman was trembling so badly that she had to lean on one of her companions.

Among these cowboys, there were some of considerable size, big enough to give a rodeo bull second thoughts about participating in a contest with them. But none of them stood as tall as Deucalion or matched his mass of muscle. They glanced at one another, and Carson thought they were wondering how many of them might be needed to take him down.

Fresh startlement raced through those assembled, gasps and murmurs, and when Carson looked at Deucalion, she saw eerie light throbbing through his eyes. The men were standing taller than they had been a moment earlier, and two more women had raised their hands to their mouths, their eyes owlish.

Carson started to speak again, sensed that the moment wasn't right, wasn't hers, might instead be Deucalion's. But the giant made no effort to intrude or explain himself. With stoic acceptance of the fear he could induce without effort, he surveyed those who gaped at him, perhaps much as he had matched the stares of those who came to see him in the carnival sideshows.

Tucking the dish towel in one of the two patch pockets on her apron, Dolly Samples came forward slowly, and no one warned her to stay back, though it seemed to Carson that the men grew more tense. Just five feet two, Dolly had to peer up at quite an angle to study Deucalion's now downturned face, and she seemed most intent on the intricate half-face tattoo and on fully understanding the terrible damage to the underlying bone structure.

"I dreamed of you," Dolly said, which was nothing that Carson expected her to say. "The most vivid dream of my life. More than two years ago, it was."

When Dolly spoke the date, Carson glanced at Michael and he at her, for the night of her dream was also the night that Victor Frankenstein, the original, had died in the landfill in highlands north of Lake Pontchartrain.

"I dreamed of your great size, the hooded

coat you're wearing now," Dolly said. "Your lovely face and your poor face, both halves exactly as they are, and the tattoo in all its detail."

Carson realized that the women with their hands to their mouths had never been stifling screams. They were guarding emotions of a much different kind, and now tears stood in their eyes.

"In the dream, I saw the light in your eyes, and at first I was afraid, but then I knew there was no reason for fear. I thought of a line from Proverbs 15—'The light of the eyes rejoiceth the heart'—and I knew that you were our friend."

When Deucalion spoke, his voice seemed deeper and more resonant than ever: "What happened in this dream?"

"We had come to the shore of a sea, the water very dark and turbulent. There were so many children with us, our own and children I'd never seen before. We were fleeing something, I don't know what, but death was coming. We were like the Israelites at the shore, and you came to us out of nowhere, one moment not there and then among us. You parted the sea and told the children to follow you, and they were saved."

"I can't part the sea and make a dry path through it," Deucalion said. "But there's something else I can do that I will show you, and then you can decide whether to entrust the children to me."

Dolly said, "I told everyone about the dream. I knew it must be prophetic, it was so intense. I knew one day you would appear among us, out of nowhere."

The other women crossed the room to Deucalion, and their men came behind them.

Dolly said, "You have suffered very much."

"And there was a time I caused suffering," he confessed.

"We all do, one way or another. May I touch your face?"

He nodded.

She raised her right hand first to the undamaged side of his face and pressed it against his cheek as a loving mother might have done. Then her fingers tenderly traced the fractured contours of the damaged side, the impossible concavity and the lumpish scar tissue.

"You're beautiful," she said. "Very beautiful."

chapter 40

At first, with three flashlight beams sweeping this way and that, revealing only portions of the glistening contours, causing shadows to swell and shrink, Bryce Walker couldn't understand what these things might be that hung from the twelve-foot-high ceiling of the school kitchen. Most were suspended over the prep tables, huge and greasy-looking and somehow obscene, but a few hung in the wide aisles.

The surface of each of these objects was mottled shades of gray. But among all the grays were silvery patches and veins that glittered like diamond dust.

Young Travis, being a reader of genres different from and darker than the Westerns that Bryce wrote, was quicker to identify these mysterious sacks. "Cocoons."

As if the word triggered a response, a slithering noise arose from the sack nearest the boy. And then the creatures gestating in the other cocoons grew restless, as well, and raised a chorus of susurrant sounds, either the friction of countless snakes coiling among one another or their hissed threats, as if this were not the Meriwether Lewis Elementary School, as it appeared to be, but was instead the bottom of the pit of the world, where the oldest serpent of them all waited golden-eyed and hungry.

"Be very still," Sully York whispered.

Bryce and Travis took the seasoned adventurer's advice, in part because, in spite of the noise, nothing appeared to move within the cocoons. The surfaces of them didn't ripple or show any strain of imminent birth.

As the slithery noise gradually quieted, Bryce looked at Travis, whose features glowed with the flashlight beam reflected back from the glimmering sack. The boy's face—his furrowed brow, his haunted eyes, his grimly set mouth—revealed his thoughts as clearly as an e-book reader presented a page on its screen. Sometimes insects spun cocoons around themselves *and* around the paralyzed but living food on which they would feed during their metamorphosis, and Travis wondered if the kitchen staff might be sealed inside these hideous bags, incapacitated but aware, his mother among them, in the embrace of some pale wriggling thing that had begun to feast.

Bryce shuddered and longed to be in an armchair, with a mug of spiked coffee and a book by Louis L'Amour or Elmer Kelton, in which the villains were nothing worse than hired gunmen or a sheriff gone bad, or stagecoach-robbing highwaymen.

When silence reigned once more, Sully York whispered, "Nice and easy . . . stay together . . . look around."

Because the kitchen was at the back of the school, the overhead lights would not have been seen from the street. Sully didn't propose turning them on, however, and Bryce supposed that might be because he feared that the residents of the cocoons would become agitated by the brightness. Or maybe he worried the shot-gun blast that had taken out the door lock would have been heard by the wrong people—who were not really people—who would cruise around the building to have a look. In unspoken agreement, they kept the three flashlights low and away from the windows.

Throughout the big institutional kitchen were signs of violence. Overturned equipment, scattered pots and pans, broken crockery. The culinary staff evidently had put up a fight.

Near a double-wide bank of stacked ovens, Bryce's flashlight revealed a severed hand. He almost turned the beam away from it in revulsion, but subconsciously he was aware that something about this chopped-off extremity was more shocking than the mere fact of its existence. He needed a moment to recognize that instead of a thumb, the hand was equipped with a big toe, not one that had been stapled to the hand by some psychotic jokester, but a toe that appeared to grow naturally where a thumb should have been.

Many hours earlier, this day had jumped off the rails of reality, and he no longer expected that two plus two would always equal four. Nevertheless, this severed hand marked a sharp turn into an even stranger realm than the one that he had been exploring ever since he had heard, in the hospital, faint distant screams of terror and pain rising from the basement to his bathroom through the heating-system ductwork.

And now he realized that the misplaced toe was not the only bizarre feature of the hand. In the meatiest part of the palm was a half-formed nose: the columella, the tip, a single nostril from which bristled a few hairs, and a small length of the bridge. The partial nose was so well detailed that he expected to see the hairs quiver in an exhalation.

He was too old for this. He was seventy-two. His wife, Renata, had died eighteen months earlier, and he was an immeasurably older man now than he had been then, ancient, exhausted. Life without her was in a way no less wearing than life without food; this was just a different kind of starvation. Finding this macabre hand, he wanted to return home, curl up in bed, lying on his side so that he could see the framed photograph of Rennie on his nightstand, go to sleep, and let the world plunge all the way to Hell if that's where it was bound.

One thing prevented him from taking that course of action—or inaction: Travis Ahern. He believed that he saw in this boy someone like young Bryce Walker had been, back in the day. He wanted Travis to live to find his own Renata, to discover the work that he was born to do and to know the satisfaction of doing it well. He and Rennie never were able to have children, but now by a twist of fate he was responsible for one.

Bryce hesitated so long over the four-fingered mutation that both Travis and Sully saw it and stood with him to wonder about it. None of them commented on the hand, not because their whispers might agitate the residents of the cocoons, but because no words were adequate to the moment.

At the end of the kitchen farthest from the point at which they entered, a door led to what Travis, having been here often with his mother, identified as a spacious walk-in pantry. A tall, heavy steel cabinet, which had stood against the wall opposite the door, had toppled into the pantry entrance during whatever melee had occurred, acting as a large angled brace that prevented the door from being opened.

"We have to look," Travis murmured. "We have to."

Bryce and Sully set aside their shotguns and together muscled the cabinet upright, against the wall where it belonged. Its safety-latched doors didn't come open, but Bryce could hear the broken contents clattering around inside.

When Travis reached for the lever-style door handle, Sully quietly cautioned the boy to wait until he had his shotgun in both hands.

Bryce held two flashlights as Travis, standing to one side and out of Sully's line of fire, opened the door and pushed it aside. The two beams played across the back-wall shelves of the deep pantry and then down to the woman sitting on the floor.

Travis said, "Mom?"

She stared at them, astonished or uncomprehending, her eyes bright with fear.

Bryce didn't know what the silvery bead was, gleaming liquidly like a drop of mercury on her left temple, but he thought it couldn't be anything good.

chapter 41

In the snow on the nearly flat roof of KBOW, Sammy Chakrabarty took up a position at the front of the building, behind the three-foot-high parapet. Between four-foot lengths of that roof-encircling wall were two-foot-wide crenellations from which a defender could, in relative safety, fire down upon attackers. He sat with his right side against the parapet, head craned forward to peer through one of the crenels, looking east toward the entry to the parking lot, where the bad guys would turn in from the street—if they came.

Sammy took some comfort in that *if,*

even though he knew in his heart that they would come.

Sometimes a cold night in Rainbow Falls was a fine thing, the chill invigorating and the town pretty in the clear, crisp air, but this was the ugly side of cold, a mean little troll of a night that had sharp teeth and a bite sufficiently venomous to numb his nose. He sat on a plastic garbage bag to keep his bottom from getting wet. For the most part, he was warm, his clothes adequate to the conditions.

But he worried about his hands. He had worn a simple pair of knitted gloves to work, the kind that didn't hamper driving, but that were not bitter-weather gear. If the replicants arrived in significant numbers, if there was a prolonged assault, Sammy feared that his hands would stiffen to an extent certain to affect his handling of the assault rifle and the shotgun. Consequently, instead of sitting with the rifle ready in his grip, he propped it against the parapet and kept his hands in the flannel-lined pockets of his jacket.

He anticipated that the replicants would have one of two strategies: either a fearless assault on the doors, with the intent of storming the place and killing everyone therein, or an attack on the broadcast tower immediately behind—and attached to—the station.

If they controlled the power company, as Deucalion insisted they did, they could black out this entire square block, but that would not put an end to Mason Morrell's clarion call for strong resistance to the revolution. The station had emergency generators housed within the building, fed by a large gasoline tank buried under the parking lot, and they could remain on the air for at least twenty-four hours on their fuel supply, perhaps twice that long.

The open-girder steel tower was of strong construction, its four legs sunk in eighteen-foot-deep concrete pylons that anchored it to the earth and that were themselves anchored in bedrock. This design ensured the tower would ride through the worst projected thousand-year earthquake that might rock the area related to a volcanic event at Yellowstone. The weakest point was the transmission cable that came out of the rear of the building in a conduit. The tower might be toppled with enough explosives, and the precious cable could be obliterated with a smaller charge. Sammy would be shooting down on any team that tried to approach the tower, and with the rapid-fire semiauto Bushmaster, he should be able to take them out long before they reached their objective, even if they were tough enough to take four or five mortal hits before succumbing.

From Ralph's home bunker, or whatever it was, he had brought not only weapons but also additional equipment that might prove useful, including four Motorola Talkabouts, walkie-talkies about the size of cell phones but an inch and a half thick. These allowed Ralph, Burt, Mason, and Sammy to speak with one another in a crisis. Sammy kept his in a jacket pocket.

The Talkabout chirruped, and when he pulled it from his jacket, he heard Burt Cogborn say, "Sammy, are you there?"

Sammy held down the transmit button, said, "In place and ready for action," and then released it.

From his post in the reception lounge below, Burt said, "If something happens to me and you take in Bobby, never ever give him any of those rawhide treats. He loves them but dogs can choke on them too easy. Over."

Sammy replied, "No rawhide treats. Got it. Over."

Before Sammy could return the Talk-about to his pocket, Burt said, "You'll want to take him out to pee first thing in the morning, again around eleven, also after he eats at three-thirty, and a fourth time just before bed. Over."

Sammy was about to respond when Burt transmitted again:

"Bobby pees four times a day, but he rarely ever poops four times. What he does is he poops usually three times a day, so if on one of his outings he doesn't poop, don't worry about it. That's normal. Over."

Sammy waited to be sure that Burt was finished, and then he transmitted: "Four pees, three poops. Got it. Over and out."

Burt wasn't finished. "Just to be sure you got it right, tell me which bunny is his favorite. Over."

"Light-green, fully floppy bunny, not just floppy ears," Sammy replied. "Over and out."

Anyone on the channel whose Talk-about was switched on could hear their exchanges. The device chirruped before Sammy could pocket it, and Ralph Nettles said, "Good thing you aren't obligated to take me in, Sammy. With this prostate, I have to pee like every half hour. Over and out."

Sammy waited for a while before stuffing the walkie-talkie in his jacket pocket once more.

As if somebody opened a door in the sky, a breeze came down to chase off the stillness. The snow seemed to fall faster, which was probably an illusion. Instead of spiraling in a waltz with the air, the flakes hurried through the darkness, bright slanting skeins in the parking-lot lamps.

Instantly the air was colder than before, and Sammy fisted his lightly gloved hands in his pockets.

chapter 42

Jocko was going to screw up. Didn't know when. Didn't know how. But Jocko would screw up because he was Jocko.

He sat on the floor. At the living-room coffee table. Wearing one of his fourteen funny hats with bells. Not his hacker hat. This was his please-don't-let-me-screw-up hat. It had never worked before. But it had to work this time. It just had to.

With a book, Erika sat in a chair by the fireplace. She smiled at him.

Jocko didn't smile. As a former tumor and a current monster, his smile was terrifying. He had learned the hard way how terrifying his smile could be.

Erika wasn't terrified by it. Erika loved him. She was his mom, adopted. But his smile frightened everyone else. Then they screamed or stoned him, or beat him with sticks or buckets, or shoved him in an oven and tried to bake him to death, or shot at him, or tried to set him on fire, or tossed him into a pen with three big, hungry hogs, or literally threw him under a bus, or tried to strangle him with a prayer shawl.

Don't smile. Don't smile.

Kneeling on the floor, across the coffee table from him, was his new friend. Chrissy.

Because he was a few inches taller than the average dwarf, Jocko was shorter than almost everyone. He wasn't shorter than Chrissy, who was five years old. He was the *big* kid here. Status. This was a first for Jocko. The *big* kid. The responsibility of his position weighed on Jocko. He was afraid he would start to sweat.

On the table were two cups and saucers. A little plate on which lay four plain-looking biscuits and six cubes of sugar. Two spoons. Two fancy linen napkins with embroidered pink roses that Jocko would have liked to make into a hat for Sundays. And a teapot.

Chrissy said, "How very nice of you to come visiting, Princess Josephine."

Surprised, little bells jingling, Jocko looked around. For the princess. Royalty. He'd never met royalty before. He might need a different funny hat. He might need shoes. But no one new had come into the room.

When he cocked his head at Chrissy, perplexed, she said, "Now you're supposed to say, 'How very nice of you to invite me, Princess Chrissy.'"

Deeply impressed, Jocko said, "You're a princess?"

"I'm the princess of Montana. My father is the king."

"Whoa," Jocko said. He began to sweat. Just a little. In his ears.

"And you," said Princess Chrissy, "are Princess Josephine of a faraway kingdom."

"I'm Jocko."

"This is tea with princesses. Princess Jocko sounds dumb. You've gotta be Princess Josephine."

Jocko smacked his mouth flaps, thinking about it. "You mean her stand-in because she couldn't make it at the last minute?"

"Okay, sure."

Jocko asked, "Why couldn't the real Princess Josephine make it?"

Princess Chrissy shrugged. "Maybe she met a handsome prince and they're gonna get married."

"Or maybe," Jocko said, "a sinister contagion has swept her father's kingdom."

Princess Chrissy frowned. "What's a . . . that thing you said?"

"A sinister contagion. A plague. A horrible, disfiguring disease. Your nose can rot off, your ears, like leprosy. Your tongue can turn black and shrivel up. Thousands dead. Thousands more scarred and deranged and crippled for life. Bodies piled up in gutters. Mass graves. Catastrophe."

She shook her head. "No. It's the handsome prince. Now will you say it so we can go on?"

Because he wanted this teatime to be a great success, Jocko smacked his lip flaps and thought some more. To be sure he did just what she wanted. To be very sure. Then he said, "It so we can go on."

Princess Chrissy cocked her head at him, the way he had earlier cocked his at her.

From her chair by the fireplace, Erika

stage-whispered to Jocko: "How very nice of you to invite me, Princess Chrissy."

Oh. He felt stupid. Stupid, stupid, stupid. Less monster than tumor, less tumor than lowly *cyst.* Typical stupid Jocko. He tried to make a suave recovery. "How very nice of you to invite me, Princess Chrissy."

"Would you like tea, Princess Josephine?"

"Yes. I would like tea."

"Isn't this a pretty teapot?"

"Yes. It is pretty. And a teapot."

"Shall I pour a full cup?"

"Yes. You shall," Jocko said.

He was getting the hang of this. It was easier than he thought it would be.

Princess Chrissy said, "Something's dripping out of your ears."

"Sweat. Just sweat."

"I don't sweat out of *my* ears."

Jocko shrugged. "It's a gift."

"It's icky."

"A little icky," he admitted. "But it doesn't stink."

As she poured the tea into the cups, Princess Chrissy said, "Princess Josephine, whose picture is on your dress? Is he a knight of your kingdom?"

Jocko wasn't wearing a dress. He wore jeans and a long-sleeved T-shirt with his hero's image on it.

"He's the one, the only, Buster Steelhammer! He's the face-smashing, butt-kicking, steroid-crazed, make-you-cry-mama *best wrestler of all time!*"

Princess Chrissy said she didn't know what a wrestler was, they didn't have wrestlers at the royal castle, and Princess Josephine, who was Jocko, was thrilled to explain. He wrestled himself around the floor. Got himself in a hammerlock. Which he could do because of the length of his arms. And the extra elbow joint. He stomped his right foot in his face, held his squished-up face to the floor. He didn't have any hair to pull. Except the three hairs on his tongue. But he'd never seen any tongue-hair pulling in any show put on by World Wrestling Entertainment. He couldn't pick himself up and body slam himself. He tried. But he couldn't. However, he could do a lot of cool wrestler stuff. Which he did. And then returned to his place at the table.

Princess Chrissy giggled. "You're silly."

Her giggle made Jocko feel like a real prince. Or a princess. Whichever.

Princess Chrissy picked up her cup, blew on it, and said, "This is the only time I ever, ever had real tea to drink for tea-time. Maid Erika brewed it for us."

"What do you usually drink at teatime?"

"Air tea," Princess Chrissy said.

Jocko drained the teacup in one swal-low. "Yuch. Blech. Gaaaah. Gaaaah. Kack. Feh. Fah. Foo." He stuck out his tongue and rubbed it vigorously with both hands. Grabbed up the fancy napkin. Wiped out the inside of his mouth. Blew his nose. Blotted the sweat from his ears. He said, "No offense meant."

"You should ought to put sugar in it," Princess Chrissy said, pointing to the four cubes left on the plate.

Jocko snatched up all four cubes. Tossed them into his mouth. Rolled them around. Better. But too sweet. He spat them in his cup.

"Wait," he said, sprang to his feet, and pirouetted out of the room. Along the hall-way. Into the kitchen. Around the center island. He liked to pirouette. When he was nervous. Burning up energy. Spinning to calm down. Oh, how his hat bells jingled!

When he returned to the living room, he

brought a silver tray with two fresh tea-cups. A two-quart bottle of cold Pepsi. A plate of whoopie pies.

"This is how we have tea in my king-dom," Jocko said.

He poured Pepsi in both cups. Didn't slop any on the table. Didn't just drink from the bottle. Threw the four plain-looking bis-cuits into the fireplace. Tossed a whoopie pie as if it were a Frisbee and caught it when it spun around the room like a boo-merang and returned to him. Totally George Clooney.

Putting her tea aside, Princess Chrissy said, "This is lovely."

"Very lovely," he agreed.

"Princess Josephine, tell me the news from your kingdom."

About to thrust an entire whoopie pie in his mouth, Jocko put it down instead. He was only Josephine's stand-in. He didn't know anything about her kingdom. Maybe he should lie. But lying wasn't right. He had often lied. But it wasn't right. He wanted to be a better Jocko.

Princess Chrissy said, "Tell me about your dragons."

"There aren't any dragons."

"What about witches?"

"Nope. No witches."

"Then tell me about your wizards."

"No wizards."

He saw she was unhappy with him. He was a bad conversationalist. Bad. Pathetic. Despicable. Horrendous.

Think. Think. Salvage the moment. Put the burden of conversation on her. "Your father, he's the king of Montana. How many heads has he chopped off?"

"Silly. He doesn't chop off heads."

"Some kings do," Jocko said.

"No, they don't."

"Some do. And torture people in dungeons."

"No, they don't."

"They rip out your fingernails."

"What's wrong with you?" Princess Chrissy asked.

"Jocko's just saying. Like in the history books. They brand you with hot irons and stick needles in your tongue."

"You have yellow eyes," Princess Chrissy said.

Now confidently holding up his end of the conversation, pleased to discover his social skills improving so rapidly, Jocko said, "They put you on this thing they call the rack, and they stretch your body until your joints pull apart."

"You got scary eyes," Princess Chrissy said.

From her armchair by the fireplace, Erika said, "Did you know that some angels have yellow eyes, golden eyes?"

"They do?" Chrissy and Jocko asked simultaneously.

"Did you know that angels have to know how to wrestle because they're always wrestling devils?"

"Is Buster Steelhammer an angel?" Princess Chrissy asked.

"He's too bad-ass to be an angel," Jocko decided.

Outside, the growl of an engine rose, like a truck pulling into their driveway.

Putting aside her book, rising from her chair, Erika said, "Why don't you talk about angels, just angels, while I see who that is."

"It probably isn't angels," Chrissy said. "Angels fly, they don't need trucks."

Erika said, "That's why I keep a semi-auto shotgun handy, sweetheart."

chapter 43

In the interest of efficiency, a Communitarian needed to adapt to setbacks whenever they occurred. With the urgent need to finish bringing more order to the disordered barn and thus do her part to destroy humankind, Nancy Potter used the push broom as a crutch and hobbled into the tack room at the back of the barn.

At the end of that narrow space stood a small desk where the real Mayor Erskine Potter had sat to maintain records of expenses related to the horses and to keep notes about vet visits and recommendations. At the desk was an old wooden office chair on wheels.

Nancy broke the back off the chair, turning it into a wheeled stool. Using a large roll of Vetrap hoof tape, she bound the cauterized stump of her left leg to the stool, which wasn't an easy task, but she persisted for the Community. Walking on her right foot, rolling on her footless left leg stump, she maneuvered out of the tack room, into the main part of the barn.

She stood over the remains of Ariel, wondering if there was anything she ought to do. This didn't look like a Builder anymore. It was like a large, mostly smooth formation of limestone in which someone had been carving faces. There were three faces at different places, all sort of resembling Ariel but distorted. She turned the broom around in her hands and rapped the end of the handle against what had once been Ariel, and it sounded like stone, too. She could not see anything she needed to do more urgently than sweep and sweep the barn floor until all the bristle marks in the dirt were aligned rather than chaotic.

As she set to work, she realized that

sprinkles of snowflakes were coming through the two holes that Ariel, in her swarm mode, had made in the roof. Because the building was heated, most of the flakes melted and evaporated as they fell. Those few that survived all the way to floor became dots of dampness that would soon dry.

The broom swished and swished, the wheels of the chair squeaked, the seat creaked. A light wind soughed in the eaves of the barn and snuffled at the holes in the roof.

The horses were calm again. Commander had not managed to kick out any portion of his stall at the height of his terror. Now and then, Queenie and Valentine nickered. A couple of times, the stallion snorted.

Entirely committed to precisely aligning the bristle marks in the dirt, replicant Nancy seldom looked up from the difficult task before her. But every time she raised her eyes, the horses had their heads beyond the tops of their stall doors, watching her, sometimes while they chewed a bit of hay, other times just staring.

They were so stupid. Like everything in

nature, they were really stupid, poorly designed, requiring too much in the way of
resources, crapping all the time, urinating
all the time, so stupid that they would just
stand and watch, hour after hour, as she
swept, just stand and watch, too stupid to
understand that she was working for the
total destruction of them and of the natural
world that sustained them.

The horses were so stupid, Nancy
wanted to laugh at them, but she couldn't.
In theory, she quite understood the psychological and emotional causes of laughter,
but laughter was for human beings, one
more indication of their lack of seriousness,
of how easily they were distracted. Communitarians could pretend laughter to pass
for the people they replaced, but laughter
never distracted them from their duties,
from their lethal crusade. Laughing or not
laughing, humans were inattentive, heed-
less, preoccupied, oblivious fools, no better
than horses.

For a while, she pretended laughter,
practiced it diligently, so that if at some
point she needed to masquerade as an
amused and distracted human, she would
sound convincing. The swish of the broom,

the squeak of the wheels, the creak of the chair seat, the sough and snuffle of the wind, and her laughter, and the snow fluttering down and vanishing in midair, and the horses watching, the stupid horses, so easily entertained.

chapter 44

A lover of history and tradition, Addison Hawk had never been afraid of change. Occasionally suspicious of the reasons behind some of it, often unconvinced about its value, but not afraid. Until now. Replications of people being pumped out in laboratories, nanoanimals instantly devouring their enemies. . . . That electrifying video made by one of the Riders seemed to support the fear that if the end of humanity had not begun in Rainbow Falls, if this battle could be won, the victory would be brief, and the end would begin elsewhere, the enemy a later generation of these creatures or something else equally post-human but even worse.

He didn't know what to make of Deucalion. The name Frankenstein had been shared with him, as it had not been shared with either the people at the Samples house or with the staff at KBOW. As an editor and a publisher, knowledge was his business, his life, but he was in danger of information overload.

When he heard they were taking a dozen of the Riders' youngest children—between four and eleven years of age—to Erika's house, he knew this must be the beautiful and self-possessed woman whom he had encountered earlier in the day outside of Jim James Bakery. He didn't know of another Erika in Rainbow Falls. He volunteered to go with Deucalion and to stay with Erika, to help her manage these kids and the others who would be brought later.

With the children on benches in the back of the truck, Addison rode up front with Deucalion. He was given to understand that the giant knew a shortcut, a way around the roadblocks, but this mode of travel—teleportation?—was just as unprecedented as all else on this day. As

Deucalion drove along the Samples drive-way, toward the street, he said something about the arrow of time being indeterminate on the quantum level, that every moment contained both all the past and all the future. And when they turned left into the street, they also and instantly turned into Erika's driveway, four miles north of town, and parked near the front porch of the house.

Evidently aware that Addison had been stunned into immobility, Deucalion said, "The universe began from an inexpressibly dense speck of matter, which was as much a thought—a concept—as it was matter. After the big bang, after expanding outward in all directions through these billions of years, that speck of matter has become the universe as we know it. But on a fundamental level, because all of time is present in every moment of time, the universe is still that dense speck, it's simultaneously both that speck and everything that it has since expanded to become. So while the universe is vast, it is also very tiny, a speck, and in that speck, all places are the same place. The Samples house is one step from Erika's place, which is one step from Hong Kong, which is one step from Mars. You just have to know how to live in the reality of the universe in both of the states that it exists."

Although he was a man of words, for a moment Addison could think of nothing to say. Then he said, "I'll get the kids out of the back."

Erika waited for them on the porch. As Addison followed the children up the front steps, she appeared surprised—and he thought perhaps pleased—to see him.

Although the cold wind chapped lips and pinched cheeks, Erika kept the Riders' children on the porch long enough to explain to them that in the house they would meet another little girl like them, but also a special little boy. This wonderful little boy, she said, had suffered much in his life, mostly because he looked so different from other children. She said he was self-conscious about his appearance, his feelings were easily hurt, and all he wanted was to have friends and be a friend to others. She was aware that all the Rider children knew about Jesus, and she reminded them that Jesus valued goodness, not appearances. He valued goodness even more than a nice ride on a fine horse. She said once they got to know this special little boy, they would love him. But she also said that after they got to know him, if suddenly he seemed very scary, that would only be because he had smiled. He had a very unfortunate smile. He would try not to smile, because he didn't want to scare people, but sometimes he just couldn't help himself. So if suddenly he looked like he was going to eat you alive, that was just silly, because he was only smiling.

Although the kids were excited about meeting this wonderful little boy and shared their anticipation with one another, Addison wasn't sure that he was as eager for the encounter as they were. Laboratory-made people, voracious nanoanimals, Frankenstein and his two-hundred-year-old creation, teleportation or something like it: Enough was enough for one night.

Erika smiled at him as she waited for the children to take off their snow-caked boots, and he decided to accept her invitation. She ushered them inside, through the foyer, through an archway, into a living room, where a pretty little girl stood beside the special little boy whom apparently Jesus

wanted them to love. The boy was immeasurably more special than Addison Hawk
had expected, and if the word *boy* actually
applied, Addison's dictionaries were so out
of date that he might as well burn them.

———

Not one of the kids screamed. That surprised Jocko. They all gasped. Nothing
more. *Gasp.* Not one of them went looking
for a bucket. Or a stick. Or an oven to
bake him in. Some of them gasped twice,
and a few smiled, sort of, smiled funny-
like. None of them puked. Their eyes were
very wide, although not as big as Jocko's
eyes. They seemed amazed, only amazed.

For a moment Jocko didn't get it. Then
he did. They weren't interested in him. Why
would they be? They recognized royalty
when they saw it.

Sweeping one hand toward his teatime
hostess, Jocko said, "It is my great honor
to present her royal highness, Princess
Chrissy, daughter of the king of Montana."

chapter 45

Listening to Grace Ahern, Sully York aspired to be the pulp-fiction hero that he'd been often before, in the best moments of his eventful life. He had been shaped by the boy's-adventure novels he began reading when he was eight years old. He'd read hundreds. As a young man, he unconsciously styled himself after the intrepid figures in those books, and when he had realized he was doing so, he decided that he would have more fun if he *consciously* styled himself after them. He was aware that some people could not abide him. But he knew at least a thousand men who modeled themselves after Holden Caulfield in *The Catcher in the Rye,* and who were all the very self-satisfied phonies they supposedly despised, so he reckoned that he had done well enough. Now, as Grace Ahern told her tale, Sully York reacted in the finest pulp tradition: He felt his blood boil with outrage, his heart pound with a sense of adventure, his spleen swell with righteous anger, his spine stiffen with courage, and his gut clench with the right kind of healthy fear, the kind that wouldn't loosen the bowels.

Just outside of the walk-in pantry, Grace, a damn attractive woman, clung desperately to her son, Travis, who was proving himself to be a gallant lad. They wanted to get her out of there, away from the cocoons, but she refused, insisting instead that they had to understand—and act.

This display of fortitude and commitment made her markedly more attractive. Even in the severe and distorting shadows created by the upwash of flashlight beams, she could quicken a stout heart, and he knew she would be lovelier in *any* other ambiance. Sully found himself watching

Bryce Walker as much as he watched this fine woman, trying to read whether the writer was smitten by her. Well, it didn't matter if they were both charmed by Grace Ahern, because they were both too old for her, and it would be absurd to think otherwise. Of course, there *were* men in Sully's family who had lived well past a hundred, still physically fit, active, and mentally sharp. Some of them even held jobs past the century mark. But that was neither here nor there. They were both too old to charm her as she charmed them, and that was the end of it.

Grace recounted how the culinary and janitorial staffs finished serving lunch the previous afternoon and were cleaning up the kitchen and the cafeteria when they were assaulted by police officers and by the principal, the assistant principal, the school nurse, and other people with whom they had worked for years. As they were overpowered, a gunlike stainless-steel device was pressed to their heads, the trigger pulled.

The others had become instantly docile, aware and alert but incapable of resistance, able to control only their eyes.

Seeing her coworkers standing in attendance like zombies waiting for some hoodoo master to give them orders, Grace proved herself as quick-thinking and as iron-nerved as she was damn attractive. The controlling probe—if that was the word—had not affected her as it affected the others. A sharp flash of pain, and then a lingering dull headache. Perhaps it angled through the skull, through bone, and never reached the brain. Or—a more daunting thought, even if it was a thin needle—perhaps the thing pierced the brain but failed to function. In any event, she pretended to the same docility that the others displayed. She stood among them, waiting for an opportunity to bolt.

The principal, assistant principal, and other conspiring school employees departed, leaving only two policemen to guard the helpless zombies. Moments later, a radiantly beautiful young woman and equally radiant young man arrived in the kitchen, of such physical perfection that they appeared unearthly, from a higher realm. They moved like dancers, seeming to float across the floor. When they spoke, their voices were mellifluous. Each said only one thing, the same thing: *I am your Builder.* The rendering began. And when one of the Builders had churned through two people, it regurgitated the matter that had spun into the first cocoon.

If Grace had attempted to flee then, she would surely have been chased down and captured. But she was paralyzed by terror long enough for a lone trucker, making an unscheduled food delivery, to enter the kitchen through the receiving room and the walk-in refrigerator. He couldn't have made much sense of what he saw, but Death was obviously in that kitchen even though the method of slaughter mystified. The deliveryman ran, and the police chased him out through the receiving room, leaving the standing zombies in the care of the busy Builders.

Grace couldn't have fled to the parking lot, for the cops would have snared her as they would surely grab the deliveryman. Likewise, she knew that if she passed through other parts of the school, she would encounter one of her fellow workers who had participated in the assault on the culinary and janitorial staffs. Her hope was to hide out only until the Builders, whatever they were, finished their horrific work, whatever it might ultimately be.

The pantry was the only place in the kitchen where she could quickly get out of sight. The Builders weren't people anymore, they were ravenous things, intent only on their rendering.

"But then," she said, still holding fast to Travis, the two of them supporting each other, "maybe the deliveryman came back with reinforcements he found in the parking lot or other people arrived unexpectedly. I don't know. But there was a struggle in the kitchen, I could hear it through the pantry door, shouts and things crashing. That cabinet fell against the door, trapping me . . . and then before long, everything got very quiet."

Travis said, "Mom, we've got to get you to a doctor."

"No, honey. I wouldn't trust any doctors in this town, any more than I'd trust a policeman."

"But what if you're bleeding . . . in there, inside your head?"

"Then I wouldn't have made it this long. Right now, what we've got to do is burn those cocoons, whatever's in them, burn every one of them."

By God, Sully liked her pluck. She had true grit. He liked her mettle. He wondered if she knew her guns. If not, he knew she could be taught to shoot, and after this mayhem, she'd want to be taught. Some martial-arts training, too. Throwing stars and chain bolos. She looked like she had the shoulder and arm strength for a cross-bow.

Bryce Walker said to Grace, "An operation this size, you must have cooking oil in five-gallon cans. We could pour a pool of it under the cocoons. The gas ovens are nearby. But I think we'll need something more flammable than vegetable oil to lead the flames down the front of the oven to the floor and to get the kind of flash fire we need. I imagine you use Sterno or some equivalent for the chafing dishes in the cafeteria. A can of that would be just the thing."

Squinting at Bryce, Sully thought, *Ah, so that's how it is, you slyboots scribbler. Well, don't think Sully York will surrender the prize easily.*

He said, "Mix the Sterno with the cooking oil on the floor. But you can't be in the room and pour it on open gas flames. The flash will take you down. With Sterno and a few ordinary cleaning supplies, I can make a Molotov cocktail, throw it from the door, and be out by the time it shatters and ignites the pool."

"Let's do it," Grace said. "Burn all of these abominations. Then find out where others have been spun, locate every one we can, burn them like burning nests of gypsy moths out of infected trees, burn them back to Hell where they came from."

By God, she was game. She knew how to nail her colors to the mast and stick fast to them. Sully had never seen intrepidity in quite so pretty a package.

chapter 46

Jocko in the study with the big guy. The monster of monsters! The legend! The big guy sitting in Jocko's desk chair! Jocko standing beside him, not just a former tumor with hyperactivity disorder, not just a screwup with hardly any butt and toad feet too big for shoes, but now *a comrade in arms*! This was better than anything. Even better than eating soap.

Jocko had tried to show Deucalion the printouts. The stolen secrets. Depredated data. Plundered, pirated, purloined by Jammin' Jocko, cyber cowboy, highwayman of the ether! But he had dropped them. Scooped them up, shuffled them into order. Dropped them again. When Jocko started shouting at the pages as if they were alive and in rebellion against him, Deucalion suggested that *he* hold the pages, review them himself, and ask questions if he had any.

Now Jocko stood ready. Waiting for questions. About Progress for Perfect Peace. Standing ready. Well, not just standing. Dancing from foot to foot. Sometimes pirouetting, but only five or maybe six revolutions at a time. Doing the boogaloo. A little bit of the funky chicken. Making propeller noises with his mouth flaps. Hat bells jingling. Sort of Christmasy.

He felt the need to talk, too. He said, "Jocko had it all done like an hour ago. Ripped it, zipped it, got it done. Then Jocko was Princess Josephine. Not the real one. Stand-in. Didn't put on a dress or anything. Stand-in for teatime. With Princess Chrissy. Her dad, I don't know. Maybe he chops off heads. Maybe he doesn't. Jocko sweated from his ears. Otherwise did pretty well. Jocko hates tea. Tea sucks. Whoopie pies are good. Better than bugs, like Jocko ate back when. When he lived in a sewer. *Way* better. No whoopie pies in a sewer. Jocko likes *Little Women,* the movie. Jocko's got every version. Poor sweet Beth. She always dies. It just rips Jocko up. Jocko cries. Not ashamed. It's a good cry. But they should remake. *Little Women.* Let Beth live. Jocko would watch it a thousand times. Unless Johnny Depp played Beth. You know Johnny Depp? Probably not. Different social circles. Jocko used to be afraid of Justin Bieber. Still is, a little. Then saw Depp. You have allergies? Jocko does. Raspberries. Face swells up. Lots of snot pours out. Well, not snot. Uglier than snot. Don't know what. Never had it analyzed. Disgusting. Jocko can be disgusting. Not on purpose though. Do you like to pirouette? Jocko likes to pirouette."

The big guy said, "You've done an excellent job here."

Jocko almost died of delight.

"Progress for Perfect Peace. No doubt this Victor Leben is the clone of our Victor. I've been to the warehouse you discovered they own. It's not where he's located. It's a center for liquidation of the people they've replaced with replicants. You found nothing that would pinpoint a location along the End Times Highway that's related to Progress for Perfect Peace?"

Jocko shook his head. Adamantly. Proud of his thoroughness. "Nothing to find. Jocko shucked every ear of data corn. Popped it, buttered it, salted it, ate it up. Peeled the online onion down to its last layer. Bit every byte of the banana. Sliced, chopped, diced, minced, mashed—and what you see is what there is. Jocko would bet life on it. Jocko will kill himself if he missed something. Kill himself brutally. Savagely. Over and over again."

"Progress for Perfect Peace," Deucalion brooded. "Knowing this name is key. Knowing it, we'll find him."

chapter 47

A mild wind came up, and Mr. Lyss called it a devil wind, not because devils were blowing around in it, but because it started to smooth away the snowmobile tracks. Just as it seemed the trail would be erased before their eyes, they saw house lights through the snow and found their way back to the Bozeman place.

The sad music was still being played. After Mr. Lyss retrieved his long gun from the workbench in the garage, he went into the house, to the living room.

Nummy followed the old man, though he didn't want to follow because he was afraid of the monster playing the piano. There was something about Mr. Lyss that made you have to follow him, though Nummy didn't understand what it was. It wasn't just that he sometimes threatened to cut your feet off and feed them to wolves if you didn't follow him or if you resisted doing other things he wanted you to do. In fact, Nummy felt compelled to follow Mr. Lyss *in spite* of the threats. Maybe at the beginning the threats were part of what made Nummy stay with him, but now it was something else. If Grandmama was still alive, she would know what it was and would be able to explain it.

In the living room, Mr. Lyss said to the piano player, "Was Bozeman the most depressive sonofabitch who ever lived, or are you just not playing the livelier music he knew?"

"Kill me," the piano man said, "and the music will stop."

"I'd like nothing better than to kill you dead as anyone's ever been," Mr. Lyss said. "I've killed every damn monster I've ever met, and there have been more than a few. But I won't be *told* to do it by the monster himself. I'm not a man who can be bossed around. Tell him that's true, boy."

Nummy said, "That's true. Mr. Lyss can't be bossed around. He gets his back up easy. If he was on fire and somebody told him jump in the water, he might not do it 'cause it wasn't his idea first."

"Hell's bells," the old man said, "where did that come from, boy?"

"It come from me, sir."

"Well, I know it came from you, I heard you say it. But it came from somewhere deeper in you than most of your jabber and prattle comes from. Not that I'm encouraging more of the same. I didn't ask you to psychoanalyze me. I asked you to confirm my simple statement for this gloomy sonofabitch."

As before, Xerox Bozeman's hands seemed to float back and forth across the keys, almost as if they weren't taking the music from the piano, as if instead the music was in the hands and the piano was drawing it out of them, like the land draws lightning to it in a storm.

Nummy felt a little hypnotized by the

floating hands, as before. Maybe Mr. Lyss was hypnotized, too, because he listened for a while without saying anything.

But then the old man said, "If you want to be dead because of what you saw when Bozeman died, why don't you kill yourself?"

"I can't. My program forbids self-destruction."

"Your program."

"The one installed in me in the Hive, in the laboratory where I was made."

"By Frankenstein," Mr. Lyss said with some scorn. "In the Hive."

"That's right."

"You're still sticking to that story."

"It's true."

"And it's not true that you're a Martian or some murderous scum from some other planet?"

"It's not true," said the piano player.

"We burned some big cocoons earlier tonight. You make those cocoons?"

"No. I'm a Communitarian. The cocoons are made by Builders. We both come from the Hive."

Mr. Lyss thought about that for a while before he said, "Earlier I wanted to kill you, but I knew for some reason it was a bad idea. I think it's still a bad idea, damn if I know why, since I'd get plenty of satisfaction from it. So I'll tell you what—I'll kill you as dead as dead can be, as soon as I feel it's right."

The music was very sad. Nummy thought a person might curl up like a pill bug and never uncurl, listening to that music too much.

"In return," Mr. Lyss said, "you come along with us, answer some questions."

"What questions?" the piano player asked.

"Any damn question that pops in my head to ask. I'm not giving you a list of questions ahead of time so you can study them and just scheme up a bunch of lying answers. O'Bannon here is a dummy, but I'm not, and you better keep that in mind. If you lie to me, I'll know it's a lie, I can *smell* a lie better than a bloodhound can smell the nearest sausage. Then I'll put you in a cage and feed you well and *never* kill you. You have to earn it. Is that understood?"

"Yes," the Xerox Bozeman said, and he stood up from the piano.

chapter **48**

The Communitarian workers in the Hive are forbidden to descend to the vacant lower floors not used by Victor's enterprise, through which he now walks in splendid isolation.

In the early days of their creation, two had come down here, been *lured* into this realm by a scientist named Ehlis Shaitan, or so he claimed, who worked in the building back in the Cold War. Shaitan had gone mad in a most interesting way, had vanished while supposedly on vacation, but in fact had been living in the secret byways of the lower floors for almost thirty years, subsisting on immense stores of dehydrated, vacuum-packed foods intended to sustain thousands of government officials who would have been brought here in anticipation of imminent conflict, to ride out World War III and the radioactive aftermath.

In certain ubersecret bunkers at the bottom of this supersecret installation, Ehlis Shaitan invented a colorful personal history that was mythological in nature. In scores of thick handwritten volumes, in elaborate bunker-wall paintings and carvings done with hand tools, he celebrated his supposedly supernatural powers and crowned himself the immortal ruler of this underworld. And acting as a prophet, he predicted his own ascension to the surface in a time of cataclysm, when he would take what riches he wanted, rape whomever he desired, kill more prolifically than any score of homicidal rulers had ever murdered their fellow men, and allow those to live who worshipped him and became his pliant and obedient servants.

In his mid-seventies, Shaitan grew weary of waiting to ascend to rule a devastated Earth, and when Victor and his original team of scientists moved into the upper levels of the facility, the bearded old man monitored them secretly. Eventually he enticed two first-generation Communitarians into his lower world of obscene, violent, grotesque murals, into rooms in which the floors were as vividly decorated as the walls and ceilings, and he made an effort to enlist them in his cult.

When Victor and his team found the two missing Communitarians, both had to be destroyed, so strange had they become. The weakness in their program was identified: certain lines of code that did not sufficiently embed and enforce the absolute need for *total* focus on efficiency. All subsequent Communitarians had functioned perfectly, of course.

Victor had personally killed the lunatic old man and ordered his bunkers sealed. There was no room for an Ehlis Shaitan in the world to come, no need for his like or his opposite.

Now Victor walks the lower floors, alone with his thoughts, his multiple cascades of scintillant theories and ideas, pleased by the prospect of witnessing the extermination of every thinking creature on the planet, down to the last finch and wren, to every smallest lizard. When his are the only eyes left to see the world, when his is the only mind left to appreciate it, how brilliant it will be to end his own existence as unhesitatingly as he had terminated Ehlis Shaitan.

He would prefer to walk in this deep retreat for hours yet, for days. But although the solitude is invigorating, his time here is necessarily limited by the absence of Communitarians to see to his needs.

He takes an elevator up to one of the floors of the Hive. In the corridor, as he approaches the first plasma screen, it sounds the three-note alert to request his attention. Scrolling up the screen comes the report that the employees at KBOW have not been entirely replaced with Communitarians as per the plan. They have become aware of the replicants among them, and they are broadcasting a warning to Rainbow Falls and, perhaps more worrisome, to communities beyond in that portion of Montana that the station serves.

This is not a gnat in the path of the Communitarian war machine, as was the failure to properly track two of the Builders. This is admittedly a larger issue, a housefly rather than a gnat, but it is not a serious setback, because there can be no serious setback in the progress of the Community. Their triumph is inevitable; and to think otherwise would credit humanity with at least some significance, when it has none, not a minim.

Victor says exactly what he said before, although he knows that his order has already been effectuated because of the well-programmed responses of the brutal Communitarian war machine. "Consult the master strategy-and-tactics program, apply the appropriate remedy, and press forward without delay."

With no destination in mind at the moment, still walking just to walk and think, he turns right at the next corridor, where the small three-legged table waits for him. On the table stands a cold bottle of water. Beside the water is a yellow saucer. In the saucer lies a shiny red capsule and a white tablet. He swallows the capsule first and then the tablet.

When next he approaches a plasma screen, it sounds the three notes. The scroll informs him that, in addition to the problem at KBOW, pockets of organized resistance have formed in Rainbow Falls.

This is expected. Resistance is futile. Even now, Builders by the score are emerging from their cocoons, and the next, more violent, phase of the conflict is beginning. Soon they will emerge by the hundreds. They are indestructible, unstoppable, and their rapidly increasing numbers will soon ensure victory in Rainbow Falls, after which they will spread out anonymously through the country and then the world, a plague of death growing geometrically in virulence day by day.

chapter 49

At the end of Erika's driveway, Deucalion turned right, not onto the county road
but instead directly into the driveway at the
Samples house, under the spreading limbs
of the towering evergreens. Through the
broken-out passenger window, he heard the
nearest sentry call quietly to a second who
was farther removed, and the second to a
third, passing the news like members of a
fire line passing a pail of water. The name
with which they announced his return wasn't
his own—"Christopher . . ." "Christopher . . ."
"Christopher . . ."—and he wondered why
they had adopted a code name for him.

As Deucalion stepped down from the truck, Michael appeared in response to the sentries' announcement. "The Riders don't waste time. The effort to make a garrison of the neighborhood is moving fast. And expanding from one square block to two as they get people to join them. Those cell-phone videos make an impression on the skeptical. And now your work at KBOW. Some local talk-show guy is getting out the word with such passion he mostly sounds convincing. And even when he sounds like a raving nut, he sounds like a nut who's telling the truth."

"More children?" Deucalion asked.

"Carson's assembling the next group in the living room."

"How many?"

"I think fifteen. They're coming over fences from neighboring houses, yard to yard to yard."

Opening the cargo doors, Deucalion said, "Jocko found a few things worth knowing. The most helpful might be the name of the organization Victor is using for cover. Progress for Perfect Peace."

"Interesting sense of irony. When all of us are dead, the peace will be perfect, I guess."

"It's not irony," Deucalion said. "It's confidence."

"I hate that guy."

"Progress for Perfect Peace. Spread the name around. Maybe someone has heard it before. Maybe someone knows about a location other than the warehouse where they were liquidating those brain-damaged people."

Carson appeared on the front porch of the house. She led a group of well-bundled youngsters down the steps and across the yard to the truck.

The children must have been briefed about Deucalion, because they showed no fear of him. Their thin, pluming breath seemed to be a testament to their fragility, to how easily they could be snuffed out, but the plumes didn't betray any terror of him. As they boarded the truck, some looked at him shyly, and other sweet, cold-pinked faces regarded him with an awe that seemed to have in it an element of delight.

He was not accustomed to delighting children. He liked it.

After Deucalion assured the kids that they would not have to endure the dark in the back of the truck for more than a few minutes, he closed the doors and said to Carson, "Why do the sentries call me Christopher?"

"Among other things, he's the patron saint of travelers, especially of children. They say he was a Canaanite of gigantic stature. Seems to me, Christopher fits you better than your current handle."

In a time when he was bitter about having been brought to life, when he was full of rage and had not yet realized what his mission must be, he named himself Deucalion as an expression of his self-loathing. Mary Shelley titled her book *Frankenstein; or the Modern Prometheus.* In classical mythology, Prometheus was a Titan, brother of Atlas. He shaped human beings from clay and endowed them with the spark of life. Made by Victor, the modern Prometheus, Deucalion was in effect his son, and he felt, back then, that he should carry the name to remind himself that he shared the shame of Victor's rebellion against all of nature.

Now he knew that the lightning of his birth pulsed in his eyes as he said to Carson, "I haven't earned a better name than the one I have now."

"Earned? Back in Louisiana, you presided over Victor's death in the landfill."

"But now he's back. Version 2.0." He started forward toward the driver's door, then stopped and turned to them. "Where did his clone get the money for this? He left New Orleans with only a fraction of my maker's fortune."

"He's like a Broadway producer," Michael said. "He found some backers."

"Backers with deep pockets," Carson said. "So deep they might as well be bottomless."

Deucalion said, "Even if these new creations can be defeated, and even if he can be killed, perhaps we ought to be worried about the reaction of his backers when they get no return for their investment."

He got behind the wheel of the truck. As he pulled out of the driveway and turned left, he tapped the horn—and it sounded as he braked to a stop at Erika's place. By the time he opened the back door and the children began to disembark, Erika and Addison appeared on the front porch to greet them.

chapter 50

Frost on foot, urgently seeking transportation, was not sure where he would go when he had wheels. If Chief Rafael Jarmillo, out there bringing a hard new kind of law to this hellish town, was not the real Jarmillo, if the real Jarmillo and his family had been ground up like Dagget, then roads out of Rainbow Falls were probably blockaded. This was the War of the Worlds or something like it, and restricting the movement of people in a captured town was always a priority in a war. To be seen approaching the roadblock and then turning away from it would invite pursuit. Frost wanted to avoid pursuit. After what he had seen, he didn't think he'd survive being chased by whatever the things were that pretended to be local cops.

As he prowled this residential neighborhood, wading along snow-mantled sidewalks, drawing steadily closer to the business district, he saw shadows moving behind drawn curtains in some houses, and he wondered what might be casting them. He definitely wasn't going to indulge his curiosity by ringing a doorbell or two. At a few houses, he saw faces at windows, people seeming to study the night, but he kept moving because maybe they weren't people any more than the brunette from the cocoon had been the beauty queen that she first appeared to be.

A car turned the corner a block away, and as its headlights swung in his direction, Frost crouched on the sidewalk beside a Lexus SUV. Maybe the driver of the approaching vehicle was someone coming home from shopping or from dining out, human and trustworthy. But if the police were not really police, and if they were patrolling with the determination to limit citizens' ability to move freely about, they might be assisted by others of their kind driving ordinary vehicles instead of marked squad cars, on the lookout for pedestrians and unauthorized motorists. Under the grumble of the car's engine, Frost heard the muted clinking of snow chains as it cruised past without slowing.

Driving might make him a more obvious target than if he remained on foot, but he continued to seek transportation. Instead of cruising around at random, he would drive directly to some parking spot where he could keep a watch on all approaches, yet where the crystallized exhaust of the idling engine would not attract attention, so that he could stay warm and gain time to think. Perhaps in the last row of for-sale vehicles in a closed car dealership, far back from passing traffic in the street. Or the big supermarket on Ursa Avenue. It would be closed now, the lot deserted, and a dark corner there might be just the place.

When he found the old Chevy—winter tires but no snow chains—in front of a house in the next block, he tried the driver's door. He dared to think that he might have some luck left, after all, when the car proved not to be locked. He had a penlight and a multifunction penknife, but luck was indeed with him; he didn't need to hot-wire the Chevy when he found the keys under the floor mat.

In spite of the cold, the car started at once. The engine sounded tuned and well maintained. He boldly switched on head-lights, popped the hand brake, and shifted into drive, half expecting to hear a shout and see the angry owner rushing down the front-porch steps. But he pulled into the street and drove away without a pro-test being raised.

The vintage car needed time to warm up before the heater would work. As he drove, Frost anticipated the first wash of hot air with no less relish than he had ever looked forward to a filet-mignon dinner—or to sex, for that matter. Earlier, he'd been daydreaming of a time fifteen or twenty years ahead, when he might retire on some tropical shore or in a desert resort where they didn't sell gloves or winter coats because no one ever needed them. Now he dared only think ahead fifteen or twenty minutes, and his goal was simple survival.

Of the choices available to him, the supermarket parking lot was the closest, and he remained watchful street after street, leery of an encounter with a patrol car. As the heat at last breathed from the vents, he realized that the Chevy offered more than mobility and heat. He turned on the radio—and discovered that the alien invasion was not as secret as he feared it might be and that it wasn't an alien invasion.

chapter 51

Nummy put his foot down. He said no to Mr. Lyss, who didn't like anyone saying no to him. Nummy said no, no, no, the monster couldn't come with them in the car. It happened right there in the living room, with the piano player standing beside the piano and Mr. Lyss holding the long gun. Grandmama taught Nummy always to be kind to people. But she also taught him not to let people take advantage of him, to put his foot down in the nicest way he could when someone insisted that he do something he knew wasn't right.

The Xerox Boze said he wasn't one of those things that gobbled up people. He said he wasn't born out of a cocoon but instead out of a machine in a laboratory. Those cocoon things were called Builders, and he was called a Communitarian, and he couldn't eat someone any more than he could kill himself.

Nummy didn't believe a word of it. Monsters were monsters, they always did what monsters did, always disgusting, never anything nice, which was why Nummy wouldn't watch their movies. If monsters killed people and ate people and did even worse things to people, then of course they would lie. Lying would be no big deal. Even a dummy knew that.

Mr. Lyss was no dummy, but he believed the monster. He said the monster saw what the Boze saw when the Boze died, and now the monster was broken somehow and couldn't do monster things anymore. Mr. Lyss said you might call it a spiritual conversion, except the monster didn't have a spirit and so couldn't be converted. He said you also might call it a born-again experience, except the monster was never born in the first place, only manufactured, so he couldn't be born again, only broken.

Nummy asked if the monster had seen the Lord, and Mr. Lyss said maybe not the Lord, maybe just Heaven, or maybe the Fiery Pit, depending on what the Boze saw. But maybe nothing like any of that, just something amazing on the other side.

So then Nummy wanted to know what the old man meant by the other side. The other side of what? Mr. Lyss said the other side of life, over where the dead go. Nummy said that was called either Heaven or Hell, it wasn't called the Other Side. And Mr. Lyss said different people have different ideas about that. The Other Side might be far different from either Heaven or Hell. It might be this world again but you're a new person, or even sometimes you're an animal, what they called reincarnation. Nummy said that was silly, nobody would believe that, Mr. Lyss must be making it up. People couldn't be animals, and they certainly couldn't be a carnation, which was just a flower. Mr. Lyss said that if he was being called a liar, he would fry Nummy's nose with some onions *and* fix him so he had to pee out of his left ear.

At that point, the piano player again asked Mr. Lyss to kill him, and right away. Xerox Boze begged for death so hard that Nummy found himself pitying him. Monsters probably couldn't cry, crying wasn't in their nature, and this one didn't shed any tears, but he sounded really miserable. Nummy felt sorry for him. He wondered if maybe he put his foot down too hard.

Nummy said to Mr. Lyss, "I don't want to be mean to him, not even a monster. Lots of meanness has come my way, so I know how bad it feels."

"There's an attitude Grandmama would admire," Mr. Lyss said.

"But I'm scared," Nummy said.

"Well, Peaches, haven't you been scared pretty much all this dreadful day, and haven't you come through all right? I've got my faults, one or two, but I've taken good care of you, haven't I?"

"We've stolen a lot of stuff."

"Tarnation, I did just say I have a fault or two. I didn't make any claim to shining perfection. All I said is I've kept you safe. Haven't I?"

"I guess so."

"Guess so? You've got both feet to walk on, don't you? You've got both hands to eat with. Your big dumb head is still on your shoulders, isn't it?"

"I guess it is," Nummy admitted.

"All right, then," said Mr. Lyss. "Let's go."

Nummy had put his foot down, but now he found himself picking it up and doing just what he didn't want to do, which was walk out to the stolen car with Mr. Lyss and the monster.

And when they got to the car, Nummy discovered that Mr. Lyss wanted the monster to drive.

As Xerox Boze got in behind the wheel, Mr. Lyss led Nummy around to the passenger side, where he opened both doors.

"It'll be all right, Peaches. If I drove, I couldn't keep him covered. This way, I'll have a pistol aimed at him the whole time, though it won't be necessary."

"I don't know what it is we're doing," Nummy worried.

"First it was alien bugs, which is just blind fate, no meaning to it. Then it was Frankenstein, which isn't fate, it's about how we try to tear apart the way things are, just to prove we can. It's still Frankenstein, Nummy, but it's something a lot bigger, too. Even a useless old hobo like me can see signs in the sky if they're big and bright enough."

Nummy looked at the sky, but he didn't see any signs, just snow coming down.

Mr. Lyss smiled, which was a surprising thing to see, and he put a hand on Nummy's shoulder in a way that made him think of Grandmama. "There's big Evil in this town tonight, son, bigger than most people will ever admit exists. When it's all over, they'll just say it was these people machines, science run amok, which is true enough but not the whole truth. Anyway, there's not just big Evil in Rainbow Falls tonight, there's something else, too."

"What else?" Nummy asked.

"From the start, things have gone our way when they never should have. We ought to be dead ten times over."

"That's because of you you're so smart."

"I'm smart enough for a hobo, but I wouldn't be a hobo if I was as smart as I said I am. Things have gone our way for a reason, and I think I know what it is. I'll explain that part later. But things went our way big-time when we found this broken monster, especially when you think about what broke him. He knows things about the monster-making machine only one like him could know, and in this war, that's invaluable information. We have to find someone who knows how to use what this broken monster knows."

"Who?"

"I don't know. But I'm going to look after you, and I'm going to do the smartest thing I know how, but I'm also going to say 'Show me' now and then, and just do what intuition tells me. Intuition is the little voice inside you that tells you what's right and wrong, wise or foolish—which is different from dumb and smart. Do you feel better about this now?"

"No," Nummy said. "Well, maybe a little better. But the Xerox Boze he's still a monster."

Mr. Lyss told Nummy to get into the backseat and slide over behind the driver. Then he put the long gun on the seat, barrel away from Nummy, and he said, "Don't get it in your head to take that and go hunting rabbits."

"I don't hunt ever," Nummy said.

"And remember it's a stolen gun."

"You stole it out of the preacher's house."

"That's right. You don't want to be part of that crime, too, considering all the other banditry you're guilty of lately."

"I'll never touch it."

Mr. Lyss closed the back door, got in front, closed that door, too, and handed the key to the Xerox Boze.

The monster started the car and said, "Where are we going?"

"Nummy," Mr. Lyss said, "this right now is a show-me moment if ever there was or will be one."

Mr. Lyss was quiet for a while. There was just the sound of the idling engine, and outside the snow sliding down the night, down and down, slanting in the wind.

Nummy sat staring at the back of the monster's head, and the monster didn't start humming sad music or anything, he just waited like Nummy.

After half a minute or more, Mr. Lyss leaned forward and clicked on the car radio.

A man on the radio was talking about a war somewhere. Then he said Rainbow Falls. Then he said people that weren't people.

Mr. Lyss said, "Thank you very much."

chapter 52

The cocoon split. She was liberated. She came forth into the courthouse basement.

A mist of millions rose from her skin. An illusion of clothes formed and clung to her as the mist clarified.

She was the revolution. She would devour the past.

Nearby another cocoon disgorged another beauty. A small, swarming portion of herself became her costume.

They would devour the past but make no future. There would be perpetual revolution until the revolution devoured even itself. Then nothing.

Another cocoon ripened to the moment of delivery. He came forth into the courthouse basement. Clothes formed: a business suit, white shirt, and tie.

He was the revolution. Only a perpetual revolution could be a legitimate revolution. What revolved must take its meaning from its motion. When it ceased to revolve, it had no meaning.

She, she, he. In truth, they had no gender. Their gender was strictly their disguise. Each was an it. A colony of many tinier its. It had two purposes: to destroy and to reproduce asexually.

Another cocoon split and spat forth. A fifth cocoon and a sixth dropped their fruit into the world. Two men, a woman: three its.

They were the revolution. They were hatred and rage distilled to perfect purity. Their hunger was as great as the gravity of a black hole, which could pull worlds to their destruction.

Other cocoons in the courthouse basement were not yet ready to deliver.

The six departed and climbed stairs to the main floor.

The courthouse stood silent. It would be silent for decades, until it collapsed from lack of maintenance.

Outside, they descended the courthouse stairs, perhaps six magazine models expecting their glamour photographer to be waiting.

They did not slip in the snow. Their shoes were in fact part of their substance expressed as shoes, so they were barefoot. But their feet were the illusion of feet, and the soles and heels that met the snow-blanketed pavement were really millions of nanoanimals gripping-releasing-gripping. Their traction and balance were such that in their human masquerade, they could never slip or stumble.

As they stepped into the street and surveyed the area, they might arouse suspicion because their faces in the lamplight were in every case exquisite, more flawless beauty on display than in an exhibition of Botticelli masterpieces. And in the cold, their breath did not smoke from them in pale plumes, because although they passed for people, they had no lungs.

The neighborhood around the courthouse offered classic old homes, mostly in Federal and Victorian styles. The six separated and went visiting.

———

Rusty Billingham sang softly as he walked home through the snow. Rusty lived to sing. He wrote his own songs, and people seemed to like them. He played guitar well, but he also played a synthesizer and could make himself sound like a combo. From time to time he did a bar gig, a wedding, a birthday party. He didn't make much money at it, but he didn't expect to make much, so he wasn't disappointed.

A booker who was scouting for talent heard Rusty one night at Pickin' and Grinnin', the roadhouse owned by Mayor Potter, and said he could get him regular work across four states. But Rusty didn't like traveling. He had gone away to war in the Mideast for a few years, and that cured him of wanting to see new places. At twenty-seven, he came back home to Rainbow Falls, and now at thirty, he planned to stay here until he needed an undertaker.

The booker gave recordings of Rusty's songs to a talent agent, and the agent wanted Rusty to come to Nashville, all expenses paid, to discuss his future. Rusty said thanks but no thanks. He had no illusions about himself. He could write music and sing, but he didn't have the looks to go big-time professional. He was as not-handsome as Montana was not-Afghanistan. In fact, he was a little goofy-looking, goofy in a nice way but goofy nonetheless. The days of non-handsome country stars were all but gone. Anyway, he could play for locals, people who grew up here, who knew him or knew his folks, but when he played for a room of total strangers, his shyness kicked in, and he couldn't look much at the audience or do patter between songs.

He made a decent living with carpentry and cabinetmaking, crafts he learned from his dad. He always had work, and there was nearly as much satisfaction to be had from doing good joinery and hand-rubbed finishes as from making music. And nobody cared what a cabinetmaker looked like. Currently he had a kitchen-remodel under way, only six blocks from home, so he could leave his tools there and walk back and forth.

As long as he could remember, he liked to walk this town, pretty as it was, but especially since he came home from war. Rusty knew men who returned with one leg or none. Every day he gave thanks for his legs, and he proved his gratitude by using them. He didn't feel guilty that he walked away from war while others were carried, but he felt the iniquity of it, the gross injustice, and sorrowed sometimes late at night.

He was half a block past the old courthouse, nearing the corner, when he thought he heard a man scream. He stopped to listen, but the cry had been brief and muffled, as if it had come from inside one of the big old houses. It might have been less a scream than a shout.

Rusty turned in a circle, studying the street in the lamplight, the houses with their deep porches, the bare-limbed trees black where the snow had not painted them. The second scream, a woman's, was not as brief, but also muffled. The snow played tricks with sound, too, and he couldn't pinpoint the source of the cry before it abruptly cut off.

No traffic moved on the main street, as

far as the falling snow allowed the eye to see. When he took three steps to the corner, he saw that the cross street was likewise deserted. The storm harried people home early and kept them there, but Montanans were a hardy lot and not easily deterred by inclement weather. With four inches accumulated, there would usually be a few people out on skis, poling along streets where the plows hadn't yet scraped the pavement, not to mention kids building snow forts or dragging their sleds behind them toward the nearest open hill, laughing and calling excitedly to one another. Rusty saw no one, heard no children.

He realized that no snowplows growled in the distance, either. The city maintenance-department crews should have been hard at work. In and around the courthouse was one of the neighborhoods where they usually started in a storm.

When Rusty first came home from war, his nerves were frayed and taut, easily strummed but slow to quiet. The peace of small-town Montana had seemed illusory. Sometimes he found it easy to believe that stealthy assassins were at work in the night, slitting throats of sleepers. And at odd moments, for no apparent reason, he froze in expectation of explosions that never came. But those days were more than two years in the past. He didn't suffer from post-traumatic stress disorder. His nerves were knit, and even when he sat up in bed suddenly at three in the morning, unsure what had awakened him, they no longer throbbed with arpeggios of fear.

He took seriously, therefore, his sense of foreboding. Something was wrong. The two muffled cries—screams or shouts—had been real. The deserted streets, the childless yards, the quiet here and the stillness even into the distance, were unusual if not strange.

He turned left, walking slowly north on the cross street, alert for any sound and for any moving thing other than the gently driven snow. A few of the lovely old houses were dark, but most appeared warm and welcoming with lights in their windows. Indeed, the street was no less picturesque, no less charming than a winter painting by Thomas Kinkade, in which every French pane was a jewel and even trees and some expanses of snow seemed to be filled with inner light.

You could call it magical, this part of town at this moment, but it didn't feel as good as it looked. He couldn't understand how a sense of menace could arise from a scene that, in its every aspect, charmed the eye. He wondered about himself, about whether he might be sliding back into the perpetual uneasiness that troubled him during the six months immediately after he left the battlefield.

When he worked late, as he had this day, he walked home by this route because it brought him past the house of Corrina Ringwald. They became best friends their senior year in high school, when she lost her little sister to leukemia and fell into a depression that neither drugs nor counseling could cure. Rusty made her well with music. He wrote songs for her, recorded them, and put them in her mailbox. He wasn't courting her, and she knew he wasn't; it just hurt him to see her in such pain. They remained best friends all these years later. Both of them wanted a closer relationship, but both of them feared that if they failed as lovers, they would feel awkward with each other and would then be less close as friends.

Their friendship was such an important part of their lives that they were loath to risk damaging it. As often as not, when he passed Corrina's home at the end of the day, the porch light was on, which was a signal to him. If the light glowed, she didn't have any prep work for the next day's classes—she was a teacher—and wanted him to come in for dinner.

Rusty was still more than two blocks from Corrina's place when he heard another scream, a woman's. This one lasted longer than the previous two and couldn't be mistaken for anything other than what it was: a cry of abject terror. He halted, turned, trying to home in on the voice, and just as the scream cut off, he decided it came from one of two houses, both with bright windows, on the farther side of the street.

He hurried across to the other sidewalk and stood there, under a streetlamp, looking back and forth from a white Victorian with pastel blue trim to a pale gray Victorian with black trim, waiting for another scream or a clue of any kind. The sole sound was the faintest oscillating shush of the gentle wind in the trees, a wind too weak to stir a bough or branch. Nothing moved except the snow unraveling from a sky unseen. This familiar street had become as enigmatic as any far, foreign place first glimpsed. So eerie was the mood that even his shadow on the lamplit snow seemed sinister, as if it might rise up against him.

In one of the first-floor rooms of the gray-and-black house, movement caught Rusty's attention. Quick past a window, someone, something, a suggestion of violent action. He followed the front walk to the porch steps, not sure what he should do: ring the bell, just try the door and enter unannounced, look more closely through the window. . . . As he reached the top of the steps, a woman called out—"Can you help me?"—but her voice came from behind him and from a distance.

He turned and saw her in the street, in the center of the nearer intersection, perhaps seventy feet north of him. In the crosslight of the four corner lamps but at the farthest limit of each rather than in the direct glow of any of them, she looked lost. She wore what appeared to be a silk robe, short and sapphire-blue; the breeze molded it to her and riffled the hem.

"What's wrong?" he asked.

"Help me," she replied, but only stood there in the middle of the intersection, as though oblivious of the biting cold and in a state of shock.

He glanced at the house where he had been about to ring the bell or try the door. Nothing moved past the windows. No sound arose from within.

Perhaps he had come to the wrong house. Perhaps the woman in the cross-light was the one who had screamed, and then had fled into the cold and snow.

Rusty descended the porch steps and followed the walkway to the street.

The thin wrap the woman wore revealed that she was shapely. The whispering breeze and the lamplight made a lambent flame of her long flaxen hair. He suspected that on closer inspection she would prove to be singularly beautiful. In the shower of snow like thrown rice, in the provocative silk robe, she might have been a vision of a bride on her wedding night.

chapter 53

The Xerox Boze parked in the KBOW
lot where Mr. Lyss told him to stop, not
near the other vehicles and back a little
ways from the building, just in case, he
said, they were being lured here by some
sneaky sonofabitch monsters who weren't
the Paul Reveres they were pretending to
be.

They all climbed out of the car, and Mr.
Lyss got his long gun from the backseat,
which was when the two SUVs roared in
from the street, one close behind the other.
They raced past the car, braked hard
nearer the building, and their doors flew

open. Six men jumped out of one, six out of the other, and though Nummy couldn't usually tell whether people were good or bad from just looking at them, he knew right away that these twelve were up to no good.

Nine of them went toward the front door of KBOW, and three of them came this way, and Mr. Lyss asked Xerox Boze if they were his people, and Xerox Boze said, "Yes. Communitarians," which of course meant monsters.

The old man fired the long gun three times fast, and it was so loud Nummy put his hands over his ears. Each shot seemed almost to lift Mr. Lyss off his feet and jump him backward an inch or two. But he must have had some practice with a gun like that, or else he was really lucky, so lucky that you could see why he was so sure the lottery ticket in his wallet would be a big winner. Each shot hit a monster and knocked him down, and Mr. Lyss hurried forward to put the gun close on one of them, at the throat, and fired a fourth time, and Nummy gagged.

The two shot-bad-but-not-dead monsters were getting to their feet, and Mr.

Lyss backed off, grabbing shells from one of his deep coat pockets and reloading as he moved. No sooner were they up than Mr. Lyss shot them down again, and it looked like they would probably stay down this time.

But the other nine, who had been walking toward the building, stopped and looked back this way. Any monster Nummy had seen, while going up and down the TV channels, was always either growling and angry or flat-out furious. It didn't matter whether they came out of a flying saucer or out of a cave from the center of the earth, or out of the black waters of a swamp, they were either ticked off or totally crazy-furious. They didn't seem to know any other way to be, and these nine coming now were no different, they sure weren't broken like Xerox Boze.

Mr. Lyss reloaded two shells even while the last two shots were echoing across the parking lot, and now he fired four times, faster than ever. Four shots did more damage than Nummy expected, but then he remembered that each shot wasn't just one bullet, it was a lot of little lead balls that could hit more than one monster at a

time. Five went down, and two more staggered off balance, but there were nine, so
two more kept coming.

Nummy wanted to run, but there was
nowhere he could go that they wouldn't
chase him right into the ground. Mr. Lyss
didn't have time even to *think* about reloading the long gun, that's how close the
two furious monsters were, so Nummy got
ready to die and he said a speed prayer.

Some guy came out of nowhere and
stepped up beside Mr. Lyss, holding a gun
in two hands, and boy could he shoot.
What seemed to happen was two shots in
the head of the nearest monster, one shot
in the head and one in the throat of the
next one.

This gave Mr. Lyss a chance to put down
his long gun and draw the two pistols from
his coat pockets, and he started shooting
the wounded monsters that were getting
up for another try at him, they just didn't
know when to quit. And the new guy was
blasting them, too. It was like July Fourth,
all the noise. When at last the twelve were
on the ground, not moving, looking as
dead as any roadkill on the highway, Mr.
Lyss and the new guy walked among them,

looking them over, shooting three or four of them who were maybe not as dead as they ought to be.

By now Nummy saw where the new guy came from. Behind Mr. Lyss's stolen car stood an old Chevrolet, engine running, driver's door open wide.

Although his ears were still ringing, Nummy could hear Mr. Lyss say, "You shoot so precise, you must be some kind of lawman from one of the more determined agencies, but I won't hold that against you."

"Frost," the new guy said, "FBI."

"Kill me," Xerox Bose said.

"Don't kill him," Mr. Lyss said. "He's one of them but special."

"One of them?" Mr. Frost said, alarmed, and backed away a couple of steps. "One of them chewed through my partner, Dagget, like it was a wood-chipper and he was nothing but balsa."

"That's a Builder," Mr. Lyss said. "This is a different kind of them. He's a Communitarian. He's bad but not as bad as them bastards, he doesn't eat people."

A hard shot cracked, and the windshield of one of the dead monsters' SUVs exploded.

On the roof of KBOW, huddled against the parapet and watching through the open crenel, Sammy Chakrabarty held his fire as the three got out of the car, waiting to see what they would do, which might tell him whether they were human or not.

One was in a police uniform, which was problematic. If the cops were co-opted, then this wouldn't be a friendly listener inspired to visit by Mason Morrell's stirring rhetoric. He seemed oddly placid, standing by the car in the snow, arms slack at his sides. He wasn't wearing a coat or hat.

One of the other two was a dumpy little guy. Something seemed odd about him, too, although Sammy couldn't see what it was through the sheeting snow.

The third was a grizzled old guy in a long coat. He fetched a shotgun from the backseat, which didn't make him either a villain or a hero in the current situation, though his hair was wild and from a distance he looked a little crazy.

When the two SUVs burst onto the scene and twelve men bailed out of them, Sammy was pretty sure they had mayhem in mind, but he couldn't be certain of their alien nature. He couldn't fire down on them until they attempted to force the front door. They never got a chance. The number of shots required to kill them proved they weren't human.

Sammy didn't know if man-made men might kill one another the same way human beings did, but he was inclined to think they wouldn't. So most likely the three that got out of the first car and the shooter who showed up in the Chevy were his kind of people, with real blood in their veins.

Nevertheless, he wanted to have a dialogue with them before he let them into the station. He got their attention with a single rifle round through the windshield of one of the dead men's SUVs, and then he shouted down, "Who are you people?"

———

When the guy on the roof asked them who they were, Mr. Frost shouted that he was from the FBI and waved some ID, but Mr. Lyss right away took offense.

"'Who are you people?'" the old man said, repeating the roof guy's question but making it sound as if it had been said in a snotty way, which it hadn't. "'Who are you

people?' You going to let in only fancy people who went to universities where every
fool wears a tuxedo and spats, only people
drink tea with their damn pinkies raised?
This town's falling apart worse even than
Detroit, and you have your nose in the air?
You're not going to let in some funky old
hobo because just maybe he stinks a little—*which he damn well doesn't!*—because
he's not wearing a top hat?"

Nummy thought that Mr. Lyss would
wait for an answer to his question, but instead the old man sort of snorted a deep
breath that puffed out his chest and lifted
him taller, and he went on in his most angry voice. His face was so hot-red in the
parking-lot lights that he ought to have
melted the snow that stuck in his eyebrows. He talked right over the poor man
on the roof, who started to say something:

"Who we are is the very people who
might save this miserable jerkwater from
the plague of monsters your fruity an-
nouncer's been jabbering about on the air.
I'm a hobo, this one here beside me is a
dummy by anyone's reckoning, and one
look at us would tell any fool we're as

human as human gets. Go on boy, do your part, tell him you're a dummy."

Nummy said, "He's right. I am. I'm a dummy and always been one. I don't mind him saying it. He don't mean it in a mean way."

Mr. Lyss said to the guy on the roof, "This creature that looks like Officer Bozeman is one of the two kinds of monsters your town let overrun it. He's not one of the people-eating kind, and anyway he's broken, he's no threat to anyone, though he'll test your sanity if you let him near a piano. All this morbid bastard wants is for me to kill him because his program won't allow him to kill himself, but damn if I'll kill him until he tells us everything we need to know to find what nest these sonsofbitches come from so we can go in and burn it out. That's *who we are,* and if *who we are* isn't good enough for you, then you can just get in your Mercedes-Benz and drive yourself straight to Hell."

Nummy realized that Mr. Lyss must have had his feelings hurt about a lot of things over the years, maybe since he was a little boy. That was really something to think about.

chapter 54

The seeming void silent and dark above, the snow materializing out of that inverted abyss, the houses bright or dark but each as still as a mausoleum, and the deserted white street from which this swaddling winter might have robbed all dimension if not for evenly spaced streetlamps dwindling toward other neighborhoods . . .

As the band and collet and prongs of a ring existed to display the gemstone, so it seemed to Rusty Billingham that everything his senses perceived in this glittering scene existed to display the jewel of a woman at the center of the intersection. From a distance of seventy feet, as he approached her, walking the middle of the street, she promised to be extraordinarily beautiful, and when he was still sixty feet from her, he knew that promise would be kept, perhaps more fully than he could imagine. Although it must be but a trick of lamplight and diamonded threads of snow, she appeared radiant, luminous from within.

Rusty was certain now that she'd been the one who screamed, because she was clearly in a state of shock. Standing there with snow well above her ankles, perhaps barefoot, wearing a short silk robe that offered no protection against the night, she seemed to be oblivious of the piercing cold. She had fled from something, out of a house into the street, but now she didn't run to him as a frightened woman seeking protection ought to have done. He asked her again what was wrong, and this time she didn't even ask him to help her, just stared at him as if in a trance.

As he closed to within fifty feet of her, Rusty realized that his reaction to her was as unusual as was her catatonic stare.

Seeing a woman in distress, whether she was beautiful or not, he would have ordinarily hurried to her, but he moved not slowly but deliberately. Unconsciously, some experience cautioned him, some reference to the past that he could not in the instant recall—and when the engine sound of a fast-moving vehicle rose from the west, Rusty came to a halt, still more than forty feet from the woman.

She turned her head to her right, peering along the cross street toward the approaching vehicle, suddenly bathed in its headlights. She made no attempt to get out of its way, seemed rooted or perhaps frozen to the pavement.

Braking, snow chains stuttering, a Chevy Trailblazer appeared and came to a stop beside the woman, its headlights now past her. Four or five people were in the SUV.

The front passenger window purred down, and a grandmotherly figure leaned out. "Honey, are you all right, you need some help?"

Suddenly Rusty knew why he'd been inexplicably cautious. Four years back. Afghanistan. A woman in a burka, only her eyes revealed. She approached a check-point with U.S. Army security. He hap-pened to be at a window half a block away when she detonated the bomb strapped to her body, out of the danger zone but wit-ness to the horror.

The blonde's silk robe revealed the con-tours of her voluptuous body so completely that no bomb could have been concealed under it—but in some way that Rusty could not comprehend, *she* proved to be a bomb. The grandmother in the Trailblazer leaned out of the passenger window, asked the courteous question, and a thick, silvery jet of . . . something like molten metal shot out of the flaxen-haired beauty, into the older woman's face, and the face seemed to dis-solve as she toppled over in her seat. The blonde and the silvery something were one and the same, and as the jet continued spewing into the SUV, she evaporated up from the street, leaving footprints in the snow, transforming entirely into that corro-sive stream and fully invading the Trail-blazer.

People were screaming inside the SUV, maybe four people very loud, but then three not so loud, and the vehicle rocked from the power of what was happening in there, creaked and twanged, bounced on its tires, springs singing a tortured song. Only one person screaming now. A couple windows cracked but didn't break, something *splashed* against the glass, not blood but maybe some blood in it. The driver wasn't in control anymore, most likely wasn't even alive, but the Trailblazer rolled across the intersection, jumped a curb, plowed into a hedge, came to a stop, canting to port. The last scream faded in a thin falsetto, but something continued to churn inside the vehicle, as if it were frenziedly feeding on remains. All was chaos in there, and Rusty could make no sense of the seething shapes he glimpsed.

He took several halting steps toward the Trailblazer as it coasted across the intersection. But by the time it shuddered to a stop in the hedge, he knew there was nothing he could do to help those people. There might be nothing he could do to save himself, either, but he broke into a run.

chapter 55

Deucalion conveyed a third group of children to Erika's place, bringing the number of refugees sheltering there to forty-two, which seemed beyond the maximum the house could handle. She insisted she could accept even more, and Addison Hawk agreed that together they could manage half again as many if they set down dormitory rules. They had enough food for the next thirty-six to forty-eight hours, and in the meantime, Deucalion could bring supplies.

When the fourth group proved to number thirty-four, however, the decision had to be made to take the kids elsewhere. With Carson's and Michael's help, Deucalion got them lined up on the benches along the walls of the cargo box and in two facing rows on the floor, crowding them together to a degree that would have been intolerable if the trip hadn't been just two minutes long. They were trying to be brave, a few crying but quietly, others actually excited by the adventurous nature of this sudden nighttime excursion.

Because every point in the world lay as close to the Samples house as Erika's place, Deucalion drove out of the driveway, turned left, and pulled into the parking lot at St. Bartholomew's Abbey, high in the great mountains of northern California. In addition to the abbey with its guest wing and church, the seven-acre property included St. Bartholomew's School, which was an educational facility and orphanage for children with physical and developmental disabilities. The monks oversaw the abbey and church, and Benedictine nuns, under the guidance of their mother superior, Sister Angela, operated the school.

Deucalion had lived here, in the guest

wing, for over two years, while considering whether to become a postulant. Over the centuries, he dwelt for extended periods in the monasteries of different faiths, where he was never considered a freak, always a brother, and to his surprise sometimes served as a mentor to those he thought were wiser than he was.

He had left St. Bart's less than twenty-four hours earlier, drawn first to New Orleans, then to the sprawling landfill in which the original Victor perished, and then to Carson and Michael in San Francisco, compelled by the sudden certainty that Victor was alive again and engaged in the pursuit of his utopia, which like all utopias was a kind of hell.

As he got out of the truck, he blew the horn twice, hoping to summon help. He went to the back of the truck, opened the door, and said, "We're here. You're going to like this place. You'll be here only a little while, and it's going to be a lot of fun."

The children clambered out of the truck, amazed to discover they were somewhere they had never seen before, not more than two minutes after they set out on this trip. In early October in these mountains, no snow had yet fallen and stuck. The night was cold but clear, a sea of stars overhead, the blizzard magically undone.

As the last of the kids disembarked and as Deucalion closed and bolted the cargo-box door, a monk arrived. The giant was not surprised that of all the confreres, the first to respond to the horn happened to be Brother Salvatore, also known as Brother Knuckles. He was Deucalion's best friend at St. Bart's, the only one who knew exactly who he was and would, therefore, be quickest to understand where these children came from and why they were in flight.

This was a day of omens, of which Brother Knuckles was one of the smallest, a day of events suggesting hour by hour that those who would stand against Victor were not standing alone, that regardless of how many died in Rainbow Falls, the world would not be allowed to become a graveyard from pole to pole. Deucalion believed that as the night progressed, events would turn ever more rapidly against Victor—as long as those who resisted him remained willing to join the fight, refused to flee, and were prepared to die for what they knew was right. Miracles were not given, they were earned.

Father Abbot came soon after Knuckles, and without question led the children toward the guesthouse, where the bedrooms and public chambers would accommodate them. They were too young to remain in the grip of fear when the threat was no longer imminent. Resilient in their innocence, they gave themselves to wonder, and their excited voices, clear and sweet, brought a kind of music to the High Sierra night.

Alone with Brother Knuckles, Deucalion said, "There's a terrible situation in Montana, a town called Rainbow Falls. It probably hasn't reached the national news yet, but the story's getting out. It'll seem too bizarre for most in the media to believe at first, but proof will overwhelm their disbelief. I haven't time to tell you, so turn on your recreation-room TV and steel yourself for the coming horror of it."

Brother Knuckles considered the truck and said, "How long it take you gettin' here from there?"

"No time at all."

"I'd love to take a ride like that."

"Maybe we'll do it someday."

Brother Knuckles studied him for a moment. "If I was still the man I used to be, bustin' heads and bettin' ponies, I think maybe I wouldn't put a bunch of money on the chance any such ride will ever come to pass. Are we gonna see you here one day again? Ever?"

Deucalion looked at the sky, the eternity of stars, and said, "Snow will be coming soon. Nine nights from now, about seven in the evening. When it's done, you'll have a foot of fresh powder."

chapter 56

After setting the Meriwether Lewis kitchen on fire, they waited outside in the falling snow, shotguns ready, to see if anything tried to escape. Flames flew up quick and bright, as jolly a blaze as Sully York had ever seen, the first flash blue from the Sterno, then white and orange as the cooking oil ignited. Faster than he expected, the windows began to blow out from the intense heat, which was a most satisfying testament to their planning of this sortie. When the kitchen was a raging inferno and no filthy space-born malefactors attempted to flee, afire or otherwise, through the door that had been left open to oxygenate the flames, their work here seemed to be done. Even with a fire-control system, the explosive beginning of the blaze was likely to overwhelm the building and leave it a burnt-out shell, eradicating any other off-world fiends that might be hanging about therein.

Sully disapproved of destruction for destruction's sake, which seemed ever more popular in the modern world, but he always took delight in burning out or otherwise eliminating Evil when Evil just couldn't keep its ugly head down and stay to the shadows, when it came right at you with all teeth bared. The world needed a little Evil, so Good had something to compare itself to, but you couldn't let it think it had the right-of-way on the road and an invitation to dinner.

As they headed toward the Hummer parked between school buses, Grace Ahern said, "If they planned to feed the elementary students to those Builders, they're planning to do the same to the kids at the high school. We've got to get in there now and burn those suckers, too."

Grace said what she meant and meant what she said, by God, and Sully York liked nothing in his life better than the sound of her voice, the common sense and never-turn-tail spirit that it conveyed. She raised young Travis alone, working hard at more than one job, and though they didn't have much, they had their pride and each other. He doubted that he would ever hear this woman complain or whine; she was as incapable of self-pity as any of the Crazy Bastards, in their day, had been incapable of running from a fight—or losing one.

Bryce rode up front with Sully, and Travis sat in back with his mom, and that was just how it should be, for several reasons. Sully would have liked to spend half his time watching the street ahead and half watching Grace in the rearview mirror, but lacking one eye, he couldn't be quite that distracted. Dash it all if he hadn't become a moonstruck lad in the autumn of his years, which would have been an embarrassment if it wasn't so exhilarating and if she hadn't been such a shining example of pluck and guts.

Of course, he was too old for her, no argument could be made to the contrary. They were both too old for her, he and Bryce, although Sully was more than ten years younger than the writer and not yet on Social Security, certainly not decrepit. Yes, he was missing one eye and one ear, and one hand, but he was also missing an appendix and a spleen, and no woman had ever held the lack of those against him. He was too old for her, nonetheless, though there was something to be said for the fact that he wasn't too old to be the male influence that Travis would need in order to grow up strong and true to his potential.

They arrived at William Clark High School and parked in the rear lot. In addition to Grace's primary job at Meriwether Lewis, she occasionally did some part-time work at the high school, evening prep for the next day's lunch, and she had a code to turn off the security system.

Switching on the lights, she proved to be as dead-on right as the prophet Cassandra and as quick to fearless action as the goddess Diana on a hunt. Worse than cockroaches infested this kitchen, more of those repulsive sacs suspended from the ceiling. Already a team with mutually understood tasks, the four of them worked together to set another fire of extermination.

Entirely splendid!

chapter 57

The plasma screens are positioned at far too many places in the Hive. Excessive care has been taken to be sure that Victor Immaculate can be informed of developments in a timely fashion. When funds are unlimited, there is a tendency to overdesign critical systems, and this is certainly an example of absurd redundancy. The screens are everywhere. They are ubiquitous. He wishes only to walk and think, to allow the invigorating torrents of brilliant ideas, theories, and analyses to pour through his singular mind. But everywhere he turns, there is a plasma screen taunting him with its three-note alert. They are annoying in the extreme.

None of the news is of any import, the usual gnats in the path of the Communitarian war machine. The Builders gestating in cocoons at Meriwether Lewis School are no longer transmitting their progress. This is not a problem with those Builders, however, but it is yet another malfunction of the monitoring equipment, which is worse than government surplus, which is government surplus *made in China.*

And now the Communitarians sent to the radio station to retake it have also ceased transmitting. Of course the problem is not in the Communitarians, for they are an unstoppable force, perfectly designed and manufactured. Any problem is here on the receiving end, the less than adequate Chinese-made monitoring equipment failing yet again, no doubt sabotaged by disgruntled laborers in Shanghai or Shenyang or Guangzhou, who don't think they should be working for two dollars a day and therefore take out their anger on total strangers who are using their products half a world away. Idiot-human economic systems.

The answer to every little glitch is the

same, and Victor moves on without repeating it, because the Communitarians are at all times operating according to that directive: *Consult the master strategy-and-tactics program, apply the appropriate remedy, and press forward without delay.*

Of the virtually infinite number of problems with human beings, one of the worst is the economic systems that they create. Whether capitalism or communism, or something between, they are all grossly inadequate, and essentially for the same reason: Every system relies on workers who expect to be compensated in some way for their labor.

That isn't the case with Communitarians. They do not need money to go to a movie or to attend a concert, or to purchase the latest novel by the current literary darling. They have no interest in such things. They don't need money for cars or for new clothes, because they just *take* what they need. And they won't continue needing and voraciously consuming forever because eventually they will all drop dead at once. *That* is a perfect economic system.

Zhonghua Renmin Gongheguo. "The People's Republic of China." The problem can be seen in the name of the place: *People.*

Another plasma screen sounds its three-note alert, and this time the scrolling report informs Victor that the gestating Builders at the house of Reverend Kelsey Fortis ceased to transmit hours earlier. Their silence has not been noticed by the monitoring system until now.

He prefers to descend again to the levels of this installation that are below those given to his work, to the peace of corridors and rooms free of plasma screens. But with no Communitarians down there to attend to him, he must remain here, especially now. After being afflicted by these unending reports of problems that aren't problems, that are only errors of monitoring, he needs perhaps more attention than usual.

When Victor turns another corner, the three-legged table waits for him. On it stands a cold bottle of water. Beside the bottle is a lavender dish. In the dish wait two burnt-orange capsules and a sour-yellow tablet as big as a dime.

He is surprised that these things should be put before him so soon after he took the shiny red capsule and the white tablet that were offered in a yellow saucer. But of course he must need them.

Not just his vital signs but also his brain waves—alpha, beta, delta, and theta—and an array of hormone levels are meticulously monitored telemetrically at all hours of the day and night. In the interest of having the fullest power of his unprecedented intelligence at his command 24/7, he developed a brilliant regimen of natural substances— herbs, exotic spices, ground roots, ultra-purified minerals—and a wide array of pharmaceuticals in exquisitely measured doses, which are provided to him as the telemetric data indicate he requires them.

The bottle of water is cold, yes, but it seems less cold to Victor than it ought to be. For burnt-orange capsules and a sour-yellow tablet, a lavender dish is inadequately coordinated. On the other hand, he has never needed burnt-orange and sour-yellow mental enhancements simultaneously, so the Communitarians programmed to attend to him were required to wing it. And, after all, they have no interest in design or art.

He swallows what has been provided. As the clone of the great Victor Frankenstein, distilled into greater brilliance than his namesake, further self-refined, he is incapable of error. Therefore the Communitarians, his creations, are likewise without the capacity for error.

After he walks a few minutes, Victor begins to feel better than he has felt for several hours. The waters of his mind are clearer and deeper and thrillingly colder than they have ever been previously, sparkling with thoughts no man or clone has ever entertained before, great schools of ideas like silvery fish darting after one another in dazzling patterns and profusion.

The plasma screens are silent for a while, but then one sounds its tones and scrolls up the news that the Moneyman has canceled his visit. In Denver on business, he has with great stealth decamped with his entourage to a safe house in Billings. From there he is supposed to come secretly to the Hive at dawn, by helicopter or in a fleet of Land Rovers if weather grounds the chopper. He is to receive a tour of this facility. He will instead return to Denver, canceling his plans because of the KBOW broadcast, which he claims is being recorded by people outside Rainbow

Falls and uploaded to numerous sites on the Internet.

Victor has planned an unforgettable reception for the Moneyman, and he is not pleased by this absurd and cowardly response to what is an easily addressed problem. Communitarians are even now applying the appropriate remedy and pressing forward without delay. The Moneyman is a mere human being, however, and even though wealthy and powerful, he is prone to errors of judgment. When KBOW is taken and its crew replaced with Communitarians, they will begin broadcasting an apology for the hoax perpetrated by some of their staff. The public is easily aroused but just as easily sold a false sense of security. In time the Moneyman will realize—though never admit—his error, and he will be more supportive than before.

Because Victor Immaculate has all the memories of the original Victor, he has known many like the Moneyman. They share the same desires and corruptions. Their behavior is predictable.

All shall be well and all manner of things shall be well in this Victor Immaculate world.

chapter 58

Rusty Billingham ran for his life along the center of the street, directly into the wind-driven snow, which had grown icy enough so that the flakes mostly didn't stick to his face and melt but instead bounced off like grains of sand. He glanced back a few times at the Trailblazer, expecting it to be reversing out of the hedge or already coming for him, driven by something no one would write a song about, at least not the kind of songs that Rusty wrote. But the SUV didn't move, and he figured the blond she-devil might need a while to digest all of those people.

That had to be the craziest thought ever to cross his mind, but he knew his eyes had not deceived him. Facts were facts, and they fit together how they did, not how you wished they would. There was one right way to make perfect dovetail joints for a drawer box, and there was no way to deny that the blonde was not really a woman, that she was some new kind of predator, ravenous. Movies trained you to think *aliens.* Maybe that's what she was, but right now what she was didn't matter. What mattered was whether more like her were in the vicinity and how many.

A chatter of gunfire from a house on the left gave him a partial answer. The rapid semiauto fire shattered a second-floor window, glass bursting onto the padding of snow on the porch roof. No one up there screamed, but fantastic shadows throbbed across the portion of the room that Rusty could see. A mere two-shot follow-up to the first fusillade suggested that either the shooter or the target had succumbed, probably not the latter.

He was in good shape, he stayed fit after the war, and he could run a mile while breathing as relaxed and as steady as if he were only crossing a room. But now he gasped for breath, heart knocking as though he'd done half a marathon. He wanted to live, but he also wanted Corrina to live, and it was the possible loss of her that wound tight the clockworks of his fear.

From a distance, out of the west, too faint for him to get a fix on it, came another scream. Then more than one screamer, three or four, somewhere to the east, maybe from the street parallel to this one. As Rusty reached the next intersection, two big German shepherds raced along the cross street, as silent as ghost dogs, too terrified to bark, in flight from something that not even dogs of their size and fabled courage dared to confront.

Running through the intersection in the wake of the dogs, Rusty saw something pulse in the sky far off to the east, a pale yellow light at first but suddenly brighter and orange. Not a mother ship descending with more storm troopers like the one who attacked the Trailblazer, not an object at all, but a fire reflecting off the low clouds and the streaming snow. Something was burning out there. Judging by the spreading glow, it had to be a large structure.

One moment he was walking home in the snow on an evening like any other, and the next moment the gates of Hell were open and the world was full of demons. He knew that other places were hells and potential hells, but not Montana. Elsewhere in the world, you could buy a thousand flavors of crazy, but only a few were for sale here.

Corrina Ringwald lived in the next-to-the-last house in this block, on the right. Look at it: not grand yet beautiful, built with loving care and maintained with pride, a place that said *home,* that said *love* and *family.* Not a place Norman Bates would live or Charles Manson, not a place where bad things should ever happen, but they could. You always had to remember that they could.

The porch light was on, amber panes in a copper lantern, her invitation to him. She had prepared dinner for them. He heard music inside, Rod Stewart singing "Someone to Watch over Me." Rusty rang the bell, pressed it again without waiting for the first passage of chimes to finish. Suddenly he wondered what he would do if it wasn't Corrina who answered the bell, if it was another one like the blonde in the

blue robe. He retreated one step, two, terrified that he was too late.

Corrina opened the door. Rusty had
never been so glad to see anyone in his
life. She was smiling, relaxed. The music
prevented her from hearing the sounds of
rising chaos outside.

As she opened the door, she said, "Our
special tonight is pot roast—" She read
his face at first glance, and her smile froze.
"What? What's happened?"

Rusty glanced back at the street. Deserted. For now.

He didn't strip off his boots, but instead
reached for her hand, crossed the threshold, closed the door, and locked it. He
switched off the porch lamp, the overhead
foyer fixture. "Turn out the lights. Every
room. They might think no one's here, they
might not come in."

Bewildered, she said, "Who?"

He went into the living room, extinguish-
ing lamps. "First the lights, then I'll explain."

"Rusty, you're scaring me."

"Damn it, I mean to. *Hurry!*"

He never raised his voice to her. She
knew him too well to take offense, and she
hurried off to do as he wanted.

Rusty clicked off the CD player and made his way through the gloom to stand beside an open panel of drapery, to one side of a living-room window. He had an angled view of the street, looking south, the direction from which he had come.

Nothing out there. No vehicles. No women who weren't women. No fleeing dogs.

Corrina returned through the dark house, into the living room. "Where are you?"

"Here," he said and guided her to stand on the opposite side of the window from him, so they faced each other with the width of it between them, neither of them directly in front of glass.

He could see her as a shadow and a pale face barely illuminated by the weak influx of the street lighting.

"I tried to call 911," she said. "The phone doesn't work."

"Keep a watch north on the street. I can see south all right."

"You've given me goose pimples. What am I watching for?"

"Anything. Tell me the moment you see anything. There was this woman, standing in the street, just standing there, like in a trance. She asked for help. That's what she said—'Help me'—and I started toward her. These people drove up in a Trailblazer, rolled down a window to ask her if something was wrong, and she killed them all."

"Oh, my God."

"If I'd been closer, she would have killed me."

"Shot them?" Corrina asked. "What? She just shot them?"

Rusty's mind was spinning, thinking what else he ought to do. "My footprints in the snow. Up the walkway and onto the porch. Maybe they won't come right away, maybe there'll be enough time for wind and snow to erase the prints on the walkway."

"They? You said a woman."

"Keep a watch on the street. Don't look away from the street. There's more than one. They're killing people all over town. Outside, you can hear it. Screams. Gunshots. Something's on fire way over to the east. But no sirens, no one seems to care, maybe because there aren't any firemen to respond."

"Rusty, you don't joke like this."

"No, I don't." The aroma of pot roast and parsley potatoes alerted him to another danger. "If they come in here, dinner nearly on the table, they'll know we're in the house. No matter where we hide, they'll keep looking until they find us. Listen, we can't hole up here. Our best chance might be to stay on the move, like the dogs, till we can find help."

"Dogs?"

"I've never seen dogs so terrified."

She said, "Here come some people, walking right up the middle of the street."

Rusty couldn't see them from his angle, but he had no illusions that the cavalry had arrived. This was moving as fast as a firefight, except this enemy didn't need guns, and Rusty didn't have one. "How many?"

"Eight. They're strange."

"Strange how?"

"Walking two by two, just staring ahead, walking but it's almost as if they're marching. Five women, three men. None of them dressed for the weather."

Leaning forward, Rusty dared to expose his face at the window and peer north.

Corrina said, "What're they, performers or something, the way they look?"

He leaned away from the window again, his heart hammering as hard as when he'd been running in the street. "They aren't human. They . . . change. I don't know what the hell they are."

Something she saw in the behavior of the eight so disconcerted Corrina that she didn't question his bizarre assertion.

"Come on," he said, "quick, we gotta get out of here, back door."

Entering the foyer behind him, jerking open the closet door, Corrina said, "I need a coat, boots."

"Grab a coat. No time for boots."

She shrugged into the coat as they followed the hall toward the back of the house.

Rusty led the way. As he crossed the threshold into the dark kitchen, he saw a figure looming on the back porch, a half-seen face at a window. He retreated into the hallway, pulling her with him. "One already out there."

As they followed the hallway toward the foyer, the door chimes sounded. One of the things must be on the front porch.

"Upstairs," he whispered, holding her hand to prevent her from falling if she lost her footing on the unlighted staircase.

chapter 59

At the Snyder house, Chief Rafael Jarmillo and his Communitarian equal, Deputy Kurt Nevis, found Warren Snyder, general manager of KBOW radio, in an armchair in his living room. The wife, Judy Snyder, and their nineteen-year-old son, Andrew, sat on the sofa. They were still because they had been told to remain so, though their eyes jittered with terror. Much earlier, they should have been picked up and taken away to be rendered by a Builder at one of the warehouses. But here they were. The son appeared to have urinated on the sofa.

Judy Snyder's replicant had been left here to oversee these three, but she was not with them. Jarmillo and Nevis found her nude in the kitchen.

The unclothed replicant was on her hands and knees beside a bucket of pine-scented cleaning solution, scrubbing the floor with a brush and various sponges. She did not look up at them but remained focused on the floor tiles.

"What're you doing?" Jarmillo asked.

She said, "There was no neatness in this house. Where there is no neatness, there can be no order. They have a cat. It sheds enough for a dozen cats. Hair, hair, hair everywhere. I'm glad we're killing all the cats, too. I swept and I swept, and finally there wasn't any more hair, though I haven't looked on the upper floor yet. I'm sure it's a mess. I threw the litter box in the trash, it was disgusting. But cat hair and kitty litter isn't the half of it. These kitchen counters needed to be scrubbed. Especially the grout. The grout was filthy. And the refrigerator, and now these floors. I'm going to be *hours* on these floors. Especially the grout."

"Why are you nude?" Jarmillo asked.

"I noticed my clothes were wrinkled. It really bothered me. I couldn't get my mind off my wrinkled clothes. I couldn't *think,* so I stripped out of them and ironed them, made them perfect, and put them back on. But you know what happened then? I hardly did anything, just a little more sweeping, and I could see a few wrinkles in them again. I had to take them off and iron them, and then they were wrinkled *again,* so I took them off and ironed them and didn't put them on, just hung them so they'll stay wrinkle-free."

"Does Warren have spare keys to the radio station? Where does he keep them?"

Vigorously scrubbing the soiled grout between the floor tiles, Communitarian Judy said, "I don't know. I didn't download the stupid bitch's memories. I didn't need to because I didn't have to pass for the stupid bitch except to set her idiot son up to be nailed by his replicant."

Jarmillo returned to the living room while Deputy Nevis remained to watch Judy scrub the floor.

"Warren," the chief said to the KBOW general manager, "do you have spare keys to the radio station?"

Warren Snyder's mouth trembled, but he didn't reply.

"You can't avoid answering me," Jarmillo said. "You have no will to resist."

Haltingly, Warren told him where to find the keys. They were in a utility drawer in the kitchen.

When Chief Jarmillo returned to the kitchen, Deputy Nevis was on his hands and knees, using a sponge to help Judy clean the floors.

"What're you doing?" Jarmillo asked.

"The only virtue is efficiency," Nevis said. "The only sin is inefficiency. You can't have efficiency in a disordered environment."

"Yes, but this isn't *your* environment. Get up and come with me."

The utility drawer contained numerous keys. Fortunately they were labeled, although not in a consistent fashion. In forty-nine seconds, the chief found the KBOW keys. In an organized drawer, he would have snatched them up in one second, two at most. He was tempted to put things right here, but then he closed the drawer.

Deputy Kurt Nevis, being Chief Jarmillo's equal in all ways as a Communitarian, decided not to accompany him to the radio station but instead to remain at the Snyder residence to scrub the baseboards. He had noticed they were in urgent need of attention.

chapter 60

When Deucalion drove out of the parking lot at St. Bartholomew's Abbey and immediately into the driveway at the Samples house, Carson O'Connor was waiting. She stopped him from getting out of the truck and spoke to him through the open door.

"Only three new kids here. Michael's keeping them entertained. Big news is the radio station. There was a failed attack against the place. They've got an FBI agent on air with Mason Morrell, some guy named Frost. And they say they've got one of Victor's new people, he's come over to our side."

Deucalion's eyes pulsed with the light of another place, another time.

She remembered when first she'd seen those eyes in New Orleans, in Bobby Allwine's apartment, where everything was black—floor, walls, ceiling, furniture. She was wary of Deucalion back then but not afraid, because she would never give anyone the satisfaction of controlling her with fear. Into her suspicion, he had said, "I'm not the monster anymore. I'm your best hope." He was right about that, and it was still true.

Looking down at her from the driver's seat of the truck, he said, "This is the moment, Carson. We'll finish it now, finish him. I've been given . . . reasons to believe this is his last day. And in case he finishes me or you and Michael—or all of us—as we take him out . . . it's been an honor knowing the two of you, being your friend and ally."

She reached up and took one of his enormous hands in both of hers. At first she could not speak, only hold fast to him. But then she said, "You will not die."

"I'm long overdue for death. Every human being is born with the dead, but I was born *from* the dead and don't fear my end. I love this world, its beauty, but there could be nothing better than to die in its defense."

"Even if you die," she said, "you will not die forever."

He smiled, and the light pulsed in his eyes, and he said, "Give Scout a kiss for me."

As she stepped back, he pulled shut the door. She watched the truck turn through a half circle—and vanish.

———

Arriving from the Samples driveway, the truck ran over dead men lying in the KBOW parking lot. They were not men, of course, but Victor's newest race, who encountered a far better armed resistance than they could ever have anticipated.

Getting out of the truck, Deucalion realized that these foiled attackers hadn't been dead for a long time, only minutes. Those over whom he had *not* driven were covered by just a thin dusting of fresh snow.

He stepped around a corpse and into the engineer's nest in the building. "You've captured one of them?"

Ralph Nettles looked up from the control board not in surprise but with a *what's-taken-you-so-long* expression. "Not me. Some cranky old guy. He's in Sammy's office with a replicant of a cop named Barry Bozeman."

chapter 61

As Rusty Billingham reached the top of the dark staircase with Corrina, the door chimes sounded again. This carillon was pleasant in ordinary circumstances, two bars of something classic, perhaps a piece of Beethoven, but now each note was icy and sinister, vibrating through him as if his spinal column were a tubular bell. Pressing the bell push twice in rapid succession, at a dark house, seemed to be a taunt if not mockery. They were saying, *We know you're in there. If you won't come out to play, we'll bring the game to you.*

Windows opened onto the back- and

front-porch roofs. But one of these killers, whatever they might be, was on each porch. No way out, only farther up.

"You've got an attic?" Rusty asked.

"Yes, but—"

"Where's the entrance to it?"

"The master-bedroom closet."

Glass shattered. The sound seemed to come from the back of the house.

"Show me the way," Rusty said. *"Quick."*

He had been on the second floor of her house only once, on a tour before dinner, each of them with a glass of good red wine, the evening thoroughly pleasant, the world so *normal* then. She knew the house better than he did, and even in the dark with only the ambient light of the night pressing at the windows, Corrina led him along a hallway, through a door, across the bedroom, and into the walk-in closet.

As more glass shattered downstairs, Rusty closed the door behind them and fumbled for the light switch. A cord hung from a ceiling trapdoor. He pulled, and the trap swung down on heavy-duty springs, revealing a folded ladder attached to it.

Corrina said, "But there's no way out of the attic. We'll be cornered up there."

Unfolding the ladder, he whispered, "I'm not going up. Just you." He loosened the simple knot that fixed the pull cord to a ring on the lower face of the trap. "Then I'll distract them. As far as they know, I might be the only one in the house. They get me, they stop searching as hard."

"No. I can't let you."

He whispered, "Stupid for both of us to die." He grabbed her by both shoulders, kissed her as he had never kissed her before in their determinedly platonic romance, and said, "Go. *Go!*"

She climbed into the darkness.

As she reached the top, he called after her, "Stay quiet."

She turned to look down, face as wan as a wafer of unleavened bread. "Until . . . when?"

"Until I come back for you."

She didn't ask what she should do if he never returned. If she had asked, he would have had no answer.

When Rusty folded up the ladder, the counterweighted trap swung shut with a soft thump that made him wince, closing Corrina in the attic. He tucked the detached pull cord onto a shelf above her hanging clothes.

After turning off the closet light, he stood for a moment with one ear to the door, listening for activity in the bedroom. All was silent, but he knew it might be the silence of something waiting for him to emerge.

He eased open the door. The master bedroom was black except for two rectangular windows barely revealed by the snow-veiled glow of streetlamps.

He crossed the threshold and after a moment identified the open doorway to the upstairs hall, which was slightly less dark than the black wall through which it cut.

If anything like the blonde in the blue robe had been waiting for him here, it would already have attacked. He vividly remembered the striking-snake speed with which she had gone after the people in the Trailblazer.

Bent forward, hands reaching out low to search for obstructing furniture, Rusty eased toward the doorway. He needed to get as far as possible from the master bedroom before calling attention to himself and drawing them away from Corrina. He felt around an armchair, past a tall chest of drawers, and reached the open door without making a sound.

His mouth was as dry as a salt lick. Stomach acid burned in the back of his throat, as it had not done since the war.

For a long moment, he stood in the doorway. The airless-moon hush suggested that the killers either had not entered the house or had already left it.

He took just two steps into the upstairs hallway and halted again, listening. No windows here. Dim light rising from the foyer windows and from a stairway-landing window below, revealing nothing.

Silence. Silence. A distant *clink-clink-clink.* He thought the sound had come from the lower floor. *Clink-clink-clink.* Wrong. Not downstairs. It issued from the farther end of the pitch-black hallway in which he stood. *Clink-clink-clink, clink-clink.* This time he got a better fix on the source: to his left, an arm's length away.

chapter 62

Nummy O'Bannon listened to radio sometimes, but he never before was inside where they made it. There were none of the musicians or singers he expected. The rooms were just mostly offices except for the spaceship controls where Mr. Ralph Nettles worked, and the desks were all stacked with stuff, not neat at all.

Mr. Lyss was watching over the broken monster, the Xerox Boze, in one of these offices, and Nummy was watching over them both. He was afraid the Xerox Boze would start doing the usual nasty monster stuff now that there wasn't an upright piano to play, so he kept an eye on the thing. He kept an eye on Mr. Lyss, too, because the old man was always doing something interesting, even if it wasn't something Grandmama would have approved.

For a few minutes, things were quieter than they had been since Nummy met Mr. Lyss, and then the biggest thing of the whole strange day happened. In fact, it was the second most important thing of Nummy's life, the first being when Grandmama died and he was left alone.

A man came into the room, the biggest man Nummy had ever seen, not fat-big but tall and with a lot of muscles, which you could tell were there even though he was wearing a hooded coat. He was bigger than Buster Steelhammer, the wrestler, and his hands were so large he might have been able to do disappearing tricks with apples the way magicians did with coins. Half his face was tattooed, but it was his eyes that made him the second most important thing ever to happen to Nummy.

When the giant looked at Nummy, light moved through his eyes sort of the way that the moving light on the machine in the hospital kept dancing across the screen that showed Grandmama's heartbeat, although this was somehow both softer and brighter than that light, not scary, either, but beautiful and calming. Nummy didn't know why the light in the man's eyes didn't frighten him, like he would have expected, especially with the half-broken face and tattoo—and then he *did* know.

Grandmama said there were angels on earth, guardian angels, but they worked in secret and weren't easy to tell from other people because they didn't have wings or halos. She said the only way you sometimes could know them was when you saw the light of love in their eyes. They were so full of love, Grandmama said, that sometimes they couldn't hold it all inside, and they gave themselves away by the light in their eyes.

Nummy never before saw an angel, and now here was one, and he said to Nummy, "Don't be afraid, son. You'll live through this night. Fifty days from now, all will change for the better."

The angel turned his eyes toward Xerox Boze, stared at him a long moment, and then said to Mr. Lyss, "You claim this replicant is broken."

Mr. Lyss must not have seen the angel light in the big man's eyes—or if he did see it, maybe he didn't know what it was. To the old man, the most important thing was one little word the angel used. His eyes bugged out, and his hair seemed to stand on end more than usual, like a cartoon animal sticking its paw in an electric socket and all its fur going *bzzzz.*

"Claim?" Mr. Lyss said. *"Claim?* Is that a weasel word so you don't have to say to my face you think I'm a lying sonofabitch? You walk in here like you own the joint, your fancy face tattooed more than some rock star's butt, and you make smarmy suggestions Conway Lyss is a liar? I've done worse things to people who call me a liar than Stalin did to kittens, and *believe me,* Stalin hated kittens. He ripped out their throats with his teeth if he caught one. This thing that was supposed to call itself Barry Bozeman is broken so plain any fool but you can see it. Look at his hangdog face, his whipped-dog posture in that chair. He's programmed not to kill himself, wants me to kill him, but I won't do it until I'm damn good and ready to kill him. *Nobody* tells me when to kill him, not even some pathetic broken Frankenstein monster!"

Nummy saw the angel react to the name *Frankenstein,* but he didn't ask if Mr. Lyss was crazy or call him a liar. He didn't say anything more at all to the old man, but he went to stand over Xerox Boze, staring down at him. Xerox Boze asked the angel to kill him, and Nummy thought the angel would say that he couldn't, that it wasn't something an angel could do. Instead, he said in the most tender way, "I am your brother. Two hundred years separate our . . . births. Do you recognize me?"

Xerox Boze stared up into the angel's eyes for a long time and then said softly, "I . . . don't know."

Mr. Lyss became upset about the brother thing and wanted to know if this was some kind of hellish monster convention. Nobody, not even Nummy, paid attention to the old man's rant.

The angel asked Xerox Boze, "What is your life?"

"Misery."

"Shall we stop him forever?"

"I can't lift a hand against my maker."

"I think I can. And will. Where is he?"

"The Hive."

"Perhaps you're not broken."

"But I am."

"Perhaps you're here to lure me into a trap."

"No."

"Help me to believe I can trust you," the angel said.

"How?" Xerox Boze asked.

"*He* didn't name it the Hive."

"No. It's our word."

"What does he call the place, the front organization behind which he works?"

Xerox Boze said, "Progress for Perfect Peace."

After a silence, the angel asked, "Do you know where that is?"

"Yes."

"Show me."

Xerox Boze got up from his chair, and the angel led him into the hallway. Nummy followed, interested in anything an angel might do, and Mr. Lyss tagged along behind, grumping about something. They went to a map on a wall in another office, and the angel said it showed KBOW's broadcast reach, whatever that was. He pointed out what was Rainbow Falls and what was the county, and some land beyond the county, and he asked the Xerox Boze to point to the place called the Hive. The monster pointed. The angel said they would go there together, and if it was the place the monster said it was, then the angel would give him "the grace of a quick and painless death," which sounded nice except for the death part.

Turning away from the wall map, looking hard at Mr. Lyss, the angel said, "Fifty days from now, you get your chance. Use it well."

Mr. Lyss was only grumbling under his breath through this map stuff, but now he got fired up again. "Damn it all, first you just about flat-out call me a liar the moment we meet. Now you insinuate—what?—that I don't usually do things well? Considering I didn't get half my face wrecked as bad as a runaway train and then try to hide it under some stupid psychedelic ink work, I suspect I take care of business a lot smarter than you do."

Instead of answering Mr. Lyss, the angel looked at Nummy and smiled. He put a hand on Nummy's head and smoothed his hair, almost exactly like Grandmama used to do, and Nummy's eyes filled with tears, though he didn't know why.

He was blinking away those tears when the next thing happened, so he couldn't be sure he saw it like it really was. But it seemed that the angel took Xerox Boze by the arm, turned with him as if to leave the room, but vanished in the turning.

Mr. Lyss let out a terrible seven-word curse that it was good the angel couldn't hear, and ran into the hallway looking for the vanished two. But he didn't find anyone.

Nummy followed Mr. Lyss back to the room where they had been watching over the Xerox Boze. They settled in chairs, and Nummy watched the old man, who sat for a while, leaning forward with his head in his hands. Nummy wanted to ask if Mr. Lyss had a headache and if he could get him some aspirins, but he didn't want to stir up the old man with a wrong word.

After a while, Mr. Lyss looked up at Nummy. "Peaches, you remember earlier when I told you this was a lot bigger than space aliens or Frankenstein, that there was a way bigger Evil in town tonight?"

Nummy nodded. "A bigger Evil and something else, too."

"I told you we should have been dead

ten times over, and I'm pretty sure I know why we aren't."

"You said you'd explain that part later."

"Well, the reason we're not dead—the reason *I'm* not dead—is because of you, and the way you are. I won't explain more now. What I want to say here is . . . for a while I forgot what I said earlier. I forgot all that about something very big at work tonight, and I just went back to being me. Well, I've just been chastened. You know what that means?"

"No, sir," Nummy said.

"I've been humbled. I've just been given to see myself as what I am, what I insist on being. Peaches, I'm going to try my best to do right by you, but when I slip back to being like what I've always been, don't pay any attention to me. I'll get better in a while. I'm a shiftless, irritable, intemperate sonofabitch and a world-class people-hater, and maybe I can change, but I can't change easily or overnight."

Surprised, Nummy said, "What people do you hate?"

"All of them. All of them I ever met. Except you."

chapter 63

When Carson returned to the house after seeing off Deucalion on what might be his final confrontation with Victor, Michael was in the living room, playing his where-have-I-hidden-your-nose game with the three young children waiting to be evacu-ated, and the kids were giggling with delight. She stood watching him, loving him, thinking about little Scout, about her brother, Arnie, back in San Francisco, until the screaming started.

Outside. The front of the property. The initial screams were followed rapidly by gunfire, a lot of it. Something had broken into the garrisoned neighborhood.

The Riders in the living room grabbed their weapons. One of them dashed to the bolted front door and dropped a length of four-by-six lumber into sturdy steel brackets that had been bolted into the jamb, providing extra resistance to an assault on that entrance.

Carson glanced into the adjoining dining room, where the ever-ready Riderettes were abandoning their culinary chores and picking up their guns.

She knew—maybe they all knew—that this war wouldn't be won with firearms. Those Builders on the cell-phone videos, in mere seconds consuming Johnny Tankredo and other Riders at the Pickin' and Grinnin' Roadhouse, wouldn't be stopped with bullets. They wouldn't be defeated with *anything* that might have brought down an ordinary assailant. At this worst moment of the storm, she and Michael and all those with whom they gathered could not fight to win but only to delay.

If they could hold their position long enough, Deucalion might have time to find his maker's rat hole and go into it after him. If the clone of Victor Helios, alias Frankenstein, was like his namesake unto a fault, which seemed to be the case, then he would not tolerate the possibility that his creations might live on after his death. As in Louisiana, killing Victor would ensure the death of every creature spawned in his laboratories.

The gunfire stopped. Screams gave way to shouts of confusion. Something slammed hard against the front door. The deadbolt and the bracing lumber held through the first impact, the second, the third.

To the left of the door, a window shattered. Backlit by a porch lamp, a young woman's blond hair registered as an otherworldly nimbus around her head, and in the outflowing light of the living room, her exquisite face seemed to absorb the light and return it in a radiance twice as bright as the lumens she received. She was without doubt a Builder, but she didn't appear calm and beatific like the Builders in the opening frames of the roadhouse videos. Her feverish blue eyes burned with hate. Her toothpaste-commercial-perfect teeth were bared in an unvoiced snarl. She appeared savage, eager, driven by some unthinkable need. The Riders had fortified the window with bars of two-by-four lumber; these infuriated her, and she clawed at them, tearing away splinters of wood. She opened her mouth as if in a scream, but what issued from her was a sound partly like a garbage disposal grinding up half-spoiled fruit and partly like a cackling animatronic witch in a carnival fortune-telling machine. From her mouth puffed a thin silvery plume, as though she had coughed out lungfuls of twinkling smoke, but then the small cloud raveled back between her lips.

One of the Riders stepped past Carson, thrust his shotgun between the two-by-fours, and pumped four rounds into the Builder's face, the thunderous crashes echoing deafeningly around the room. She received the deadly pearls of buckshot with no more effect than they would have caused if fired down into a still pond: a froth of emulsified flesh, brief holes, turbulence in her tissues, and then the smoothness of the surface reasserted.

The Builder vomited what appeared to

be a mass of wet ashes brightened with silver sequins, which flowed around the smoking barrel of the shotgun and tore it from the hands of the startled Rider, who fell back and scrambled out of the way. Like a tentacle, the repulsive gray mass retracted through the two-by-fours, taking the weapon with it, seeming to dissolve it even as the walnut stock clattered against those wooden bars and vanished into a sucking maw so grotesque that Carson would no longer be able to think of the creature as "she," regardless of the form in which it might choose to manifest.

In fact, the Builder didn't return to its Miss Universe mode, but in a frenzy of rage—assuming any human emotion could be assigned to it—the thing entered the house as a swarm. It churned between the two-by-four bars in three streams, but the three coalesced into one in the living room.

Michael herded the children into a corner. He offered himself as a human shield for them.

As the swarm ascended to the ceiling, Carson returned to her husband's side. They both held Urban Snipers, which could stop cold a charging bull—but couldn't halt a Builder.

The swarm of nanoanimals circled overhead, buzzing and hissing, exploring the limits of this space, as if the billions of them were conferring about what to devour next.

Intuition seemed to have brought the same message to everyone in the living room, to the Riders as to Carson and Michael: The swarm might be attracted to movement, and whoever moved first might be the first to die.

chapter 64

Deucalion and the Bozeman replicant arrived on the End Times Highway in driving snow. A straightaway swept down from the crown of a hill behind them and faded ahead, westward, still white lanes dwindling into falling white flakes, all the whiteness flowing into a darkness that at this moment seemed eternal. On both sides of the road were great dark formations of evergreens, like the rising walls of some vast castle, their boughs not yet fully flocked, the faint scent of them almost sweet in the crisp, cold air.

No tire tracks cut through the blanketed pavement, which wasn't surprising, considering that no one lived along these twenty-four miles of road. The night lay as quiet as if, back in the day, the Cold War had turned hot, atomizing and irradiating all humanity into oblivion, leaving a world where the only significant noises were of occasional seismic events, moving water, and wind.

"Where?" Deucalion asked the replicant whose arm he gripped.

"Directly north, into the forest at least two hundred yards. Three hundred might be better."

"Take the step with me," Deucalion said, and transported them into the forest.

Gloriously wild and vast, yet intimate in its every tree-defined space, the forest might be a cathedral by day, though it was a series of chapels by night. This must seem to be a blind-black wilderness to the replicant, but to Deucalion it was an array of chambers receding one into the other in every direction, the air scented and flavored by the natural incense of pines and alpine firs. Because during the day little sunlight reached the forest floor, no brush obstructed, and until the weight of the limb-borne snow caused boughs to bend sufficiently, only flurries of flakes found their way through the evergreen canopy to plant small cold kisses on his face.

"Where?" he asked again, and the replicant said, "Down."

Deucalion stared at the earth underfoot until he sensed solid strata, dense and deep . . . but then hollow spaces farther below, a kingdom of strange chambers.

"Turn with me," he told the replicant, and in the turn they stepped out of the chapel forest and into a long corridor with white walls and a gray floor.

The silence here was more profound than that in the woods above, as if the queen had long abandoned this hive, her workers and her drones swarming in her wake.

Within a few breaths, however, Deucalion knew he had arrived in Victor's lair: Victor Leben now, clone of Victor Helios—in spite of all aliases and all eras, Frankenstein forever. The telltale scent that came to him was not a trace of pheromones and nothing at all of sweat and blood. He smelled instead the damp stone walls of the old windmill that had been converted to the great man's first laboratory in faraway Europe, the ozone created by leaping electric arcs between the poles of arcane and primitive machines, the malodor of his own recently dead flesh that lingered even after the moment of successful reanimation. His maker roamed this vault of secrets, near and nearer.

"Kill me," the Bozeman replicant pleaded, and Deucalion gave him that grace, breaking his neck and lowering him gently to the floor.

———

The screams and thudding feet overhead were of no concern.

Addison Hawk worked with Erika in the living room, rearranging sofas and armchairs and footstools, which would serve as beds, to open more floor space for makeshift mattresses made with quilts, moving blankets, towels, heavy winter coats, and other items.

As they worked, they got to know each other. Addison could remember no other woman with whom he ever talked so easily, in whose company he had felt so comfortable. He was not a ladies' man. He was to Don Juan what tinfoil was to silver leaf. Yet this beautiful woman so enchanted him that he chattered away, less self-conscious than he had ever been with one of the fairer sex.

A multitude of footsteps thundered down the back steps, toward the kitchen, accompanied by much squealing and shrieking.

Erika's beauty was of course the first thing that dazzled him, but soon her looks mattered hardly at all when compared to her many other qualities. She was calm and competent, seemed to know just what to do at every moment, as these bizarre events unfolded. She had an air of worldliness, as though she had traveled everywhere and seen everything, but at the same time she remained humble without being compliant, modest without being coy, gentle but not meek.

A merry jingling of tiny bells arose in the downstairs hallway.

Addison found Erika to be deeply layered to such an extent that she was mysterious. How she could be so approachable and forthcoming yet remain enigmatic, he didn't know. She inspired in him both wonder and curiosity. Something about this woman was recondite, remote from ordinary perception, almost mystical.

Beyond the archway, Jocko appeared in

the downstairs hall, in one of his fourteen belled hats, leading a conga line of children, some of whom were wearing the other thirteen hats. "Step to the left, step to the right, forward hop, hop. Step to the left, step to the right, forward hop, hop. *Pirouette!*"

Erika paused in her work to watch the procession. Her gentle smile was a curve of kindness, sweetly maternal. Addison wanted to kiss that smile, not just Erika but that *smile,* to taste and to receive the serenity of it.

Jocko reached the front stairs and started to climb. "Three steps up, one step back, slap your butt cheeks—*whack, whack, whack*! Advance three steps, now retreat one, snorting like a pig is *fun, fun, fun!*"

As the children ascended behind Jocko and all the whacking and snorting receded, Erika said, "They'll sleep well tonight."

"Especially Jocko," Addison said.

"Oh, Jocko rarely sleeps. Sometimes he sticks a fork in a wall plug and knocks himself out for an hour. I don't know why it doesn't kill him, but it doesn't, and I've learned to live with it."

———

Rusty in the lightless hallway, just outside Corrina Ringwald's bedroom, knew something was near him, an arm's length away to his left, and he assumed it must be another of those abominations that had killed all the people in the Trailblazer. *Clink-clink-clink.* He couldn't hear the thing breathing, but maybe their kind didn't breathe. *Clink-clink.* He expected it to surge forward and dissolve him or do whatever it was they did to people like those in the SUV, but the creature just loomed in the velvet blackness. *Clink-clink.*

He considered fleeing to his right, stumbling through the dark toward the dim glow rising in the staircase from windows below. But he clutched when he thought another of the things might be waiting there to receive him, that they were bracketing him, that he must be doomed no matter which way he turned. He was too long from the war, his nerves civilianized, and he could not in such short order armor himself against mortal fear to the extent that he had overcome it on the battlefield.

After no more than half a minute, Rusty knew that light would be preferable to continued darkness, no matter what hideous presence might be revealed. He felt behind him, along the wall beside the bedroom door, and he found a plastic cover plate, the notched head of a screw, and then the switch in the center. He hesitated for a moment, revelation awaiting his command, and as a shudder of dread, as cold as dry ice, passed through him, he turned on the overhead hallway lights.

Nothing waited to his right, as he had feared, but immediately to his left stood a man in a business suit, his face bristling with shards of broken glass. In fact, his face *was* broken glass, no flesh or features, just hair above and ears on the side, a thin jawline, the point of a chin. The entire face itself was formed of bristling spears of clear window glass, which shifted in a way reminiscent of the colored fragments at the bottom of a kaleidoscope: *Clink-clink-clink . . . clink-clink. . . .*

As Rusty stood frozen in terror, the well-tailored business suit turned to vapor, a mist that the thing appeared to absorb, revealing not a human body but the mere form of a man shaped from some mottled gray substance with veins of twinkling silver bits. Abruptly, glass blossomed from the body at several points, sharp-petaled flowerlike forms that glittered with scores of cutting edges.

Rusty remembered the sound of shattering glass rising from the ground floor earlier, and he sensed that rain of ringing fragments was related to this weird display, though he didn't know how or why.

From where the mouth ought to have been in that spiny face, several spear-point shards spat out, whistling past Rusty's head as quick as arrows from a bow. They shattered against the wall at the end of the hallway.

Rusty ran for the stairs.

———

Overhead the swarm circled, circled, buzzing-hissing, and Carson couldn't repress the idea that every human being in the room was but an item on an all-you-can-eat buffet. The dense cloud of gray and glittering nanoanimals, needing fuel to create, was considering its options, matching its selection to its current craving. Presuming those billions of tiny creatures possessed the equivalent of taste buds and culinary preferences was absurd, of course, but this colony was so alien in its nature that Carson could not imagine how or why it decided to do anything it did, and she could try to analyze its actions and predict its next move only by thinking in terms familiar to her, even as useless as those terms might be.

The theory that movement would attract a ravenous assault proved false. The swarm abruptly began to swirl, a glittering spiral nebula winding itself into a rapidly tightening form. From the center of the mass, something like a funnel cloud formed, struck down at one of the Riders, who had been as paralyzed as everyone else, and sucked him apart as if he had been little more than gelatin, feeding him up the tornado into the cumulonimbus form overhead, leaving no morsel of flesh or scrap of clothing.

————

Leaving nine cocoons ablaze in the high school, Sully York and the new Crazy Bastards climbed into the Hummer and went looking for trouble.

Riding shotgun once more, Bryce Walker was more involved, more *alive,* than Sully had seen him in eighteen months, since his Rennie had died. Something in Bryce died with her, which was understandable, because their long marriage had been not just a matter of piling up the years in a mutually agreeable relationship but also an expression of true love. Love was everyone's to experience if they opened their hearts, but *true* love was a rare and sterling thing, damn if it wasn't, a sterling thing that required the intervention of destiny: two hearts fated to be as one, finding each other among the billions of the world. *True* love, by God, was the Excalibur of emotions, and if you recognized it when you saw it, if you drew that noble, shining blade from the stone, your life would be a grand adventure even if you lived it entirely in one small town.

Sully had known love but never true love. True love wasn't defined as being willing to die for the one you loved. That was part of it, but the smaller part. Hell, he had been willing to die for women he loved, for women he didn't love, and even for a few dreadful women he disliked, which was how he ended up with one eye, one ear, and one hand. *True* love meant being willing to *live* for the woman who was the other chamber of your heart, to work yourself threadbare for her if necessary, to know her mind as you knew your own, to love her as you loved yourself, to cherish her above all earthly things unto the end of your years. *There* was the valiant and exhilarating life, more thrilling than ten thousand expeditions up ten thousand Amazons!

Sully looked at the rearview mirror, at Grace Ahern in the backseat with brave young Travis.

"What's this?" Bryce asked.

When Sully glanced at the writer, he thought the question must be a challenge to his quite innocent attraction to Grace. But Bryce leaned forward, squinting past the sweeping windshield wipers and through the driving snow.

Ahead in the street stood a man and a woman, side by side but about six feet from each other, blocking both lanes. They were not properly dressed for the weather, she in a simple black cocktail dress, he in a tuxedo. They possessed a theatrical air, as if the street were a stage and they were about to perform an amazing act, he an illusionist and she his about-to-vanish-in-a-flurry-of-doves assistant. As Sully braked to a stop less than twenty feet from them, he saw that they were, even in the hard light of the headlight beams, remarkably good-looking people, more luminous than movie stars

From the backseat, Grace said, "More of the same. They're like the two in the Meriwether Lewis kitchen, the ones who said 'I am your Builder,' then destroyed everyone, and spun the cocoons."

"We don't want this fight," Bryce said.

Sully shifted into reverse, checked the rearview mirror, and damn if there wasn't a similar couple in the street behind them. Four Builders, one for each of the Hummer's occupants.

———

Waste and void. Waste and void. Darkness upon the face of the deep. Thus it was; and thus it will be again.

The spirit moved upon the face of the deep, and there was light. The sun does not respond to Victor Immaculate's demands, and so light will remain in the world. But after the Community, there will be no eyes to see it, no skin to feel its warmth.

Brought to new heights of intellectual clarity and power by the burnt-orange capsules, by the sour-yellow tablet, Victor walks to think and thinks the world into its death. Ultimate visionary that he is, he peers forward to a time when nothing flies and nothing walks and nothing crawls and nothing slithers and nothing swims, a time when little grows and what still grows does not thrive, a time of empty skies, barren lands, dead seas.

In these high spirits, he arrives at the room where he would have had a most interesting meeting with the Moneyman if that fool had not mistaken one small setback for catastrophe. Here, with the bodyguards in another room, they would have met, just the two of them—at first—to discuss what additional equipment, matériel, and funds would be needed in the months ahead.

The room is approached through a small vestibule and two pairs of pneumatic doors that whoosh—one, then the other—into the walls. It is circular, thirty feet in diameter, with a dome. The thick concrete walls and domed ceiling are covered with sound-proofing board, as many layers as phyllo, and over the board is gray-felt upholstery and thousands of six-inch-long felt-covered cones. In the days of the Cold War, paranoia was deemed necessary to ensure survival; even in this deep, blast-proof facility once staffed by the most reliable patriots, the architects felt obligated to provide a chamber from which not a word could escape to a hallway or an adjoining space, where a shotgun could be fired without drawing attention. In here, a shout sounds like a murmur, but even words spoken in a murmur are as clear as a shout.

Victor expects to see the wheeled eight-panel gray fabric screen standing toward the farther end of the room, but he does not expect the three-legged table with another prescription only minutes after the previous offering. It waits just inside the door from the vestibule, bearing a cold bottle of water and a black saucer. In the saucer are two small white capsules, one larger yellow capsule, one five-sided pink tablet, and one blue ball the size of an M&M candy.

This is an unprecedented number and variety of intelligence-enhancing supplements to be presented in the same saucer. Victor Immaculate assumes, therefore, that his magnificent brain waves and other physiological data, always being transmitted telemetrically, have alerted his staff to the fact that he is at the brink of a mental breakthrough, about to surge to new heights of perception, perhaps rising to a realm of thoughts and ideas so revolutionary and so profoundly wise as to surprise even him, though he is not easily—if ever—surprised. He chases all five items with cold water.

Happily anticipating the effects of the ingenious supplements, Victor crosses the room to the screen and rolls it aside. Lying on a gurney is a naked replicant, eyes closed, in a kind of stasis, waiting to be called to duty. It is identical in appearance to the Moneyman, who would not have left this room alive. For all his wealth and power, the fool seems never to have grasped that, with as little as one of his hairs, he can be duplicated and made redundant. Why snivel before him and beg for more funds, for more support, when replacing him with an obedient Communitarian ensures that everything needed will be swiftly supplied?

From behind Victor, a deep voice, perhaps rough but smoothed into a crystal-clear murmur by the room, says, "I am satisfied."

———

Hoping to draw the bizarre glass-faced, glass-spitting creature away from the master bedroom and the consideration of the attic where Corrina hid, Rusty plunged down the stairs. The hall light was behind him, ahead only the blizzard-filtered glow of the streetlamp pressing against the ground-floor windows but not through them. As far as he knew, he might be descending into the arms of the blue-robed woman or one like her, or one unimaginably more strange.

In the foyer, he didn't hesitate to switch on the lights. He found himself alone.

The glass-faced thing came down the stairs in pursuit of him, and Rusty stepped to the front door, almost unlocked it, but shrank back when he saw the face of a man at one of the sidelights flanking the door. Matinee-idol handsome, the guy had a smile so appealing that it could sell anything to anyone, even hope to the dead. Rusty had no doubt that this was one of the eight he'd seen marching in the street earlier.

At the staircase landing, the glass-faced thing fell, shattered, and Rusty turned to see glittering fragments of the creature spill down the lower flight of steps. As the pieces tumbled, they somehow became miniature glass men of various sizes, scores upon scores of them. Their limbs snapped off as they tumbled and lay vibrating on the treads. A dozen made it intact to the foyer, where they crawled or tottered this way and that, perhaps seeking him out but blind to his position, until they collided, cracking, splintering to pieces.

War never brought Rusty Billingham near to the brink of madness, but minute by minute the impossible events of this night pushed him farther from the calm center of sanity toward its periphery. He knew he was not hallucinating, yet what he saw defied reason and suggested delusion if not delirium.

Glass figurines could neither crawl nor walk, as these did. When they shattered against one another, the fragments should not twitch like the bodies of snakes after their heads were cut off, but that's what these glass limbs and torsos and heads did, fracturing into smaller and still smaller pieces, until abruptly they were still.

If the glass-faced monstrosity had been a killing machine like the woman in the blue robe, something seemed to have destroyed it.

The door chimes rang.

Rusty meant to follow the hallway into the kitchen, hoping to leave by the back door and lead those things away from the house. But something stepped out of the dark living room, blocking his escape.

His mind moved from the suburbs of sanity to the borderline.

———

Victor Immaculate possesses all the memories of the original Victor. He knows, therefore, the meaning of the words that have been spoken behind him: *I am satisfied.*

More than two hundred years earlier, shortly after Deucalion murdered Victor's bride, Elizabeth, on the shores of Lake Como, the great scientist and maker of men had returned to Geneva. There, as he knelt in a cemetery at night, vowing vengeance, his creation spoke to him tauntingly from the darkness: *I am satisfied, miserable wretch! You have determined to live, and I am satisfied.*

Deucalion had meant that now his maker's anguish would be as intense as his own, and both of them would suffer the rest of their lives, Victor for what he had lost by his pride and his imprudent researches and Deucalion for being forever an outsider, alone of his kind.

Victor Immaculate turns and sees the giant that had come to life centuries before he himself had risen to replace the original Victor in New Orleans. No slightest fear afflicts him. Rather, his singular intellect is engaged, his curiosity as keen as a scalpel.

Deucalion says, "So long ago, you told your story to Robert Walton, that man aboard the icebound ship in the Arctic. His letters and journals were what Mary Shelley employed to tell her tale. Walton said you died on the ship, and he fabricated a loathsome story about my visiting your deathbed and expressing remorse to him. How much did you pay Walton to say that you perished on that vessel?"

"Not me," Victor Immaculate replies. "Your maker paid him, and handsomely. You forget that I'm not the one who made you. I'm only his clone."

"You are him as ever he was," the giant insists. "He is in you, all his knowledge and all his sins. You are him in concentration. By using the gullible Walton, you presented yourself to the world as a flawed but compassionate, loving, noble figure, much put upon and so determined to put right the wrong you did. Every time I've read your words, the pages *stink* with your false humility, expressed at such length its insincerity is evident in its redundancy."

As the creature approaches, he seems

larger step by step. But Victor Immaculate does not retreat. He does not know how. Besides, he is invulnerable to this one.

Deucalion says, "The pages *reek* with your bottomless self-pity so poorly disguised as regret, with the phoniness of your verbose self-condemnation, with the insidious quality of your contrition, which is that of a materialist who cares not for God and is therefore not true contrition at all, but only despair at the consequences of your actions. For centuries, I have been the monster, and you the well-meaning idealist who claims he would have undone what he did if only given the chance. But your kind never undoes. You do the same wrong over and over, with ever greater fervency, causing ever more misery, because you are *incapable of admitting error.*"

"I've made no error," Victor Immaculate confidently assures him, "and neither did your maker."

Looming, the giant says, "*You* are my maker."

"That's an error of *yours,* which you seem unable to admit. I'm not Victor but Victor Immaculate."

Deucalion places his hands upon

Victor's shoulders, gripping with such power that it is impossible to shrug loose or pull away.

"I was once a monster, as you made me," the giant says. "Full of rage and hot to murder. But on the lightning, I was given free will . . . and have remade myself through the centuries. I am not a monster anymore. But you are the monster you have always been."

"Release me," Victor demands.

The giant says nothing, but a strange light pulses through his menacing eyes.

"Look at your face in a mirror," Victor suggests. "Would you like the normal half to be as disfigured as the other? Or should I instead make your skull implode and finish you forever?"

"You don't have that power over me, as he did."

"Oh," Victor disagrees, "I am quite sure that I do."

———

The funnel cloud of nanoanimals sucked the Rider off the floor, dissolving him as he rose, and incorporated him into the swarm that blackened the air near the ceiling, spiraling ominously above more of the living room than not, enlarged now by the mass of the ingested victim.

Yet Carson and the others remained paralyzed, still fearing that if they moved, they would make targets of themselves.

The swarm churned as before, darker and seemingly as saturated as thunderheads pregnant with rain. Then the cloud began to eject things, as if spitting them out: a human foot with a mouth across its bridge, teeth gnashing; what seemed to be a pair of kidneys saddlebagged across a beating heart; a grotesquely large nose with wiggling fingers protruding from its nostrils. . . . A hand fell to the carpet, and on the back of it, set high like those of a crab, were eyes that appeared all too human.

The hand scuttled across the floor, toothless yet unsettling nonetheless, and Carson cried out—"Michael!"—but he had the same idea that motivated her cry. He was already hustling the three children into the adjacent dining room.

If they could get into the kitchen, there was a door between it and the dining room, another between it and the downstairs hall. They might be able to keep the swarm out, and hope to make a stand there.

They were halfway across the dining room when aproned women began to crowd through the door from the kitchen. Another Builder had gotten into the back of the house.

———

After the failed assault on KBOW, Sammy Chakrabarty was not in a mood to celebrate. He knew worse would be coming. He relentlessly circled the roof, maintaining surveillance on every side of the radio station.

He was most worried about the back of the building, where the broadcast tower soared into the falling snow. Fifty yards beyond lay a small woods, past which was a meadow and then a motel. He could see neither the lights of the motel nor the meadow beyond the copse of pines, but he thought it might be easy to approach KBOW on foot, through the cover of those trees.

As he stood peering through the open girders toward the woods, a truck roared into the parking lot. He hurried across the roof to his original position, dropped to his knees behind the parapet, and through the crenel saw men—or things like men—pouring out of the cargo box of another blue-and-white truck. Some of them had weapons, and they began to spray the building with bullets.

Sammy opened fire on them with the Bushmaster.

———

Chief Rafael Jarmillo and Deputy Nelson Sternlagen, equal in position as all Communitarians were equal—therefore neither of them quite leading, neither of them quite following—brought two Builders through the pines behind KBOW. Jarmillo had Warren Snyder's spare keys, but he would relinquish them without hesitation to Sternlagen if for some reason it became more efficient for the deputy to be the one to unlock the back door.

They paused at the edge of the woods, waited until they heard gunfire, then hurried through the snow toward the broadcast tower.

———

The two Builders in front of the Hummer began to move toward it, as did the two behind. They approached not snarling and at a run but smiling and with an eerie leisureliness that suggested they were certain of triumph.

Sully York had never been the kind to defend his position if he had any chance of attacking from it. No one was deader than those who didn't risk all when all was at risk.

As if he'd written deeply into the minds of enough Western-novel heroes to know the intimate workings of Sully's thought processes, Bryce Walker said, "Go for it."

Even though these were killing machines of some kind, not people, as they appeared to be, Sully chose to run down the man in the tuxedo rather than the woman in the black cocktail dress, because chivalry was not easily set aside when it was the habit of a lifetime.

Confident of the Hummer's exceptional traction and bad-weather handling, Sully tramped the accelerator, and the big SUV shot forward without a spinning of tires. The tuxedoed sonofabitch didn't try to dodge out of the way, like most chickenhearted pretty boys would have. The Hummer hit him hard, jolting everyone in it, and then something happened that seemed to prove that he must be the stage magician he appeared to be.

The Builder wasn't knocked down, stood his ground, and the SUV parted around him, *dissolved* around him. The engine gave out, maybe ceased to exist, the headlights died, and the vehicle shuddered to a halt. The Builder stood now directly in front of the windshield, in an apparent Hummer vise of steel and truck parts, smiling in a snarky sort of way, as if to say the impact had been a damn treat, thank you very much. It placed its hand flat on the windshield, and Sully York thought for the first time in his life of adventures that the end had come: The glass would craze, the Builder would burst inside, they would all be liquidated and cocooned.

Instead the handsome magician frowned, opened his mouth, seemed to gag, and from him spewed a tangle of fan belts. On the windshield, his hand transformed into a conglomeration of spark plugs and wires. His tuxedo shimmered away, and he lost all human appearance a moment later. He morphed into what appeared to be a hard gray mass, roughly manlike in shape, although from it protruded all manner of engine parts, as if this were a sculpture of a man made from automotive odds and ends.

Sully knew intuitively that the Builder had ceased to function, as any machine might freeze up if its cogwheels were immobilized by metal filings that clogged their teeth. They were saved.

On the other hand, the Hummer was useless now, and three more Builders were circling them.

———

The nude woman who stepped out of Corrina Ringwald's dark living room, into the foyer, wasn't a blonde, like the one in the blue robe, but she was a brunette of even greater beauty, more unreal than any airbrushed photograph of any plasticized and Botoxed Hollywood star. After she had come into the light and given Rusty a moment to admire her physical perfection, her nose collapsed into her skull, her face puckered around that hole and then raveled inward, and her head sank out of sight into the stump of her neck.

Behind Rusty, as he tried to hold fast to his sanity, the door chimes sounded again.

The brunette's face formed in the abdomen of her headless body, her breasts now like horns on her brow. Her eyes were green and fierce, and her voice was both seductive and triumphant when she said, "I am your Builder."

———

In Deucalion's grip, certain of his power over the giant, Victor nevertheless decides to change his tack:

"Why be a defender of their kind? They're less than you. They're of the same species as one another, all of the human community, and yet they hate one another, conspire against one another, *war* against one another."

"And some are willing to die for one another," Deucalion says.

"Yes, for something called duty and something called love—which are concepts, not realities. You can't deny they live for lust, for greed, to envy and to justify violence with their envy, to seek power over one another and to apply it ruthlessly."

"Most of them are not that way," the giant says. "But among them are enough like you, Victor, to lead them astray again and again, to be their conniving politicians and their self-sickened intellectuals, their self-satisfied elites who seduce them away from their better natures. There is a serpent in the world, and having signed a pledge with it, you spent your life—your lives—spreading its venom."

Victor knows he has the right side of this

debate, and he does not hesitate to press forward, face-to-face: "They think themselves exceptional, a part of them eternal, but consider the world they have made, a sewer of vice and self-interest, of worm-riddled bread and grotesque circuses that become more macabre year by year. They make a claim to lives of meaning, yet they pursue nothing but meaningless thrills."

"Because it is your kind among them who bake the worms into the bread and write the scripts for the circuses. You repeat the same tired argument."

"But if for no other reason," Victor Immaculate says, "surely one as ancient and wise and intelligent as you must hate them for their riotous individuality, every personality different from the other, the whole vast, tumultuous sea of them, not a fraction as organized as the lowly crawling ants, seething with eccentricities, with an infinite variety of passions and prejudices, likes and dislikes, schemes—"

"Hopes and dreams," says Deucalion.

"—quirks and useless idiosyncrasies—"

"Charms and talents," Deucalion says, "gifts and graces."

Waiting for his mental power to soar to

unprecedented heights when the latest round of supplements kicks in, Victor Immaculate does not attempt to break free of the giant, but raises one hand to the undamaged half of the brute's tattooed face, touching it tenderly, much as a loving father might touch it, and Deucalion doesn't shrink from the contact.

"Surely you see," Victor says, "that they will never be as one, work as one, unite without qualification in a quest for greatness. They will never sacrifice their individuality for the betterment of the race, will never bend their billions of minds and hearts to the same goal and thereby conquer nature and the universe forever."

"God spare them that," Deucalion replies.

And then a surprising and unpleasant thing begins to happen.

————

Deucalion didn't know how the execution would transpire, only that this Victor, this self-proclaimed Immaculate, would perish and all of his foul work with him.

The end arrived when he began to be aware of the pulses of light passing through his eyes. Previously, he had seen the phenomenon only in mirrors or in pools of still water. Now, cold white waves of light passed across Victor's upturned face. In the clone's frightened eyes, incandescence throbbed, too, although it wasn't an inner luminosity but a reflection of his executioner's eye-shine.

In his mind's ear, Deucalion heard the storm—and more—on the night that he had been born from the dead: the escalating crashes of thunder that shook the heavens as if to bring them down like vaults of quake-shocked stone, the burr and buzz of arcane machines echoing off the walls of the old windmill, his anguished cries as he resisted his creation, his maker's shrieks of triumph, a mad cacophony. And in memory, he saw once more the first thing that he had seen when opening his eyes on that distant night: the colossal bolts of chain lightning turning the night to blazing day beyond the mill windows and crackling down the cables by which Victor induced it into his demonic machinery, not the usual lightning of an ordinary storm, but lightning of unprecedented explosiveness, light *alive.*

Now he felt that same raw power surging through him, along his arms and into his hands, into the body of this Victor Immaculate. The madman's clothes smoked and burst into flames, but the flames didn't burn Deucalion's hands. Victor's skin blackened and peeled, his eye sockets splashed full of fire, flames licked from his mouth, and in mere seconds, he collapsed out of Deucalion's grip, reduced to ashes and fragments of charred bones.

More than two centuries of scheming toward utopia were at an end. The only thing of significance that Victor achieved was a death toll in the many thousands, and even that appeared insignificant when compared to the work of Hitler, Stalin, Mao, and others, who murdered in the tens of millions. Under all his names, Leben and Helios and Frankenstein, Victor was a small man of small ideas, large only on the silver screen in the theater of his demented mind.

On a nearby gurney, the naked body of a replicant struggled to rise as Victor burned, but shuddered and fell back, dead. Until now, Deucalion had not realized that this particular Communitarian was a duplicate of the President of the United States.

———

As the three Builders approached the disabled Hummer, Sully York said, "Damn if

I'll let it end like this. Bryce, let's me and you give these sonsofbitches such a case of indigestion that Grace and Travis will have time to run."

He threw open the driver's door and, issuing a muttered war cry, clambered out into the falling snow with his gun and with a lifetime of experience surviving hopeless situations. He heard Bryce getting out of the passenger door, and he thought, *By God, it's always good to give the blighters what-for with a good man at your back.*

He was almost disappointed when, before the battle could begin, the Builders collapsed simultaneously into apparently inert piles of what appeared to be, but certainly wasn't, gravel.

———

With the rattle of gunfire at the farther end of the building, Chief Jarmillo and Deputy Nelson Sternlagen reached the back door of KBOW, the two Builders immediately behind them. Jarmillo handed the key to Sternlagen—he wasn't quite sure why— and Sternlagen handed it back to him, and they both stood for a moment, staring at the key in the chief's hand. They never did get it in the lock.

The face in the abdomen of the headless woman declared, "I am your Builder." The mouth stretched wide, and from it came a jet of silvery gray sludge—that halted inches from Rusty's face, quivered in the air, and fell to the floor, as did the headless woman. This once phantasmagoric and threatening figure was now an apparently harmless pile of . . . something.

Heart racing nonetheless, Rusty noticed that the fragments of the glass-faced man had continued fracturing until they now formed little mounds of what might have been sand but probably wasn't. And the door chimes were not ringing.

He switched on the porch lamp and hesitantly put his face to the window. The porch seemed to be deserted.

When he opened the door, the handsome man with the I-can-sell-you-anything smile was gone. Nothing remained but another strange pile of . . . something.

Rusty stood in the cold, on the porch, listening to the night. He heard no gunshots. No screams. No cadres of models were marching in the street. The handsome pair of German shepherds appeared, no longer fleeing in terror, wandering aimlessly, smelling this and that. One of them abruptly dropped and rolled onto its back in the freshly fallen snow, kicking its legs joyfully in the air.

As suddenly as the nightmare had begun, it was over.

Returning to the house, Rusty called, "Corrina, Corrina," all the way up the stairs. By the time he reached the master bedroom, he was *singing* her name.

———

At the core computer in the Hive, in a room littered with the bodies of Victor's people, for several hours Deucalion worked as a man possessed, which in a way he was. In his state of possession, he performed miracles with the trove of data, eliminating everything that revealed *how* Victor had created his Communitarians and Builders, while leaving ample proof of *what* he had done.

Unlike those in Rainbow Falls, the telephones in the Hive still functioned. With an ease that further suggested that he did not work unaided, Deucalion was able to make online contact with a trustworthy reporter at a major cable-news network, to whom he opened all the many digital files that he had just redacted.

———

Carson and Michael had to get out of that house of grief, in which four members of the Riders in the Sky Church had died— two men, one woman, and a child. Carson knew, as did Michael, that they could not have saved the little girl, that no one could have, not when their enemies were two colonies of nanoanimals against which no weapon could defend.

They walked together in the post-dawn shadows under the immense evergreens that shrouded the Samples property. Early light, clear and golden, speared down here and there between the laden boughs of the trees, spotlighting those portions of the ground where falling snow had reached, leaving dark those areas carpeted with dead needles.

The storm ended before first light. Now the chattering rotors of a helicopter grew louder, louder, and passed overhead, out of sight above the trees. She supposed the aircraft must be from the Montana State Police or another state law-enforcement agency. Soon the sky would be full of helicopters and the highways into town choked with the vehicles of first responders and the media.

Carson was inexpressibly grateful to be alive, hand in hand with Michael, but as never before in her life of close calls, she felt to a degree guilty for having lived when so many perished. Her sweet and thoughtful husband, usually quick with a funny line, was unable to amuse her now; but she would have been lost entirely without him at her side.

They passed between the massive trunks of two alpine firs, and ahead Deucalion walked toward them where he had not been walking an instant earlier. They met in a shaft of light.

"It's over forever this time," the giant said.

"We thought so before," Michael reminded him.

"But this time, there is no slightest doubt. None whatsoever. I feel myself being . . . called back. I should have realized after New Orleans that if it was really over, my journey on this world would have come to an end, as well."

"And now it will?" Carson asked.

"It is ending even now," he said. "I've only

returned to put your minds at ease, to assure you that Frankenstein is history and that your lives will never again be braided into his. Be happy, be at peace. Now I must go."

Michael reached out for Deucalion's hand.

The giant shook his head. "I didn't come to say good-bye. There is no such thing as parting forever."

A cloud occluded the shaft of sunshine, and shadow fell upon them.

Deucalion said, "Until we meet again," and turned away from Carson and Michael.

She expected him to vanish in the turn, but he didn't take his leave in his customary fashion. He walked away into the early-morning gloom beneath the trees, although he did not fade as a shadow into shadows. Instead, as he receded through the woods, a luminosity rose in him, soft at first but then brighter, brighter, until he was a shining figure, an apparition of pure light. When he reached a shaft of sunshine in the distance, he melded with it—and was gone.

chapter **65**

Nine nights after Deucalion delivered the truckload of children to St. Bartholomew's Abbey, and five days after they were bused home, shortly before seven o'clock on that cold October evening, Brother Salvatore, also known as Brother Knuckles, went into the yard outside the guest wing and stood staring at the night sky, where no stars twinkled. Snow began to fall precisely on the hour. He stood in it for a while, feeling no chill.

———

The five weddings were in early December. Originally, they were supposed to be separate ceremonies, but in the wake of 3,298 deaths, the town of Rainbow Falls needed to be lifted up and motivated to get on with life. Who first suggested a group ceremony and how it came to pass, no one could quite remember. Clergymen of different faiths agreed on the manner in which the rites would be administered, the church was filled to capacity, and over two thousand gathered in the square outside to listen to the portable loudspeakers that had been set up to share the moment with them.

Sully was too old for his bride, a fact no one would dispute, but neither of his best men—Travis nor Bryce—would tolerate anyone saying so aloud, which no one did. All the brides seemed beautiful, not least of all Grace, and Addison Hawk's Erika. By God, Sully's favorite moment of the whole affair—aside from Grace's "I do"— was when young Rusty Billingham sang the song he had written for Corrina.

———

Because he was one of the heroes—and so colorful—Mr. Lyss was in demand for interviews. People wanted to pay him to tell his story, but he told it for free. This made Nummy proud of the old man.

They sold Grandmama's little house. When it was learned that Mr. Lyss once was something called a certified public accountant and hoped to return to that work, Grandmama's attorney, who looked after Nummy's inheritance, wasn't so suspicious of the old man. Besides, Mr. Lyss cleaned up really well. Sometimes Nummy thought Mr. Lyss almost didn't look like Mr. Lyss anymore, but kind of like Mr. Chips in that old movie about a boys' school.

So first Mr. Lyss took Nummy to see somewhere warm, with palm trees and everything, which was called California. They stayed in a little motel where everything was amazing to Nummy, until Mr. Lyss bought a lottery ticket. He'd always said he had a winning ticket in his wallet, but that was a lie. No surprise. Mr. Lyss tried not to lie anymore, and mostly he didn't. But he didn't have to lie when the new ticket won. The giant at KBOW told Nummy everything would change in fifty days, and it sure did, when Mr. Lyss won more money than Nummy could count if he lived a thousand years.

Mr. Lyss bought a house with a view of the sea. He and Nummy spent a lot of time on the patio, talking about just everything, which was nice. Mr. Lyss bought Nummy a real dog, instead of the stuffed dog he used to have. This one didn't talk to you when you pushed the button behind its ear, but it was a lot more fun than the stuffed one. Maybe the best thing of all was when Mr. Lyss brought Grandmama's body all the way from Rainbow Falls and buried her again in a cemetery with palm trees, close enough so they could go visit her every week.

At the little service, when they put Grandmama in the ground a second time, Mr. Lyss said something that Nummy didn't understand and that Mr. Lyss wouldn't explain. The old man looked down at her coffin in the grave, and he said, "Ma'am, I can never thank you enough for what you did for me. Nobody in my whole life ever did as much. Any joy I have, as long as I live, is because of you."

This made no sense to Nummy because Grandmama died before Mr. Lyss came to Rainbow Falls. She never met the old man. But Mr. Lyss meant what he said so much that when he said it, his eyes were full of tears.

It was what they called a mystery.

———

When the reporters came, Jocko thought his life would be all sticks again. Sticks and buckets and clubs. People beating him with umbrellas. Didn't imagine he would become the star of a TV show for kids. Famous coast-to-coast. *Jumpin' with Jocko!* Nicest part—they filmed it in Rainbow Falls. Brought the studio to him. Didn't have to move out of the pretty little house to Hollywood. Hollywood: *Yuck. Blech. Gaaaah. Gaaaah. Kack. Feh. Fah. Foo.* And hats! He had hundreds of funny hats with bells, each of them funnier than the others! He lived with Erika and Addison and Princess Chrissy, as he always would. But now he had his first best friend, who was also the producer and director of his hit TV show. Sammy Chakrabarty! TV genius! One hundred thirty pounds of fabulous entertainment ideas! Hard to believe Jocko was once a tumor. Once lived in a sewer. Once ate soap. Life is strange. And wonderful.

———

In March of the following year, as she turned out her bedside lamp, Carson said to Michael, "Sweet dreams. Oh, and we're pregnant."

He sighed. "And I look so stupid in a maternity dress."

ABOUT THE AUTHOR

DEAN KOONTZ, the author of many #1 *New York Times* bestsellers, lives in Southern California with his wife, Gerda, their golden retriever, Anna, and the enduring spirit of their golden, Trixie.

www.deankoontz.com

Correspondence for the author should be addressed to:

Dean Koontz
P.O. Box 9529
Newport Beach, California 92658